Maybe a bar was exactly what he needed.

And what about Tess?

It didn't matter if she was pretty. If his body had some different idea of her than his brain did. Because his body was kind of interested in her body. His mind? It found her irritating as hell. Besides, she was practically his superior.

Marc glanced up from locking his door to see Tess leaning against the rail at the top of the staircase. She'd changed. Jeans, long-sleeved T-shirt, leather jacket slung over her shoulder. Her hair was still pulled back, but in a looser way than it had been when she'd been in uniform.

There was nothing sexy about it. Nothing. But *sexy* was the first word that popped into his head anyway.

Trouble. Plain and simple. And he'd never done anything remotely resembling trouble. Was that why it seemed so enticing?

Dear Reader,

Marc and Tess's story ends my Bluff City series (I mean, probably—you never know!), which is my first series with Harlequin Superromance.

I think more than anything I've written, the books in this series are about the ways love holds us up when times are tough, and that is one of my favorite themes to explore. I'll miss Grace and Kyle, Jacob and Leah, Henry and Ellen, and Marc and Tess a little extra for the milestones and firsts that came along with them.

I hope their stories bring you some of the joy and hope they've brought me.

If you're on Twitter, so am I (probably more than I should be). I love to talk to readers: @NicoleTHelm.

Happy reading!

Nicole Helm
nicolehelm.wordpress.com

NICOLE
HELM

Falling for the New Guy

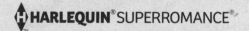

HARLEQUIN® SUPERROMANCE®

Recycling programs
for this product may
not exist in your area.

ISBN-13: 978-0-373-60901-7

Falling for the New Guy

Copyright © 2015 by Nicole Helm

This edition published by arrangement with Harlequin Books S.A.

For questions and comments about the quality of this book,
please contact us at CustomerService@Harlequin.com.

® and TM are trademarks of Harlequin Enterprises Limited or its
corporate affiliates. Trademarks indicated with ® are registered in the
United States Patent and Trademark Office, the Canadian Intellectual
Property Office and in other countries.

Printed in U.S.A.

Nicole Helm grew up with her nose in a book and a dream of becoming a writer. Luckily, after a few failed career choices, a husband and two kids, she gets to pursue that writing dream. She lives in Missouri with her husband (the police officer who, sadly, does not go by Captain Quiet) and two sons (who are also extremely *not* quiet).

Books by Nicole Helm

HARLEQUIN SUPERROMANCE

Too Close to Resist
Too Friendly to Date

HARLEQUIN E

All I Have

Visit the Author Profile page
at Harlequin.com for more titles

To my husband. For answering my endless (and somewhat disturbing) questions without batting an eye, and for being the love that gets me through all the rough patches.

CHAPTER ONE

MARC SANTINO PLACED a box in the corner of the empty apartment along with one other box. Add the two his sister and her boyfriend carried, a bed, a bookshelf and a few folding chairs, and it made up all his worldly possessions. That hadn't seemed quite so little until he put it into the apartment, tiny as the space was.

"Are you sure about this place?" Leah asked, dropping her box and then skeptically kicking loose baseboards and poking at electrical outlets.

Marc had to bite his tongue to keep from telling her to be careful. She was an electrician—she knew what she was doing.

But what kind of lunatic so casually ran her fingers over outlets?

He didn't say that, though. He was not going to ruin whatever weird equilibrium he and his not-at-all close little sister had managed over the past few months with his—some might say—paranoid worry. He liked to call it concerned with safety.

"It's a little rough, but I'll have plenty of time to clean it up. Besides, the price was right."

Leah and Jacob shared a look. Marc wasn't a big fan of when they did that. Unfortunately, the brief time he'd spent visiting in order to facilitate this move to Bluff City, Iowa hadn't given him any insight into what those shared looks meant.

"Jacob and I could move into the big house," Leah said, referencing the large house Jacob's company had restored and used as an office. But Marc knew they were trying to sell it, and living in Leah's house was more practical for them. Or more private, anyway.

"I want a space of my own. Somewhere small that I don't have to clean."

Leah let out a pained sigh. "I don't think Mom will like this."

Marc ignored the bitterness that coated his stomach. He'd made strides with Leah over the course of the past few months, but his relationship with their parents, Mom especially, remained complicated.

He didn't want to analyze it, or to feel that bitter asshole part of himself that, even at thirty-two, was jealous of his sister. A sister whose health problems had been the center of his childhood.

No, his entire life, as evidenced by him being here right now.

"Mom won't care." She only cared about Leah. "Besides, by the time she visits I'll have it looking better."

Another pained sigh from his sister. "That doesn't fix what the outside looks like."

"Mom won't care," he repeated, keeping the snap out of his tone by sheer force of will, but she seemed to get it. Instead of arguing further she leaned against Jacob.

"We should go."

Marc liked Jacob well enough, but since the guy was in love with Leah he always got a little prickly over Marc's terse way with her when they got on a topic like this. Which was great, as it should be and all that.

But sometimes Marc wanted to give the guy a shove. Which he would never do. He was a cop. He'd dealt with people a lot more annoying than a protective boyfriend, and he always kept his temper in check. Always, even when the guys he worked with lost their cool. Marc kept it under control.

That was him. So he simply nodded. "Thanks for the help."

"Anytime, you know. Anytime." Leah offered an awkward wave and a paltry smile and he did his best not to scowl. Until they were gone, and then his mouth did that of its own accord.

Scowled at the closed door. Dingy, a little rust around the doorknob. Leah was right that he couldn't fix what the whole complex looked like, but he had no doubt he could have his apartment looking decent in a week or two.

His new job at Bluff City Police Department might start tomorrow, but he had no life in Bluff City. All he had was a sister he was childishly resentful over.

So why the hell did you agree to this?

Though his mind poked him with the question on a fairly regular basis, he knew the answer. His parents had asked him to, and he didn't say no to them. Ever.

Pathetic, Santino.

No doubt. But they wanted to move near Leah. They wanted their little family to be a real close-knit one. And Leah had built a life for herself here. So he'd gotten a new job, moved from his place in Minnesota, and Mom and Dad would be moving as soon as they could.

Because of Leah. The motivation for every Santino family decision. Even when she'd run away. Even when she hadn't given the family an ounce of her attention, Leah had been the center of Mom and Dad's wants and needs, and he was nothing.

He glared at his boxes, ready to tackle the task of unpacking. A task that wouldn't take long at all, but would at least take his mind off all this shit. Dumb shit.

A loud thumping from out in the hall caught his attention before he made any progress unpacking. Followed by muffled cursing. Yeah, the walls weren't exactly thick, were they?

He walked to the door, wondering if he should get his gun out of its safe first. The peephole was murky and he couldn't make out much. Still, as run-down as this apartment complex down by the river was, it wasn't grab-your-gun-before-you-check-out-the-hallway bad.

So he opened the door. And, okay, he strategically placed himself to be ready for whatever situation he might find.

He did not expect a woman standing at the top of the stairs, cradling one arm, leaning against the wall, cursing as though her life depended on it. Cursing really creatively.

"Are you—"

Her head jerked up, hand coming off her arm long enough for him to notice a bloody piece of fabric beneath.

"You're hurt." He moved toward her, his initial reaction. Someone was hurt, you moved in to help.

"Yeah, I noticed," she muttered, staring down at the bloody fabric on her forearm before squeezing her hand over it again.

"Let me help." She stiffened when he reached toward her, so he did his best to seem unthreatening. "It's okay. I'm a cop. I can show you my badge if you'd like."

She snorted and pushed herself away from the wall, very much ignoring and avoiding his outstretched hand. "Yeah, well, I'm a cop, too, buddy. Badge and all. Which means I can help myself." She walked past him to the door at the end of the hall, then turned around.

"Wait. I know you."

He was pretty sure he'd remember eyes like that.

Which was a weird-ass thing to think, but they weren't really blue, instead nearly gray. He'd never seen gray eyes before. Paired with the half assessing, half go-screw-yourself expression in them, he was pretty sure he'd remember her.

"New guy. San…San…San Francisco?" She flashed a grin, some of the go-screw-yourself fading.

The corner of his mouth inched upward against his permission. "Santino."

"Right. Right. Matt Santino."

"Marc."

"Yeah, that's what I said, right?" She half smiled at him and he felt like a dumb teenager scrambling to say something. Something that might impress her.

Idiot. If she knew him and was a cop, she had to work at BCPD, which meant no impressing.

"Tess. Tess Camden." She nodded at his open door, blood starting to drip onto the hallway floor. "You live here?"

"Um, yeah." He moved toward her again, gesturing at the next blood drop threatening to fall. "Don't you think you should—"

"Good. That'll be convenient."

"Convenient? What do you—"

But she'd opened her door, was stepping inside. "See you tomorrow, San Francisco." With a wave, she slammed the door shut.

Marc wasn't sure how long he stood there in shock. Sure, it hadn't been a seriously painful injury or she'd probably be screaming or going to the hospital or something. But she'd been dripping blood in the hallway, and that wasn't good. At all.

But it was none of his business, and surely if she was a cop she knew how to take care of herself. Still, the image of that bloody scrap of fabric stayed with him, and he didn't think he'd shake it until he knew what all that was about.

TESS WISHED SHE could muster some anger. Frustration. Determination. But all she could feel with her arm stinging under the spray of her morning shower was defeated. Hollow. Sucky.

She stepped out of the shower, shivering against the cold morning, and gingerly dried off before winding the new bandage around her gash and shimmying into underwear.

She really was lucky it hadn't been worse. The bottle that had shattered when her father had flung it at her could have actually hit her. Or more pieces of flying glass could have caught exposed skin. It could have done enough damage she'd have to call in sick to work.

But it hadn't.

Damn it, how was he getting the alcohol? He didn't drive. Had alienated all of his friends. She'd long since stopped bringing him anything that could be remotely used to trade.

Every time she thought she'd gotten him weaned off, every time she thought he was on the path to recovery and forgetting everything…they ended up back here.

On a sigh, she pulled her hair back and began to braid, pulling as tightly as she could. It was a severe look, one she didn't go for every single day on the job, but she needed to feel severe today.

She needed answers. Why couldn't she find the answers?

She glanced at the clock and groaned. She was running late, and she didn't like to be late on a good day, but with her first day training…San…San…oh, whatever the hell his name was, she didn't want to set a bad example.

She hurried through putting on her uniform. Some days it was a little constricting. The Kevlar, the straight lines, the shiny name tag. But other days it was armor. Today was definitely one of those days. There were rules and order in the world, and she was the woman to enforce them.

She grabbed her bag and headed for the door, pushing her feet into boots. She'd save lacing them up for when she got to the station.

She caught the glimpse of her trainee at the top of the stairs. "Hey, San Francisco?"

He didn't reappear right away, but after a few seconds his head popped back around the corner. "Marc," he said in that same low, measured voice he'd used last night when he'd wanted to help her.

"Sure. Listen. I'll give you a ride."

His dark brows furrowed together. "I'm not—"

"Obviously you didn't get the memo," she said, approaching the stairs and him with a smile. "I'm your FTO."

"You're my...you're my field training officer?"

"In the flesh." She could get all bent out of shape at his shock. If she were a dude he wouldn't be all fumbling and surprised. But if she got irritated by every sexist jerk, she would have left police work a long time ago.

"That's why me living here is convenient."

He followed her down the stairs and she kept her eyes straight ahead, voice neutral. "Indeed. The beauty of a small town. Only so many places to live off a police officer's salary. There's another guy on the top floor, but he's a school resource officer. Don't see much of him."

He didn't say anything to that and they walked out into the chill of an early March morning. She'd forgotten her coat, but she'd just deal today. She wasn't about to seem as though she didn't have it together for the new guy.

She pointed to her patrol car. "I'm sure they explained it to you, but to refresh, two weeks in, you'll get your own take-home car, but right now, you're watching me. I'll be with you for the whole three months, one with each shift. Last two weeks we'll do a shadow with me in plainclothes and you handling all the calls."

"Sounds good."

She glanced at him then. He was a big guy. Tall

and broad. The uniform with vest underneath made him look even broader than he had last night in the hallway. He had a neutral expression on his face, but he had that chiseled jaw, a sort of impassive, serious resting face.

She was always jealous of guys like that, who could look intimidating without even trying. No one laughed at them when they told them to get out of a car and spread 'em.

Of course, she'd been doing this for ten years now. She'd learned how to wield herself in a way that kept most people from messing with her simply on the grounds of her being female.

But it'd be nice to not have to work so hard. Mr. Football Player Shoulders and Ruggedly Handsome—

Whoa, whoa, whoa. None of that. She didn't cross lines like that. Never had. Never would. Besides, from their encounter last night, he seemed like the compulsive-helper type. I'm-a-cop-and-I'm-here-to-help type.

In other words, so not her type. She wasn't interested in anyone's help. Especially someone whose uniform was so freakishly unwrinkled it looked as if nuns had slaved over pressing it all night.

"Man, where'd you take your uniforms?" she asked, opening her driver's side door.

"Take?"

"Yeah, what dry cleaner? I'm not sure I've ever seen one so crisp." She slipped behind the wheel and he did the same in the passenger seat. Filling up that entire side in such a way *she* felt cramped.

"Well, it's new."

"But you had to press it, right? It comes all creased in the package." She looked at him, got tricked into looking him in the eye. Kind of a really light brown. Like amber or something. Mesmerizing.

You are not serious right now, brain.

He looked away. Thank God. "I did it myself."

"You? You?"

"It's a lot cheaper than getting it dry-cleaned."

"Well, yeah, but jeez. What'd you do? Intern at a dry cleaner? That's unholy."

He didn't say anything, just watched the grungier side of town get a shade more sparkling as they drove up and away from the river, toward the police station.

She concentrated on the road and he was silent. This was only her third time field training someone, but the other two guys had been different. Talkative, easygoing. Even if she'd wished Granger'd shut up most of the time, silence was weird. She wished for Granger's grandstanding BS in the face of heavy, awkward silence.

"So, um, what brings you to Bluff City?" She flicked a glance at him to gauge his reaction. Nothing on his face changed, but as she moved her gaze back to the road she noticed his hand had clenched around his knee.

Hmm.

"Family," he said at length. He didn't say it in a way that made it sound positive. Well, that she understood.

"You grow up around here?"

"No."

That was it.

Man, it was going to be a long three months.

AFTER NINE YEARS of being on the road, three months of field training was frustrating. Marc understood why it was necessary. Different laws, procedures, protocol.

But sitting shotgun in a patrol car that smelled like…hell if he knew. Something feminine and flowery. All shoved into an uncomfortable seat he couldn't recline because of the cage in the back. Being pelted with questions by Chatty McGee FTO lady.

He would prefer clawing his way out and jumping from the still-moving vehicle.

Was everyone at BCPD going to be so damn chatty? At his old department there'd been a group of guys who were chummy, but they'd let him be. He was respected. Maybe a little feared, but he preferred that kind of distance to Tess's cheery interrogation.

"Soooo." She drummed her fingers against the steering wheel, eyes on the road. She'd driven them around their zone, talked about landmarks and the like. Things he'd already known because he'd memorized the Bluff City map. Because he wasn't some rookie who didn't know how to handle himself.

"We don't have to talk, you know."

She frowned over at him. "We're going to be sharing a lot of space here. You want to sit in silence for three months?"

"Silence is better than…"

"Than?"

He shifted uncomfortably. This woman put him at some serious unease. Small talk was not something he'd ever excelled at. He preferred quiet. Assess a situation, a person before weighing in.

He preferred being careful and not making people damn uncomfortable. Tess did not have the same beliefs, it seemed.

So, turnabout was fair play, right? "Okay, you want to chat? What happened to your arm last night?" Because he didn't give a crap about her taste in music or her favorite restaurant, but he was kind of desperate to know what the hell happened to her arm.

As he'd predicted, she closed right up. Gaze hard on the street. Fingers tightening on the steering wheel. "It was nothing."

"Sure, everyone goes home at night crashing into things, cursing, bleeding onto the hallway floor."

Her mouth quirked at the corner. "Well, I thought so." She glanced at him again. "So, Mr. Stiffy has a sense of humor?" She closed her eyes, cheeks blotching pink. "Oh, that sounded…not how I meant."

Only then did he get what she was embarrassed about. Only then did he feel a matching embarrassing heat flood his face.

This was turning out to be a hell of a first day.

"Anyway. I was visiting my dad. Glass broke. Caught me in the arm."

He wondered if she had any clue what a shit liar she was. First of all, the story was too vague. Second, the tenseness in her shoulders meant she wasn't comfortable with the subject. As did the way she restlessly pushed the car into Reverse.

"Let's go grab some lunch, huh?"

He didn't verbally respond, just gave her a nod. He wondered if his chatty FTO was in trouble, and if it would affect him.

Unfortunately, he was all out of patience with other people's lives affecting his, and he had a bad feeling about Tess Camden.

CHAPTER TWO

"CAMDEN. FRANKS WANTS to see you." The radio crackled and then shut off.

Tess glanced at Marc, who was, of course, still staring out the window. She'd switched tactics from trying to be friends with the guy to focusing on work. Third day in, he still barely said a word and barely seemed to listen.

He did catch on quick, though, which was kind of a pain in the ass.

Tess grabbed the radio and muttered into the speaker, "En route." To Marc she said, "Should only take a few. You can poke around the station. Check out the gym or something."

He nodded.

She really hated that nod. His silence. His stoic blankness. She hated that it made her wonder. No personality? Woman hater? Deep dark secrets?

She had enough on her plate without trying to figure out Mr. Stiffy. Yeah, she'd said that back on the first day. Jeez. Maybe she needed to practice some of this guy's stoicism.

And quick, if Franks wanted to see her.

She pulled into the station lot, rolling her shoulders to rid herself of the heavy rock of dread knotted between them. Franks rarely called someone into his office for anything positive, and she really hadn't done anything to garner positive lately.

"You know where everything is?"

Another nod, no other verbal response. Seriously, who was this guy? Some kind of monk? Only allowed a certain number of words a day?

She didn't have time to think about it. She had to do the dead-man-walking trek to Franks's office.

The door was open, but she knocked anyway. She'd never been taken to task before, but she knew. She just knew.

"Yes?" Captain barked.

"You wanted to see me?"

"Camden. Yes. Come in. Close the door."

Nope. Not good. But she did it, because, as with a lot of things, what choice did she have?

"We've had a few rumblings after last week."

"Last week, sir?"

"You disappeared fifteen minutes before your shift was over. And you're behind two reports from last week, as well."

Tess tried to swallow the mortification so it didn't show on her face. "I'll have the reports turned in tonight before I leave."

"Good. Good." Captain Franks ran a hand over his balding head, looking moderately uncomfortable which was rare. "I know your father is...sick."

But because she declined to say exactly what kind of sick, there was skepticism. She hated this treading-water feeling that was creeping up on her. Dad was getting worse and her life was starting to suffer. But the water kept lapping at her mouth, and she couldn't find a way to swim toward the shore.

"It's been a rough month. I'll get it under control, Captain. I just…we don't have anyone else." She didn't entertain tears, or her voice breaking, though both battled for prominence. Luckily she had a lot of practice fighting those things into submission.

"I know, Camden. You're an excellent officer, but we're also seeing our crime rates rise with the Dee's Factory closing, and I need to know my men are on top of things."

"I am. I am."

"No more disappearing then. No matter how close to the end of your shift. No more late reports. I don't want to have to write you up, but I can't let things slide just because…"

Because she was a woman. Because her whole life was spinning plates on poles and she was so damn tired of spinning. But what other choice did she have? "Absolutely."

"Have the reports in tonight."

She nodded. The reports were both nearly done, but she'd had to leave them unfinished last night when Dad had called, not making any sense, minutes from getting himself arrested or worse.

"If things get really bad, you can always consider

taking a leave of absence, but you can't slack off when you're here."

"I understand. It won't happen again."

"That's good to hear, Camden. How's our new officer?"

"Good. Quiet, but seems to know what's what."

"Good." Franks nodded to the door. "I have every confidence you'll train him right."

Tess nodded back and headed for the door. For some reason, Captain's confidence only made her feel worse. The man had given her more praise in a dressing-down than her father had in years, and yet she was risking this to keep her father out of trouble.

He doesn't mean it.

Tess closed the door behind her and forced stiff legs down the hall. Once she turned the corner, she leaned her forehead against the wall, her eyes squeezing shut.

She had to find some answers, or she had to let whatever happened to Dad…happen.

You can't do that. Not when he's the way he is because of you.

She hated that voice in her head. Because it was lies. Irrational lies. Mom had left because, well, who knew? But no matter how obnoxious a kid Tess had been, neither she nor her father had deserved being deserted.

It wasn't Tess's fault.

Why couldn't you be a good little girl, Tessie? Why'd she have to leave because of you?

She hated that voice, too. Dad drunk and weeping. Shoveling all the blame on her shoulders. It wasn't her fault. It wasn't. But the guilt, no matter how irrational, plagued her. She'd been seven when he'd first said that to her, and she'd done everything she could to make it not true.

Twenty-some years later, it was still true in her father's eyes, and even when she was able to remind herself it was all crap, the fact of the matter was, Dad had no one else. So what could she do?

She let out a long breath. Just like always, she was the only one who could find an answer, fix things. And, just like always, she would. She had since she was that seven-year-old girl. She pushed away from the wall, straightened and then cringed when she saw Santino standing a few feet away.

"Bad meeting?" he asked, sounding almost sympathetic.

San Francisco really had some timing, didn't he? "No. It was fine. I've got some reports to finish up real quick. Is it asking too much if we stick around for a few minutes? Thirty, tops. You can order some dinner, on me. Use the gym. Walk around."

He shrugged, which she couldn't read. Was he put out? Okay with it? She sighed. "I'm finishing up reports. You want to see how we do it?"

"Sure."

Want to say more than one word? Have emotions of any kind? Small talk like we're colleagues? Oh, she was cranky and she knew it, but seriously, the guy could give a little, couldn't he?

She marched to the computer room and plopped on a chair. She brought the computer to life and went through the report, how they did them, when they were due. Every last boring detail as she transcribed the rest of the events from her two incidents into the system.

"Any questions, San Francisco?"

"I'm not answering to that anymore."

"Why not? It's a hell of a lot better than some of the other nicknames I could come up with."

"California is a hellhole."

She snorted. "Do you have a secret sense of humor in there?"

"Nope."

"I think you're lying." She sent her reports to the printer. Maybe the guy was just shy. Even after three days. She'd have to work on him some more.

"Camden."

Tess looked back at Berkley and Granger standing in the doorway. "What's up, guys?"

"We wanted to meet the new guy. Had to thank him since we're not the rookies anymore."

"He's still got a bunch more experience under his belt than you two dipshits." She nodded to Marc. "Santino. This is Berkley. Granger. They're full of shit. Don't believe anything they say. Ever."

"Aw, come on. We're not that bad."

She smiled at Berkley. Even though they made

her feel old. Kids ten years her junior were wearing badges now. She felt motherly toward them. Might as well start walking with a cane.

"Franks rip you a new one?"

"Nah, he loves me." She tried to smile, but with Marc looking at her so seriously and her phone buzzing—which was pretty much only ever Dad on a bender or someone calling about Dad on a bender—she mostly felt sick.

What she needed was to be around people. Not go back to her place and be alone, because when she was alone, all the guilt twisted until she couldn't stop herself. She'd help Dad and screw herself in the process.

"Shit." Granger grumbled about reverse sexism but it was mostly just a buzz in Tess's head.

She needed a distraction. She needed to not be alone. Which was usually when she organized a department outing. That's exactly what she needed. Dipshits complaining about her preferential treatment and making her feel old. Much better than dealing with Dad.

"Hey, you guys busy tonight?"

"Never too busy for you, sweetheart."

"Screw off, Granger. We're having a get-to-know-the-new-guy get-together at Good Wolf. See who else can go, huh? Meet up at eight."

"Sure."

She turned to Marc, determined not to care that he was scowling and obviously not happy that she'd created some fictional get-to-know-him event. The department had to be a family, and she needed a distraction so she didn't screw up work with Dad again. Lucky for Marc, he was her new distraction.

THERE WERE A LOT of ways Marc could play this and not have to go. A lot of ways, and yet every time he thought of one, he inevitably thought about the look on Tess's face when he'd found her after her meeting with the captain.

Lost.

It was uncomfortable, the urge to help that surged through him. It had always been uncomfortable, and that's why he'd gone into police work. You could help without being too involved. The badge, the uniform, it all got to be a barrier.

You didn't have to get wrapped up in someone else's problems and lose sight of everything else in the process. You got to fix what you could fix under the law and move on. Not be constantly stewing in things you had no control over.

That barrier was kind of there with this, but not enough for his liking. It all felt too personal. Going for drinks with a bunch of people he didn't know. All because he couldn't say no to a woman who was his FTO and, as far as he could tell, a bit of a mess.

She did command a certain amount of respect around the station though. Even with the asshole "sweetheart" comment, people seemed to look at her and see fellow officer first, female second.

There weren't a lot of guys who had felt that way at his last department. Still, respect or not, he didn't want to go hang out at a bar with a bunch of people he didn't know. Even if they were going to be his colleagues. Bars, laughter, people. He hadn't done much of that. He'd always been so focused on doing what needed to be done, what was expected of him.

What might garner him some love and attention.

Yeah, well, even if he had moved here at his parents' directive, it didn't mean he was that same young kid desperate for their attention.

He scrubbed a hand over his face before shrugging into his jacket. This was his new life. Fresh start. No one knew him here. He didn't have to be all closed off and stoic. Didn't have to toe the line. Mom and Dad were a whole state away and that wasn't changing for months.

And it wouldn't matter when they got here. They'd be so wrapped up in Leah and her boyfriend, the fucking amazing Jacob, what Marc did wouldn't matter.

Never had. Wasn't going to change.

Christ. Maybe a bar was exactly what he needed.

And what about Tess?

He yanked his door open. It didn't matter if she was pretty. If his body had some different idea of her than his brain did. Because his body was kind of interested in her body. His mind? It found her irritating as hell. Besides, she was practically his superior.

Three days. He'd been at work three days, with

a two-day break in between, and he was already screwed up. That was impressive, even for him.

"Thought you'd chicken out."

He glanced up from locking his door to see Tess leaning against the rail at the top of the staircase. She'd changed. Jeans, long-sleeved T-shirt, leather jacket slung over her shoulder. Her hair was still pulled back, but in a looser way than it had been when she'd been in uniform.

There was nothing sexy about it. Nothing. But *sexy* was the first word that popped into his head anyway. Something about her heavy top lip, the look in her eyes, the sly smile on her face. As if she was queen of the world and she knew it.

Trouble. Plain and simple. He'd never done anything remotely resembling trouble. Was that why it seemed so enticing?

"Not exactly my first choice of evening activities."

"Really? What would be?" She started walking down the stairs and he followed.

His gaze strayed to her ass, the jeans she wore perfectly molded to—*nope*.

"Let me guess. Something that requires silence? Meditation? Building creepy serial-killer shrines."

"I'm not creepy."

"You're not exactly Mr. Warm and Friendly."

"Quiet doesn't equal serial killer."

"But it can."

"I'm a cop."

"It doesn't make us perfect."

"Why am I doing this?"

She stopped at an old, junky sedan, jamming her key into the door. "I don't know. Why are you doing this?"

"You seemed…" It was probably too direct to admit the truth, but he wasn't very good at white lies. He could keep his mouth shut, but he didn't lie well when faced with a direct question. "Like you needed it."

That queen-of-the-world expression disappeared, replaced by confusion. A hard-edged, brows-together confusion he didn't want to mess with. "What do you care what I need?"

"I don't. Or shouldn't."

"Superhero complex." She shook her head as if that was a bad thing. "You gonna ride with me or what?"

"Need a sober driver or something?"

"I don't get drunk."

"Ever?"

"Nope. Besides, we have an early morning."

"So why are we doing this?" His shoulders were already tense from all this back-and-forth. How was he getting pulled into this verbal sparring? He never did that.

"You need to understand, I don't know how your old department was, but here we're a family. We have to trust each other. We don't have to all be best friends, but we need to know that if someone gets in a jam, someone else is going to be there backing us up. Being the quiet guy in the corner isn't going to fly."

He understood that, to an extent. In his rookie days he hadn't gone out and partied like most of the guys he'd gone to the academy with. He didn't step out of line. Not one drinking-and-driving incident, hell, not even a speeding or parking violation. Even if he'd gotten one, he would have paid it rather than flash his badge.

He believed in right and wrong. Because doing the right thing would be noticed and rewarded.

Joke's on you.

But he'd been friendlier then. Smiled more. Hoping for some kind of belonging that had never materialized. No one liked a guy who wouldn't bend the loosest of rules.

"Getting in or what, Captain Quiet?"

"Captain Quiet?"

"It's my superhero name for you."

"I'm not answering to that, either." But he got into her glorified rust bucket. Why? A million reasons that didn't make sense. At least not without some deep introspection he wasn't in the mood for.

"That one suits you, though. You'd probably even look good in a pair of superhero tights."

He frowned over at her as she pulled out of the parking lot. Was she...flirting?

He didn't have much time to ponder. The Good Wolf, an old, dilapidated place on the riverfront, was a short drive from their apartment complex. It was brick on the outside, showing its age, a vintage neon sign buzzing Open in the big window.

Inside it was dark and smoky, but not as dingy as he'd expected. Tess waved to a couple other guys and suddenly he was being introduced, maneuvered into a seat, beer placed in front of him.

Social hour. He was so damn rusty with this he felt like an awkward teenager again. But Tess didn't let him stay that way for long. She prodded him into a long, drawn-out conversation about the old Superman movies.

Then she foisted him off on a middle-aged guy who turned out to be all right once they found some common ground talking cars. Still, Marc found himself watching Tess even as he chatted and drank.

She was an odd figure. A leader of sorts, but more like a mother. Which was a weird thing, because half the guys were her age or older. Weirder still because he didn't think most of the guys staring at her ass thought of her as a mother hen.

But she stepped in. Cut a guy off when he'd hit his limit, separated one of the young guys from a clearly uninterested woman. Every time Marc thought he escaped her notice, she pushed him into conversations about cars with one guy, baseball with another.

She was everywhere, subtly maneuvering people away from what they shouldn't do and toward what they should. It was all kind of mesmerizing.

"She doesn't fuck cops."

Marc jerked his head toward one of the guys from

earlier who was leaning against the table next to him. Granger. He'd been the first one she'd had to cut off, and he wasn't falling-over drunk but definitely impaired.

Marc kept his tone bland even though the out-of-nowhere comment pissed him off. For a lot of reasons. "Excuse me?"

"You're staring awful hard at our Camden." Granger gestured to where Tess was laughing with two older guys, covertly handing off their not-empty drinks to a waitress. "The thing is, every single guy in the department, and probably some of the not-so-single ones, have tried and failed. She doesn't fuck other cops."

"Not why I was watching her, pal."

"Chill, man." He held up his hands. "Not trying to warn you off, just giving some information. We're all friends here."

"So I've noticed."

Granger slapped the table. "Keep it in mind."

Marc rolled his shoulders. The kid, and he was just a kid, was right. Friends. He needed to make friends. Sure, not lifelong buddies, and certainly not anything involving fucking, but it wouldn't kill him to remove the stick from his ass.

He was free. Until Mom and Dad moved, but even then. He'd already done his duty by moving here. Leah was back in their lives. Why was he still trying so hard? He didn't matter. Never would.

It was long past time he started living for himself.

CHAPTER THREE

TESS WAS IN TROUBLE. Of two very different kinds. Sadly, they both involved drunk men she felt responsible for.

The first she was going to ignore. She had to. She had to be up early and couldn't risk another bottle-throwing incident on a work night. At some point, once in a while, she had to put herself first.

The second bit of trouble, well, she was 100 percent responsible for the second, and kind of enjoying it. Typically, she didn't like drunk men, but she'd also been around enough to know everyone handled their liquor differently.

Some got belligerent, like many of the drunk drivers she dealt with on the job. Some got violent. Hello, dear old Dad. Some, well, some just got goofy. Buttoned-up, strong silent type Marc Santino got goofy.

It made her grin, and feel oddly light. Both things her father's drunkenness never made her feel. Everything about Marc's normally tense, ramrod straight posture had relaxed. He was smiling, head bobbing along with whatever Stumpf was telling him.

He did shake off an offer for another beer, which was more than half the guys in their little group would ever do. Which was why she tended to spearhead these little gatherings and moderate some of the looser cannons.

Most were making noise about leaving, so she made sure none of the worse-for-wear guys were planning on getting behind the wheel, then she approached trouble. Hot trouble, which was nothing to smile about at all.

But she couldn't help herself. "You ready to get going, San Francisco?"

"You know, Mother Hen, which is my new nickname for you, I have never even been to California." He didn't slur, but his words, his demeanor, were all loose. So different from usual.

"I thought you said it was a hellhole."

"Seems like it would be, anyway. Can't even pay their own damn bills."

"Yes, Grandpa. Now let's get you up and out."

"I can walk." He got to his feet. No weaving or tripping, but there was a difference in his gait. Not that measured, stiff walk he usually had. This walk was a lot more wiggly.

But he followed her, and even though he was definitely inebriated, he watched her as she made sure the rest of the guys were out the door, too, and she got the weirdest feeling he was silently judging her for it.

Well, let him. He'd obviously come from a department where having each other's backs was not important. That was not how BCPD worked. Period.

Her phone buzzed and she closed her eyes for a second before slipping into her car. Maybe when they got home she'd call Dad and try to talk him down, but she wasn't giving in and going over there, and she certainly wasn't talking to him with Marc in the car next to her.

"So, what were you and Stumpf talking about?"

"Aliens," he said, deadpan.

"You were not."

"Oh, yes. He was trying to convince me he's seen a UFO. To which I said N-O."

Tess laughed and shook her head. "I hate to encourage drinking, but you're a lot funnier with a few under your belt."

"Maybe that's been my problem all along."

Her first instinct was to poke and prod and figure out what problem he thought he had. She liked to fix problems. But something about the way he looked grim and stiff again made her clamp her mouth shut as she pulled into their apartment complex parking lot.

Her phone buzzed. Again. She didn't bother to look this time. Just clicked the ignore button through her pocket.

She should have turned off the phone. Sure, it wouldn't stop Dad from calling, but it would stop her from the stab of guilt after each ring.

"Seriously, what's the constant calling about?"

Marc asked, gesturing at her pocket as he walked leisurely toward the door.

When she laughed, he squinted at her and his hand missed the handle of the complex door. "What're you laughing at?"

"Aboot."

"Huh?"

She giggled again. "Your Minnesota shows when you're drunk."

"I'm not drunk! I've never been drunk in my life." He stepped inside and then promptly tripped over the mat, barely catching himself on the wall.

"Never?" She offered Marc her shoulder and he grumbled something before using her as a bit of a steady crutch on their way up the stairs.

"Not once. Didn't even touch a drop until I was twenty-one. I am a perfect citizen through and through."

"You really are a superhero."

"The world loves superheroes. They have women and families falling all over them telling them how great they are. Well, when their parents aren't dead. Still, I am no superhero."

Oh, don't have hidden hurts. Please don't have hidden hurts. She was such a sucker for hurts of any kind. She wanted to soothe. Then there was the whole fact Marc was all muscle. Yummy, chiseled muscle leaning against her.

That leaning was enough to bring a little sanity into the equation. She couldn't juggle someone else who needed to lean on her. Dad took all her be-someone-else's-rock strength.

So she gave Marc a nudge so he leaned, with an ungraceful thud, against his door.

He squinted down at her, and even with the squint and the slightly glazed-over eyes, the color had impact. He had impact, and she did not have the time or energy to be impacted.

But there were certain parts of her body not getting that memo.

"Sleep it off, buddy. You don't want me storming your gates in the morning, because it won't be late and I won't be nice."

His gaze dropped. A quick, odd, up-and-down once-over. The kind she usually got in a guy's face for, but because he was drunk and that was kind of her fault, she let it go.

Totally had nothing to do with the fact she liked it from him. *You are one sick puppy, Camden.*

"Drink some water. Take some aspirin and get some sleep, Captain Quiet."

"Night, Mother Hen."

She gave him a mock salute and then walked to her apartment and slipped inside. She pulled out her phone. Twelve missed calls. Six voice mails. All from Dad.

It took a lot of willpower. A lot of thinking about her meeting with Franks earlier today to delete the messages unheard. She knew what they'd be. The first would be sweet, ending in crying. Increasingly belligerent with each message.

She got enough of him calling her a bitch to her face—she didn't have to deal with it via message. Not tonight.

Are you sure you want to delete all messages?

She stared at the little pop-up, not sure for how long, then clicked yes with more force than necessary. He would not get her in trouble again. Police work was the only thing she could count on in this life, and no amount of crappy guilt or biological duty was going to make her screw that up.

MARC STARED AT the coffeepot slowly spitting out dark liquid. Scowling was probably a better word. Glowering.

He felt like utter shit. Head pounding, dizzy, queasy. All from a few too many beers and one weird cocktail Stumpf had talked him into. How did all those people who'd rolled their eyes at his two-beer limit over the years enjoy this?

The pounding at the door made him wince, then growl. Then groan because, damn it, that all hurt.

The pounding started again. Moving gingerly, Marc walked to the door and jerked it open. "Do. You. Mind?"

Tess's sunny smile only served to irritate him further. "Morning, sunshine." She was in her uniform, like he was, and her hair was back in that tight work braid. Which reminded him of how loose it had been last night, how tight her jeans had—

"I'm just waiting for coffee," he grumbled, turning away from her. "No thanks to you, I feel like I'm going to die."

"Hey, I didn't force-feed you any of those beers. Didn't buy you any, either."

"It was whatever concoction Stumpf convinced me to drink. I'm sure of it. But I wouldn't have been there to drink it if not for you." He poured his coffee into a travel mug before flipping off the coffeemaker and unplugging it.

"Sorry our welcome was so unwelcome."

He turned to face her and found her looking around his living room. "Sparse. Stark. Why am I not surprised?"

"Am I going to come home some day when we're not in each other's pockets to find you've mother henned your way into sneaking throw pillows on my couch and frilly curtains in the window?"

She laughed, a full-bodied, sexy laugh.

This attraction thing was getting really annoying.

"If you ever see my apartment, you'll know why that's laughable. Now, can we get going, or what?"

"I'm not late."

"We will be if you keep chitchatting."

"I'm never late."

"Never late. Never drunk. Boy Scout Captain Quiet to the rescue."

"You're irritating in the morning."

"You're hungover."

"You were irritating yesterday morning." She would be irritating every morning. What with the cheery demeanor, smug grin and smelling-like-flowers shit.

And he talked too much around her, under the influence or not. That needed to stop. So he waved her out of his apartment, grabbing his utility belt, going into his closet and unlocking his gun safe.

Tess, of course, watched instead of shooing out like he'd asked her to.

"Man, I know a lot of cops who own a lot of guns and I've never seen anyone keep them locked away like you do. Code *and* key?"

"Safety."

She shook her head, finally taking that stupid flower smell with her as she stepped into the hallway. "I'm pretty well versed in gun safety. That, my friend, is what we call gun paranoia."

"Well, you and my sister can share your penchant for unlocked firearms sometime. I will remain staunchly prosafety."

"You have a sister, huh?" She side-eyed him as they walked down the stairs.

Talked. Too. Damn. Much. Why did she have that effect on him? No one had ever had that effect on him. Top-heavy mouth, queen-of-the-world attitude, really amazing ass or no. He was a bastion of silence.

She was screwing that all up and it had only been about a week.

She slid into the patrol car and he placed his travel mug in the console before attaching his gun belt and sliding into the passenger seat.

Just had to get through today and then he got a break from her. Then four more days until he'd at least have his own car, even if she was there. He hated this two-week watch thing BCPD did. He wanted to be behind the wheel. In charge. Maybe then he would feel as though he had some control, because today, with headache pounding and mentioning Leah, all he felt like was a helpless…amoeba.

"So, what's she like?"

"Who?"

"Your sister. I always wanted one, and I can't picture you doing a lot of playing with a sister. Although, in fairness, I can't picture you as a kid."

"Leah and I didn't do a lot of playing."

"Big age difference?"

"No."

"You're too macho and manly to have played with girls?"

"No." He squeezed the coffee cup and lifted it to his lips. He wouldn't engage. Not on this. He was not elaborating on his pathetic family situation.

She picked up the radio, seeming to have given up on him explaining. "Ten forty-one," she said into the speaker.

Now they were officially at work, which meant he

was officially not thinking about her mouth in any way aside from official officer-to-officer…mouth things.

He focused on the window. He drank his coffee and kept his mouth otherwise firmly shut. She whistled, off tune, to some terrible '80s power ballad in between answering some minor calls.

Luckily his headache subsided, the sloshing in his stomach abated. He felt almost human by lunchtime.

Just as they were about to take lunch, a call came through the radio. "Domestic disturbance at the Meadowview apartment complex on East Main. Front yard. One of the participants is armed."

Her whole demeanor changed. Granted, so far all the day shift calls they'd run together had been easy, nonthreatening. A fender bender. Blown-out tire blocking the road. Disturbances with weapons were a lot more serious, so it made some sense, but there was something about her expression that made him wonder.

She clutched the radio. "En route." She flicked a glance at him then back at the road as she turned around. "When we get there, I'm going to need you to field this one," she said, a kind of steely, grave note where usually nothing but ease lilted.

"Not that I'm complaining, because I have been a cop for almost as long as you." He shifted, trying to get a read on her expression. "But why the sudden change of heart about my week of just watching?"

She flipped on the siren, eyes and mouth grim. "Because it's my father's apartment complex."

Marc didn't have a clue what to say to that, so he didn't say anything. Since she didn't seem surprised and was having him handle it, it meant she thought her father was involved, and since she didn't seem panicked, he had to guess her father was the one armed.

Yeah, really didn't know what to say about that, so he just watched the road and tried to figure out how he was supposed to handle the armed father of his FTO.

CHAPTER FOUR

TESS TRIED TO keep her limbs steady and her expression strong and impenetrable as she pulled onto the street in front of her father's place. A crowd had gathered in the tiny parking lot, and Tess's stomach turned.

This was bad. Like high school when Dad had been locked up for three days bad and she'd been so sure that was it. She was on her own. Forever.

"I'll handle it."

Odd that Marc's calm assertion was a touch comforting. She couldn't remember anything ever being handled for her. Ever.

Which also made it uncomfortable. But there wasn't enough time to analyze her feelings here. Not enough time to do much of anything except lean over and lay a hand on Marc's arm before he could get all the way out of the car.

He waited, eyes resting on her face. Serious and unreadable, the exact expression she was trying to affect and probably failing at.

"If…if possible, see if you can talk everyone out of filing charges."

He paused, then gave a curt nod and was gone, disappearing into the crowd.

Tess tried to breathe through the panic swirling in her gut. This was her dad and she was letting some guy she barely knew take care of it. Some guy she'd practically had to browbeat into introducing himself to the department.

How could she do that?

Because right now, she wasn't Thomas Camden's daughter, she was a police officer. The fact she had no doubt it was her father out there, drunk and armed and so damn out of control, meant her objectivity was skewed and she had to be strong enough to keep herself out of the equation.

Why can't you help me, Tessie?

Tess had to squeeze her eyes shut against her father's imploring voice. He did that so well, sounding like someone in desperate need of help, a help he refused to see he had to give himself.

But the way he pleaded, desperate and sad, always pulled against reason, coiled around her heart until her brain shut off.

Sometimes she thought she was as bad as he was. Sometimes she was certain of it.

She watched the clock, counted seconds, did everything to keep herself from pushing out there. She would not be able to go out there and handle things the way they needed to be handled, because no amount of armor would make her not that man's daughter.

She was bound to him, to this, and if there were any way out she would have found it by now.

The finality, the heavy, depressing realization was too much. She had to get out of the car. She had to act. Because if she didn't, she'd cry, on the job, and that was worse than losing her objectivity.

The crowd had dispersed somewhat, and Marc was standing in between her weaving father and a skinny young man who had drug user and/or dealer written all over him.

Tess's stomach sank farther. Dad had only gotten into drugs once, and it had been bad. Lately things had been bad. But how would she have missed that? She would've picked up the signs, the signals.

"I can search you if you'd like," Marc said equitably to the jumpy guy while Dad stood, arms crossed over his chest, face mottled red.

"He attacked me!"

"Witnesses say you started—"

The moron started swearing, but one hard look from Marc and he was swearing his way across the yard and to the door on the corner of the building.

"That little punk stole from me. I want what's mine," Dad demanded.

"I think you've had enough excitement for one day, Mr. Camden. He may have started it, but witnesses weren't singing your praises, either. You did have a deadly weapon."

"It's a butter knife." Dad stumbled toward Marc. "I want it back, you thief!"

"Dad."

Her father jerked, bobbled as he turned to face her. He scrunched his face up at her uniform. "I thought I told you not to come here like that, Tessie."

"I've told you not to have cause for any of us to come here." She took his arm, forcing herself to look at Marc in the most professional way she could muster. "No charges?"

He merely shook his head.

"Then I'll get him inside. Be back in five." Tess forced herself to act like a police officer, not like a daughter. She was in uniform, and she would make sure he got inside and didn't have anything in his apartment and then...they'd go right back to work.

No tears. No guilt. No pain. This just was what it was.

Marc didn't say anything, he just looked at her. With that hooded, unreadable expression. Then his gaze dropped to her arm and she knew he was putting two and two together. He wasn't the strong silent type because he didn't know what to say—it was because he sat back and watched and understood uncomfortable truths.

Her father was the source of the gash on her arm last week. A purposeful, violent outburst. And here Tess was helping the man who'd physically attacked her—a whole lot more than once. She refused to let the quiver of self-disgust into her voice. "I'll be back in five."

He nodded, then handed her the butter knife,

handle first. It took a few seconds for her brain to engage enough to take it, but when she did, he headed for the patrol car without a word. Tess swallowed down the tears and led her father back to his apartment.

"Why can't you fix this, Tessie? Why can't you make it all right?"

She wished she had a clue.

MARC HADN'T KNOWN what to say the rest of the day, and one thing the incident with her father had done was shut up Ms. Chatty Pants.

He wished he could feel glad about that, but there was an uncomfortable weight in his gut. The weight of knowing Tess was every bit the mess he'd expected, and instead of being able to judge her for it, he felt sorry for her.

Her own father was not only a total ass, he'd hurt her. After witnessing the violence in the man this afternoon, Marc had no doubt the broken-glass excuse was bullshit. Tess's father had hurt her on purpose.

It made him sick, and he didn't know what to do about that. He'd seen a lot of crappy things in his career, worse than a lousy father, worse even than an abusive one, but what little he knew about Tess and seeing the way she'd carefully helped her father back into his apartment—yeah, it really made him nauseous.

She pulled her patrol car up to the apartment complex and Marc still didn't know what to say. What he was supposed to do.

Maybe nothing. If he'd been the one in her place he'd want nothing except for her to pretend it had never happened. She hadn't said anything since aside from the basics that had to be said to get their job done for the day.

She stepped out of the car and he followed suit, stomach tightening uncomfortably in the face of a situation he had no idea what to do with. He tried to avoid that feeling at all costs. It had been such a damn constant growing up, he'd found all the ways to distance it from himself.

But none of his self-preservation instincts kicked in. He felt drawn to the feeling inside, into figuring out some way...some way to help.

This is not the kind of thing you fix.

He knew way too much about those things.

They reached the top of the stairs and Tess slowed her pace as she pulled her keys out of her pocket. "Well, it was an interesting day." She didn't meet his gaze, which was unusual for her. This closed-off, shifty way of standing, looking. Discomfort.

"Yeah," he said, his voice coming out oddly hoarse as he stood by his door.

"Thanks." She finally met his gaze and the way she oozed embarrassment and pain had him stepping toward her. For what? He had no idea.

"Anyway, good night." She gave a little nod, looking at the floor, but the slumped posture and the defeat in her spine made him act against every sensible thought in his head.

"Tess." He didn't reach out to her, but that's what he wanted to do. Why the hell did he want to do that?

"The fact of the matter is I'm going to have a good cry, and if you don't want me to do that all over your shoulder, you better get in your apartment ASAP." She tried to smile, but it wobbled and the tears were already shimmering in her eyes.

Yes, he should get inside the safety of his apartment. He wanted nothing to do with a crying woman who was his coworker and kind of flinging her life all over his. Her this-precinct-is-a-family edicts and this stuff with her father and making him talk when he normally wouldn't and…everything.

But he didn't move to his door. Instead he reached out and touched her shoulder, because there was only so much visceral pain he could see in someone else without trying to help.

Not at all smoothly, he pulled her into a hug. He figured it'd be awkward. In the grand scheme of things, he'd never found hugging people anything but awkward.

But she leaned into his shoulder, resting her head there, her fists trapped between his chest and her collarbone. Her breath hitching occasionally.

He wasn't sure anyone had ever cried on his shoulder before. In particularly tragic situations he dealt with at work, he'd occasionally offer a hand, a shoulder pat, something solid to hold them up.

But never like this.

"A pity hug from you. I am pathetic." But she didn't pull away—she sniffled into his shoulder, and it was such a strange sensation. Holding and comforting someone he barely knew. He couldn't remember the last time he'd done this for someone he *did* know.

"How long has he been like that?"

She stiffened. A question she didn't want to answer, and inevitably the question that got her to pull herself together and step away.

Because the impulse to touch her face, wipe away the tears there, was shockingly strong, he shoved his hands into his pockets. There was something all wrong about this whole exchange, and it wasn't her crying or pulling away. It was him. His reaction to it. The wanting to understand and fix wasn't unique; he felt that a lot.

But he never felt compelled to act. Never acted against the voice in his head telling him to put up a barrier or step away. He had learned his lesson from childhood, damn it.

"Look, um, thanks. Really." She wiped her face with her palms, let out a shaky breath as she looked around. "Can't say I've ever broken down in a hallway before."

"Where do you usually do your breaking down?"

"Alone."

Christ.

"But those big broad football shoulders are good

for crying on." She ran her fingertips down his chest, and this was a completely inappropriate time to think of anything sexual, but he could not force himself to be appropriate.

She pulled her hand away and the way she looked at him, he had to wonder if she felt it, too. The little zing of heat and inappropriate attraction.

She took a full step back, eyebrows drawing together. "Anyway. Hopefully you won't be put in that position again. It isn't...normal."

"It isn't?"

The vulnerable bafflement on her face immediately changed, blanked. "Enjoy your day off tomorrow, Marc. You earned it."

"I only did my job."

She cocked her head. "You did a little more than that, Captain Quiet."

Before he could argue with the obnoxious moniker again, she stepped inside her apartment and shut the door.

He found himself here far too often, wanting to understand more, with a door shut in his face. When he should feel nothing but relief, he felt the exact opposite.

CHAPTER FIVE

TESS SCOOTED FARTHER down into the cooling bath-water. It was her day off and she didn't want to face it. So much so, she'd taken a bath, something she almost never did. Infrequently enough she didn't even have bubbles. She'd squirted some shower gel in there and now she was lounging in tepid, bubble-less water.

It seemed terribly appropriate.

At least she didn't have to face Marc. Small mercies. Her embarrassment wasn't likely to fade anytime soon, but maybe she could get a better handle on it with a day in between sitting in a car with him for eight hours.

Eight long hours knowing he'd seen through her so easily. All the bravado, all the work she'd done to create this persona, and it'd only taken her father threatening someone with a butter knife and her asking Marc to keep people from pressing charges.

Marc saw her for what she was. A scared little girl with daddy issues so wide no submarine could cross.

She thought about the way she'd cried all over his shoulder then commented on the broadness of said shoulders. It was so out of character. At the very least when she flirted with a guy she didn't do it in the middle of a good cry.

And she did not flirt with cops. Attraction didn't matter. She'd seen enough to know if she got together with one cop, all the hard work she'd put into building her reputation would be for nothing. It was rare these days someone rolled their eyes at her simply for her gender.

She wasn't undoing all that work for an impressive chest. Except she'd already done it with tears and Dad.

It *was* an impressive chest. What was the harm in a little fantasy when he wasn't here, and she was in the bath, and—

Nope. Whole lotta harm. Because she had to share a damn patrol car with the guy for weeks upon unending weeks, and she did not need actual fantasies in her head.

Which was enough impetus to get her out of the bathtub. The only problem was—now what? She should go see Dad, check his place for signs of drugs, figure out what was going on.

She should. She should. What else might he do if she didn't?

I don't care. I don't care. I don't care.

She was over the crying and the hurting. So she'd do the only thing that ever helped that—run her ass off.

She pulled on her running gear and slipped her

apartment key in her shoe. She purposefully left her phone on the kitchen counter, strapped her MP3 player to her arm and stepped into the hallway.

There was Marc.

Well, hell.

She mustered her best I-did-not-wipe-snot-on-your-shirt-last-night smile.

"Morning."

"Um, morning." He cleared his throat, looking around the hallway at everything but her. "I was, um, going for a run."

She could see that. Despite the cool March temperatures, he was in shorts. Showing off legs. Long, muscular, powerful, strong legs. A whole lotta adjectives for legs.

She had to stop looking at his legs. "I was, too." Run till her brain exploded. Hopefully her libido, as well. But not in the fun way.

"Ah." He nodded, looking at some point behind her on the wall.

"Yeah." She scratched her head, pointed awkwardly at the stairs. "Um, after you."

He gave one of those little Marc nods. She could not think of anyone else who could pull off that terse, distanced demeanor and still be something of a marshmallow on the inside.

Marc Santino had hugged her while she'd cried last night even after she'd given him a total out. No getting around that marshmallow move. Which was not something she had a lot of experience with. Which meant she should be wary, not interested.

"I should...get to it."

Tess nodded. *Not interested. Not interested. Not interested.* Her eyeballs weren't getting the message, because they were homed in on his butt as he walked down the stairs in front of her. Granted, in the loose athletic shorts she couldn't get a good butt vantage point, but she'd seen it plenty in his uniform pants.

And had apparently unwittingly committed to brain space that it seemed very tight and firm and— *yikes.*

He paused at the bottom of the stairs. "Do you know any good...running routes?" He was so stiff and uncomfortable, not making any eye contact.

Tess gave up. "Pretending last night didn't happen is way more awkward than acknowledging it."

"I wouldn't bet on it," he muttered.

"Well, maybe it's just as awkward, but you're being too weird. I can't take it."

"How am I being weird?"

"You're staring at a light fixture."

His frown deepened and he purposefully moved his gaze to her. And, *zowie*, she needed to stop dwelling in Attraction Land. But his eyes were all light brown and mesmerizing and...

Briefly, his gaze dropped, not to the floor, but more like boobs, floor, then quickly back to her face. Wait. Had he just checked her out?

Oh, they were in some trouble.

Focus on the running thing. Now. "I usually run down the waterfront then up the bluff. There's a path, pretty secluded without being creepy and a nice view."

"That's got to be at least four miles."

"Run until your legs fall off." She forced a sassy smirk. "Surely you can handle it?" Because there was no doubt about Marc being in fantastic shape. His T-shirt was loose enough in the stomach area, but around those arms? And the shoulders, perfect for snot crying?

Yeah, she had ample view of his shapes.

She seriously, *seriously* needed to cool the heck off. "You're welcome to follow along if you want. Unless four miles is too many for you."

Again he did the little boob-floor-back-to-face look, and if she wasn't totally warped, she could swear his cheeks were a pinch pink. As if he was blushing.

Anyone else, she might adjust her sports bra right there and give him something to really blush about. But no cops. Especially not ones with marshmallow centers.

"All right," he finally said, gesturing toward the door. "After you."

She forced a sunny smile and sauntered out the door. No, she wasn't sauntering. She was walking. Like a normal human being.

Swaying those hips like you want him to stare at your ass.

Okay, that, too. She kicked her leg out behind her, pulled her toes up to her butt. "Do you stretch beforehand?"

When she glanced over her shoulder, she saw him still standing in the doorway. Until the door smacked him because he hadn't been paying attention. *You will not bend over and touch your toes. You. Will. Not.*

But, oh, it was tempting. A hell of a lot more fun than trying to run her conflicted thoughts about Dad away.

But also way more dangerous. She wasn't into danger. She was into finding a way to build some kind of stability in her life.

Ha. Ha.

Marc stood to her side, where she couldn't really watch him stretch. Which was probably by design.

They stretched in silence, and it was hard work to maintain the silence. Just like she couldn't stand his weird awkwardness, she was no good with his distancing silence.

She was no good with all of it. *Maybe you're just no good.*

"Ready?" she asked, eager to run that asshole voice in her head to the ground.

TESS'S PONYTAIL BOUNCED. She bounced. Every spandex-clad inch of her. This was some circle of hell. Run with the hot woman in spandex who is your FTO and also going through emotional shit you want nothing to do with. Circle five? Had to be higher than that.

Once he'd tried to get ahead of her, but she'd taken it as a challenge and never let him pass.

So he had to run behind her on the narrow path and try to focus on trees and shit. They'd run down the waterfront and up the bluff, and Marc slowed as a familiar house came into view.

"Don't tell me you're running out of steam."

He looked at the big fancy house along the bluff. He'd only been here once, and it had been a weird visit. Christmastime. Mom harassing Leah and him stepping in. One of those rare moments with Leah when he couldn't hold on to his usual detachment. "That's where my sister works."

"Oh, yeah?" She stopped her running, bending to one side and then the other. Spandex. Ass. Breasts. Spandex. Fucking damn it.

"Are you going to stop by and say hi?" she asked, completely unfazed that he was dying.

Saying hi to Leah was the absolute last thing he wanted to do. Scratch that, the last thing he wanted to do was keep jogging with an erection because Tess's ass in those spandex running pants was not fair.

Life was not fair.

"Yeah, um…" How did he phrase this so he made it clear that even if he did go say hi to Leah, he didn't want Tess tagging along? Doing it alone was bad enough—adding this woman to the mix had disaster written all over it.

"I'll go up to the top of the street, turn around. If you're not done by then, I'm sure you'll catch up or I'll just see you later."

"Yeah. Great."

She bent backward, fingertips splayed across her back, then bent farther, giving him an ample look down her shirt.

Abruptly, he turned toward MC Restoration's office. He wouldn't go to the big house—not all sweaty and...other things he was denying.

He'd knock on Leah's little workshop door, hope to God she wasn't there, and be on his merry way. Far away from the sight of Tess in spandex.

He refused to look back at Tess as he strode through the backyard of MC. He was focused on his destination. On safety. He knocked, held his breath and hoped no one answered.

"Marc?" Leah's eyes were wide as she opened the door. "Hey, is everything o—"

"Yeah, yeah, good. I was just out...running." He gestured toward the ring of sweat around his shirt collar. "Passed by and thought I should say hi, I guess."

Leah blinked at him, but then she smiled.

Which was conflicting. A part of him felt as though he should be making bigger strides in the big brother department. Trying to figure out some relationship they could have or maneuver that wouldn't be all heavy with what came before.

But Leah had spent too long as the driving factor of his life. Spending days on end in hospital waiting rooms, scrimping so Mom and Dad could pay off her medical bills, listening to bickering and arguments, trying to tread the waters of his parents' separation.

Then, when they got back together, doing everything in his power to be whatever they needed.

Most of that wasn't Leah's fault. Her health had been beyond her control, though her rebellious streak had landed her in the hospital more than necessary after her heart transplant. Which had also been the source of Mom and Dad's discontent and...

This, *this* was why he didn't seek out Leah. Even if she was the most wonderful person in the world, she made him think about things he'd much rather not think about.

"You sure everything is okay?"

"Yeah, sorry. I was kind of trying to avoid a weird situation."

"Weirder than this?"

"Ha. Maybe. I don't know." This was pretty weird, after all. He didn't know much about how to start conversations with Leah. Conversations that wouldn't irritate him or make him feel like crap, anyway.

"Well, come on in." Leah moved out of the doorway and into her little shed of a work area. It was a mess. Tools and light fixtures and wires everywhere. Not much room to move around, either.

"What exactly were you avoiding?" she asked, picking up a few wires and studying them.

"Just avoiding someone, and there your place was. So I said I needed to come say hi to you."

"Wow, you must have really wanted to avoid them. They trying to sell you something?"

"Oh, no, we live in the same apartment complex and were going for a run at the same time and she's nice, really, I just…it was…I'm not good with small talk."

Leah put the wires down, eyebrows raised. "She?"

Shit. "Well, yes. I work with her, actually. She's my field training officer." He didn't like the way Leah was looking at him, all considering, and he really didn't like the way he was fidgeting and the way his face was getting hot.

"What does field training officer mean?"

"Basically she's observing while I learn the ropes of a new department." Marc backed toward the door. Hopefully Tess would be out of sight by now and he could slip out and—

"Ah."

He scowled. "What does that *ah* mean?"

"Oh, nothing."

"Good."

But then Leah grinned. "Must be a Santino trait."

"What?"

"Lusting after the boss."

"She's not my boss." Shit. "And I'm not lusting. Also, please don't ever use that word in my presence again."

Leah chuckled. "Fair enough." She studied him for a second before returning to a workbench scattered with tools and debris and a bunch of things he wouldn't even begin to know how to make sense of. "You can hide out here as long as you want."

"Thanks."

"And, you know, that's an open invitation sort of thing. Not just for hiding out, either."

"Thanks." Even though he didn't feel thankful. He felt guilty. Guilty for not being the kind of brother he should be. Guilty for moving here but not making any overtures toward Leah.

Guilty because even knowing he should make an effort—he didn't want to. His hand grasped the doorknob. "I should head back."

Leah's smile was small, not much of a smile at all, really. "Sure thing."

"I'll, uh, see you soon."

"Sure." She focused on her wires and, well, he was a dick. Plain and simple.

"Um, you know, I work all weekend, but maybe we could go out to lunch...or something sometime next week."

She stopped fiddling with her wires, surprise written all over her face as she looked at him. "Well, sure."

"Great. I'll call you."

The corner of her mouth quirked up. "That's a brush-off in dating code, but I'll give you the benefit of the doubt in sibling code."

"I *will* call you."

"Yeah, you're a stand-up kind of guy, Officer Santino. That field training lady doesn't stand a chance."

He scowled. "Not happening."

She made a considering noise and stood, crossing over to him before hesitating. "I was going to go for a hug but...not my forte."

"Yeah, not mine, either." Though hadn't he done an admirable impression of it last night? With a woman not related to him. A woman he barely knew.

A woman who was an adult and basically still abused by her father.

"We should try," he said, his voice uncomfortably rough. His family had its issues, deep uncomfortable ones, but they certainly didn't physically or purposefully hurt each other.

"Really? Because—"

It was awkward, and ridiculous, but it felt necessary. He reached around Leah and gave her an uncomfortable one-armed squeeze. "There."

"Please. I'm begging you. Never again."

"No promises."

She groaned. "Ah, so this is the brother torture everyone else complains about."

Thirty years, and she was just now experiencing some stupid little thing normal brothers and sisters did all the time. It wasn't anything near as bad as

Tess's father's treatment of her, but he felt guilty all the same. As if he'd failed.

"Don't get all…whatever. You can't exactly torture the little sister when she spends all her time in the hospital or running away. It is what it is."

"No, I know." But Leah had been healthy for a lot of years now, and she'd been talking to the family regularly for the past year and a half. He had been the one to not make any overtures.

Changing that filled him with dread, but ignoring the fact it was his duty wasn't an option. "I should get back, but I will call you about lunch next week."

"All right, but if there's hugging involved, I won't be held responsible for my actions."

"Noted." Marc turned the knob. He'd save the dread and discomfort for later. For right now. Right now he was just doing the right thing, and that was all that mattered.

He stepped outside, grimacing when he saw Tess's form jogging up on the path. Not quite long enough.

"That her?"

"Yeah."

Leah laughed and gave him a shove. "Go get 'em, tiger."

"I'm not—"

But Leah shut the door before he could argue. He wasn't going to go get Tess. He wasn't.

He wasn't.

CHAPTER SIX

TESS WAS SURPRISED to see Marc trudging across the expansive yard he'd disappeared toward. He hadn't been subtle about wanting to get rid of her.

She had a hard time blaming him for that. Where she'd spent years upon years successfully keeping friends and coworkers firmly in the dark about what a mess she was, she'd known Marc a week and he knew. He'd seen.

That was extraordinarily difficult to deal with, because someone knowing what a mess she was made it seem more true. Less something she could muscle her way through. He didn't believe that tough shell she donned every day.

She just wished the seer of her weaknesses wasn't so hot. Or so sweet, in a weirdly uncomfortable, gruff way.

Shit balls.

Marc fell into step kind of half next to her, half behind her. It was only then she realized she'd purposefully slowed her pace as she'd come close to the giant old house. Because she'd wanted…

It was best if she didn't think too hard about what she wanted.

"Hey."

"Said all your hellos?"

"Yeah, she's working. Didn't want to take up too much of her time."

"What exactly is that place? I'm not familiar with it."

"Restoration company. They fix up old houses for people. She's an electrician."

"I do love a woman in a traditionally male-dominated field."

Marc puffed out a chuckle. "Yeah, you two'd probably get along."

It wasn't an invitation to meet his family—obviously he didn't want that—but it made her wonder. Marc already knew so much about her life, and all she knew was he was from Minnesota and had a sister. Electrician for a restoration company sister.

"Do your parents live back in Minnesota?"

"Yes."

"Did you move here to be closer to your sister?"

He was quiet for a while. So much so, she had to glance back to make sure he was still behind her.

His expression was grim and something she couldn't read. Maybe as if the superhero let everyone down.

"You could say that."

Which was such a strange answer, purposefully vague and a little cryptic. Marc definitely had some issues of his own. People weren't so tight-lipped about their lives if they weren't hiding something.

Tess would know.

Was it a bad something, like a parental monkey on his back, or was it innocuous? Embarrassing, but not like hers. Not painful and potentially life damaging.

It would be best not to know.

"You said you didn't have a sister, but any brothers?"

Before yesterday she might have considered that question making progress. He so rarely asked her for more information than she willingly gave. But yesterday had changed things, because today he was asking not out of curiosity or the desire to get to know her better, but because he wondered about her relationship with her father. If there was someone to step in and save the day.

"Nope. Just me." In more ways than one.

She shouldn't give him any more than that, should be as terse and tight-lipped as he always was, but there was a too-big part of her that wanted him to understand, or see, or something. This thing with her father, as pathetic as it was, wasn't something she chose.

"Mom left when I was little, so it's always been just Dad and me."

She wouldn't say more than that, because it was all that needed to be said. Maybe he would understand, and maybe he wouldn't. But she'd given him enough information to know this wasn't pathetic.

They really were all each other had, and she was the responsible party.

Whether she wanted to be or not.

Marc didn't say anything, so she focused on running. Hard. So her muscles would be nothing but jelly and hopefully her brain would follow suit.

When they reached the apartment complex, Tess was breathing hard enough talking would be difficult, and she was gratified Marc was in about the same shape.

"Christ, how often do you do that?" He huffed.

Tess grinned, bending to the side to stretch before her Jell-O muscles got tight. "Couple times a week. Depending." On Dad. A few months ago it had been once a week tops. This month? Three to four times per week.

Things were bad.

You need to help him. Fix this. You cannot ignore him. You're all he has. This is your responsibility.

But she didn't want it anymore. For once in her life she wanted to make a decision not based on her father's fragile mental state.

Forgetting the rest of her usual stretches, she pushed inside the building. She felt too raw to have Marc's scrutinizing eyes around.

"No wonder you're in such great shape," he muttered, and she had a feeling she was not meant to hear that, as she was inside when he'd uttered it. Which managed to cheer her a little. Pathetic, yes, but, hey, she deserved a little pathetic.

She glanced back at Marc following her, and though he tried to hide it, he'd very obviously been staring at her ass.

Pathetic isn't all you deserve.

No. No, no, no cops. Not some arbitrary edict. It was necessary for career survival. So Marc could stare at her ass and be nice and hot and whatever. Her reputation was way more important than some guy.

Regardless of the size of that guy's shoulders. Or thighs. Or biceps. Mmm. Biceps. *Get a grip, Camden.*

She reached the top of the stairs, probably only a few feet from her tired legs giving out completely. "Well, thanks for the company. I needed it." She looked at her door, dreading facing the phone on the other side. Dreading the weakness inside her that would grow, fester, until she'd give up and go over there. Until she'd lose at convincing herself she couldn't help him.

"I'm buying a chair," Marc said out of nowhere. "Maybe a table. You…"

She turned to stare at him. "I?"

"If you're looking for something to do." He shrugged those big yummy shoulders she really needed to distance herself from. "I could use some help. I've never picked out furniture before."

Tess's throat got tight, but she swallowed through it. "Has anyone ever told you you're a marshmallow?"

"No," he said, so seriously, so disgustedly, she

had to laugh despite the warmth of gratitude clogging behind her eyes as tears.

"Well, you are, and I appreciate it. I'll even buy you lunch."

"Look, to be clear…"

Tess had a feeling she knew where this was going, and if she were noble she might have saved him the discomfort, but a mess of a girl needed a little something to make her feel a pinch in charge of her life. "Clear about?"

"It's not…it's not a date. That's not what I'm… Friends. We should be friends. Not dating…things."

"God, you're cute."

"Tess."

"No worries. I don't date cops, even if I want to. So you're safe no matter how much you're nice to me." Though she couldn't resist one little flirt. "Or how many lusty vibes crop up."

"I'm really starting to hate that word," he grumbled. "Noon. I'll meet you at my truck."

Tess nodded and did her best not to saunter to her apartment door, not to swing her hips or bounce her steps, no matter how tired her legs were, but she could feel his eyes on her, so it was hard.

Well, welcome to life. Hard.

"Pivot."

Tess started giggling, which was not pivoting so they could get the damn couch up the stairs. A couch she'd somehow talked him into. He didn't plan on having company. It was just him. Why would he need a couch? A chair would have sufficed.

"Why are you laughing?" Marc grumbled, the bulk of the weight of the couch resting on his shoulder. Though he'd never admit it to anyone, that run this morning had kicked his ass—physically and emotionally and whatever feeling was ignoring your hot neighbor/coworker's hotness.

Something akin to wanting to crawl out of one's skin. Or sex. Sex would be good.

He gritted his teeth and Tess got a better grip on the couch. "I take it from the grumpiness you never watched *Friends*. You know, Ross yelling at everyone to pivot in the stairwell?"

"No, I've never seen it."

"How is that even possible? I'm not sure I can trust someone who's never seen *Friends*."

"I'm not big on TV."

"Strike two, Santino. Next up you'll tell me you don't like dessert and I'll be forced to hate you forever."

"Depends on the dessert." Which was *not* sexual innuendo. And it didn't sound like it, either. Not to her. Not to him. Nope.

"Okay, so what's your favorite?" They got the couch around the stairwell turn.

Sexual innuendo? Oh, no, dessert. "Cannoli."

They reached the top and Tess dropped her end. "Ooh, Santino. Cannoli. Italian. Is your family in the mafia? The Minnesota mafia. And you're a dirty cop!"

"No. Apparently you watch too much TV."

"No fun."

No, he wasn't. But she was. He'd pity invited her on this shopping outing, one he'd mostly been dreading since picking out crap and spending money were two of his least favorite things, and she'd made it fun. He'd laughed.

He was so inherently screwed.

He unlocked his door, twin urges surging through him. One was the one he should listen to. The one to tell her she'd helped, and now she could leave, because he really wasn't sure how much longer he could pretend he wasn't dying.

The other was to ignore that urge. Let her come in. Comment on his apartment again. Infiltrate on some crazy chance they both knew they couldn't let happen.

"Thinking awfully hard there for a door opening."

"Just thinking about how I was swindled," he lied, poorly. Ill-advisedly.

Tess laughed, picking up her end of the couch again. "Oh, my God, you did not just say *swindled*. Are you living on the prairie?"

"It's a legitimate word," Marc grumbled. He didn't need her help to get it in the apartment, but he didn't say anything. Except, "I could make my own damn chair for half the amount of this stupid couch you talked me into."

Tess snorted. "Sure, Ron Swanson."

"Huh?"

"You, sir, need an education. *Friends, Parks and Rec, The Office.*"

"I prefer reading, thanks."

"Strike three. You're out," she puffed out as they maneuvered the couch into the apartment. They dropped it in the general area in front of the TV. "Besides, if you prefer to read, why do you have a TV?"

"Sports."

Tess rolled her eyes. "Oh, be a little less stereotypical."

"My e-reader is full of romances."

Her eyes got comically wide. "Really?"

"No. I actually prefer nonfiction. Biographies and stuff like that, but that's probably stereotypical."

She collapsed onto the couch, throwing her arm dramatically over her forehead. "Oh, and here I got all excited you had some secret poetic side to you." She peered out from under her arm. "You know, I should hate you for not paying the delivery fee and making me help."

"I should hate you for talking me into a couch when I only needed a chair."

She stretched her long legs out. She was wearing loose jeans with random rips across the thigh and knee—which actually looked like use, not some attempt at fashion. All he knew was, on more than one occasion it had given him a glimpse of skin.

On more than one occasion, he'd had to tell himself to stop staring so damn much.

"You can't stretch out on a chair," she was saying, folding her arms behind her head. "You can't nap or curl up with a fascinating biography of…" She looked at him pointedly, as if he was supposed to supply an answer.

"Lyndon Johnson."

"Ugh. Worst president ever."

"I think worst is a bit of an exaggeration."

"I watched this show once that gave evidence to how he was behind the JFK assassination. It seemed pretty legit."

"Please tell me you are not serious right now."

"Okay, this right here is another reason I should hate you—I'm lying on your couch debating about history. That is the last thing I ever want to be doing on a guy's couch."

"And what's the first thing?" *Danger. Accident ahead.* Like a flashing sign, only he couldn't backtrack and take back those words, so he had to stand in uncomfortable…uncomfortableness.

"Hmm." Her smile went sly, reminding him of that first night he'd met her in the hallway. Despite bleeding and being pissed, she'd smiled as if she had the world in the palm of her hand.

She could smile like that even though it was so obvious she didn't. He couldn't understand that. He was having a hard time resisting it, too.

"Pizza?"

She pushed herself into a sitting position, and glanced at the door. "I never say no to pizza."

"You can go, if that's what you want."

Her eyes moved from the door to him, all sly smiles and confidence gone. Just gray eyes wide and something he was having trouble resisting, too. Like what paltry help he offered mattered, meant something.

He helped a lot of people, but it never felt as though it…resonated. People moved on, people kept focusing on other people. Having someone see the effort he was making was…why did that make him feel ridiculously good?

That probably made him a dick, because helping was supposed to be something you did without the hope of thanks or retribution, but he couldn't deny he was desperate for a little thanks, a little gratitude.

Christ. Pathetic to the extreme. At least that was another reason not to like her. Chatty *and* made him consider uncomfortable truths about himself. Too bad he couldn't get that message through all the ways he did like her. He swallowed and opened his mouth to speak, to get out of Pathetic Land, but she beat him to it.

"I know, I should get out of your hair."

"No, I wasn't saying it because…" Jeez, now he really sounded pathetic. "You were looking at the door. You are welcome to stay, but I don't want you to feel obligated. I have eaten many a meal on my own. It's not half-bad."

"I just…" She looked down at her hands, pressed her palms together before looking back at the door. "I need to stay away from my phone. If I can do that for a little while longer."

Marc felt as though he'd done an admirable job keeping his mouth shut—he was damn good at it, after all—but the trepidation in her voice, in her movements made him realize keeping quiet went against everything he stood for.

He didn't let people get hurt if he could help it. While Tess was an adult and her father was her business, even if he did hurt her, Marc couldn't stand by silently if she was afraid.

"Does he harass you?"

She went completely still, presumably because he'd broken the silent agreement not to discuss what had actually happened and what it meant.

"It's not like that," she said lamely. She got off the couch, pushing her hair back and linking her hands behind her head before letting them fall at her sides. "He calls and asks for help. I need…" She shook her head. "He's an alcoholic, Marc. He's sick. I'm all he has. It's sometimes a bit much and I need a break."

"You…" Part of him was desperate to keep his mouth shut, to keep out of this, to help in only the most peripheral ways possible, but it wasn't a big enough part of him to keep his mouth shut. "I know it's none of my business, but him having a fight with that scrawny guy at his apartment complex? It may not just be alcohol."

Her shoulders slumped and she turned away from him. "I know. That's new. Kind of."

"Kind of?"

"I don't want to talk about this, Marc. I know it doesn't secm like it, but I have things under control." Her head bobbed as if she was nodding to herself. Then a sound escaped her mouth—not really a laugh, not a sob. He wasn't sure what the noise was.

"God, what a joke. I don't have a damn thing under control anymore. I'm not even fooling myself." She sniffled. "I'm not doing this again in front of you. I'm going home. Look, I'm sorry. I need to get out of here." She moved for the door, but he was— thankfully—faster and got there first. Blocking it.

What the hell are you doing?

He had no idea. He only knew he couldn't let her leave. "Tess."

Even though she'd sniffled, she wasn't crying. Yet. Her eyes were shiny with tears. "Marc, let me go, okay? I'll handle everything. I always do. I… have to." She pressed her fingers to her eyes, hands shaking.

The little voice in his head kept repeating the same question over and over—*What the hell are you doing?* Only it didn't seem to change the fact he was doing it. He reached for her shoulders, fingers curling around them. Even though her body trembled, she felt so damn strong under his hands he just wished he had answers.

He could only do his best, which would never

be good enough, but maybe it could be something. "Surely there's someone who can help—"

"I don't have anyone who can help us," she choked out, dropping her hands from her eyes, a mix of determination and defeat. How did she do that?

A few tears had escaped her eyes, and he hated the feeling in his gut—helplessness. As though there wasn't a thing he could do to fix this.

A very familiar feeling. One he couldn't seem to shake no matter where he went, and yet the words that came out of his mouth didn't seem to understand that. "I can help."

"How?"

"I don't know. I really don't." How long had he been trying to help only to fail? But…she made him feel as if this could be different. "Honestly, my choice method of help would be arresting the kind of asshole that would hurt his daughter." Without permission from the rational side of his brain, his hands moved from her shoulders down to her arm, where she'd held a cloth over a cut that first night he'd met her.

"I can't—"

"So, I can't fix anything. But I can help. You need to be away from your phone. I'm right next door. Well, almost. I don't have much of a life, considering I just moved here. The point is, if you need someone to distract you, I can do that." Which sounded… "I didn't mean…"

She smiled, which was nice to see. "Why don't

you order the pizza, Captain Quiet? That'll be enough distracting...for now." Then her expression went soft, and there was that fleeting feeling he'd been chasing for most of his life, the feeling that he'd helped, that he'd done something.

Tess rose to her toes and brushed her lips against his cheek. "Thanks," she said.

He swallowed, because a kiss on the cheek—a friendly thank-you kiss on the cheek—was not something to get all worked up over. But that's exactly what he was. Worked up. Tied up. Ridiculously pleased that someone had recognized his effort.

Also, screwed. Very, very screwed.

CHAPTER SEVEN

TESS BLINKED HER eyes open to a strange ceiling. There was no faint watermark from that one particularly nasty storm three years ago. And someone was tugging her foot.

She leveraged up onto her elbows and was met with Marc. Oh-so-yummy Marc. Who apparently attracted her tears and breakdowns like a damn magnet.

"Um, didn't know how much time you needed to get ready in the morning."

"Morning?" Tess looked around the dimly lit apartment. "What time is it?"

"Five."

"In the morning?"

"Yes, that's kind of what I was getting at."

Tess rubbed her eyes trying to get her sleepy brain to engage. So, they'd ordered pizza. Watched... hockey. Yes, that was why she'd fallen asleep. Apparently kept sleeping long after she should have.

"I slept all night on your couch."

"That must be some comfortable couch you picked out. Once you were out, you were out. And snoring."

"I do not snore."

"Oh, right, that must have been a mouse." He grinned. Like an actual, full-blown pleased-with-himself smile and God, he was so damn hot. And sweet. Nice and helpful and yes, it seemed about right that the first guy to trip her trigger in a long time was completely off-limits.

And the only one in…ever who'd stepped up to help. But that was her own fault. After that incident between Dad and her boyfriend right after high school, she'd given up any hope of help. She kept friends at enough distance so they didn't know what was going on.

Work was her life, coworkers her family and her dad this secret little piece of herself no one saw.

So sure, like this guy, have the hots for this guy and be completely incapable of doing anything about it.

Well, not incapable.

Oh, no, no, no. None of that. Because giving up all she'd built to scratch an itch or get some help was idiocy. Marc's help would be minimal and short-lived. Her reputation at the station needed to last her through retirement.

Period.

"You want some breakfast?"

"Um, thanks, really, thanks for everything, but I didn't plan on spending the night on your couch.

I need to make sure I have a pressed uniform and clean socks and all manner of things."

"Sure, no problem."

"I…I'm not usually this much of a mess." She pulled her tennis shoes on. "Really. It…really." She had a desperate need for him to understand that. He was catching her at a bad time. Usually she had no trouble juggling everything. This was abnormal. He was catching her at a bad time.

He had to believe that. *She* had to believe that.

"I believe you."

Tess laughed. It wasn't exactly a happy laugh, but a laugh nonetheless. "Honestly, Marc, I don't know why. I have given you absolutely no reason to believe I have any of my shit together."

"Actually, most of the time you seem like you have everything infinitely together. The blips make you human instead of…"

"Instead of what?"

"Nothing," he grumbled, turning away from her and walking toward the kitchen.

"Oh, no, you have to tell me. Come on. I'm the pathetic girl who cried on you for the second night in a row and slept on your couch. Give me something to boost my deflated ego here."

"Your ego is fine. You make me talk too much." He fiddled with his coffeemaker, rinsing out the carafe with more precision than necessary.

"That cheers me up almost as much as the

thinking-I've-got-it-together thing." It really did. She didn't feel so pathetic, and she got a kick out of making him grumbly. "You don't talk too much, by the way. Everything you say is…" She let out a sigh. Awkwardness wasn't something she felt too often, but in trying to give him an honest compliment, she felt it dig in.

"Anyway." She forced an easy, confident smile. She'd learned a long time ago how to pretend. *Except when he's all nice and you fall apart like a total loser.* Ugh. She crossed to him and held her hand out. "Thanks."

He stared at her hand for a few seconds before lifting his gaze to hers. Grrr, it was so unfair she couldn't throw herself at him.

"You don't have to thank me."

"Don't get all—"

"We're friends. You don't have to thank friends. It's just what we do. Okay?"

She realized he was uncomfortable, possibly as awkward as she felt. Maybe he was as bad at taking gratitude as she was at expressing it. Well, hey, that would come in handy.

"Okay," she said with a nod, dropping her hand. "No thanks. Just friends helping friends."

Marc nodded.

"Well, friend, I'm going to go get ready to cart your ass around today, and if you want to bring your friendly FTO a cup of coffee to go, she would not say no."

Marc's mouth quirked, that little half smile he had. Nothing compared to the full-blown smile during the snoring conversation, but it was enough. Enough to make the unwelcome attraction flutters come out.

"Sure thing."

Tess gave a little nod then turned toward the door. She didn't want to face her phone and the likely bazillion messages from Dad, but she felt stronger. Better equipped to deal with them than she had yesterday.

She wasn't sure if she would give the credit to Marc believing she had it together or just the offer of his help. Either way, it made her a little itchy. Help wasn't something she'd ever had.

"Tess?"

She looked over her shoulder. He didn't look up from his coffee preparations even as he spoke.

"Just to be clear, my door's always open for... whatever."

Not sexual, Camden. "I appreciate that." And she did. More than she probably should. Because even if Marc was her friend and her coworker, she couldn't always ignore helping her father. She couldn't always distract herself from it. More, she couldn't always count on Marc to drop everything for her. Eventually he'd build his own life here.

She stepped into the hall, closing the door behind her. Maybe Marc wouldn't always be around to help, but for the time being, it wouldn't be the worst thing in the world to take a little bit.

AT THE KNOCK on the door, Marc's heartbeat kicked up. "Moron," he muttered into the empty apartment. An apartment that hadn't felt all that empty until he'd come home from work this afternoon. Empty had been his way of life—it had felt like solitude.

It was not normal or okay that Tess had whirled into everything and made it feel like a void instead. Like the quiet was too quiet and the alone was too alone. He had spent the entire day working side by side with her. He'd had two hours of alone time this evening.

But he'd told her he could help. He'd told her they were friends. So he opened the door and tried to not look irritated. Besides, he wasn't a total asshole. He could definitely be her friend without also wanting to get her naked.

Or at least he wouldn't act on it.

"Brownies!" Tess said cheerfully. "Now, I'm no culinary genius, but I have mastered the art of the perfect box brownie." She waltzed her way in as if she belonged. As if that was something people normally did in his life.

Hell, his mother didn't even waltz into his place like that, and she was the overbearing sort—just more focused on Leah.

"Brownies, huh?"

"Since friends don't say thank-you for helping each other out, they bring brownies. Also, I wanted brownies, but if I keep this whole thing in my apartment I will eat it all tonight."

He was spared having to respond to that when his cell phone rang. Since the caller ID read *Mom*, Marc had to think whether or not to ignore it.

"Go ahead," Tess said with a wave, already in his kitchen drawers, presumably rooting around for a knife to cut the brownies. Hopefully a plate, too. Because if she ate without a plate, there would be brownie crumbs everywhere and—

"Answer it," she insisted.

Right. He clicked Accept and stepped toward his bedroom. He wasn't sure he wanted Tess to be able to hear his conversation. He wasn't sure he hid his pathetic mommy issues so well when he was actually talking to his mother.

"Marc? Is silence how you greet your mother? Because I know that phone of yours tells you who's calling."

Marc stepped into his room, gingerly closing the door and hoping Tess wouldn't notice.

"Hi, Mom."

"Much better. Now, I need to talk to you about next Friday."

"Next Friday?"

"Your father and I bumped up our trip. I'm hoping if we get a house lined up it might spur your sister or Jacob on in the engagement process."

Marc closed his eyes. A weight settled in his chest. A helpless feeling that he'd moved here for nothing. Mom wasn't ever going to look up and say,

"Why, Marc, you've been a kind of exceptional son. Thank you for that."

Because all that mattered was Leah. Now Leah and Jacob.

Which shouldn't be something he got so tied up about. He should be adult enough to accept it and move on. But he was here, so the likelihood of that was slim at this point.

"Marc?"

"I was looking at my schedule. I can't take off, but I'll still be on days, so I'll be free after four every day. How long are you staying?"

"Two weeks. More if I can finagle it."

"Okay, well, I'll have Monday and Tuesday off."

"That's fine. Leah said she can take off whatever days we're here. Your father and I can always entertain ourselves, or Jacob said MC's doors are always open. But of course we'll want to have you come over for some family meals, too."

We. Come over. To Leah's house. Even though he'd moved here because they'd asked him to so they could be one big happy family, and being the idiot he was, he'd thought that would put him on equal footing. He'd thought that meant he mattered.

But he was being invited to dinners like an outsider while they stayed with Leah and Jacob.

He needed this conversation to be over. "Yeah, sure. Just keep me up-to-date."

"Have you spent any time with your sister?"

"I stopped by MC the other day, and we're going

to have lunch next week." Although with Mom and Dad coming maybe he could get out of that. Hell, maybe he could get out of the whole damn thing. Maybe he'd moved here for them, but if they still didn't want to see him…maybe he didn't need to be seen.

"I've got company, Mom. Gotta go."

"Oh, what kind of company?"

"A friend from work."

"Oh." Mom's disappointment was palpable, but at least that was something. If he really wanted her to care, he could probably mention the friend from work was a woman. A very attractive woman.

But as desperate as he was for his mother's attention, he wasn't that bad. "I'll talk to you later."

"Sure, sweetie, love you."

"Yeah. Love you, too." He clicked End and tossed the phone on his bed. Maybe Tess had the right idea about ignoring the parental phone calls.

Yeah, because her father is an abusive jerk, not because she's pathetic and desperate for attention like a four year old.

Years of self-flagellation didn't change the fact that he was always looking for the crumbs of attention his parents deigned to throw his way. Could he break the habit now? Maybe he should try.

Maybe he and Tess could be each other's distraction. Not sexually. If he reminded himself of that enough, maybe he'd believe it. He stepped out of his room, leaving his phone inside.

"Sorry about…" He blinked at the empty kitchen, then looked around the living room. She'd…left?

He should not feel disappointed. Then he looked down at her pan of brownies, a generous chunk missing, a little note on top. *Had to run out for a bit. See you tomorrow.*

He should let it go. This was none of his business. He was the distraction friend. He didn't need to be more than that. Maybe he was overreacting to think she was going to see her father. Maybe it was something else. He didn't know everything about her life.

But all the rationalizations in the world didn't stop him from shoving his feet into his shoes and jogging out the door, not even bothering to lock the dead bolt, which was unheard of.

He took the stairs two at a time and pushed out the building door to the parking lot. Tess was just opening her car door.

"Tess!"

She stopped and looked up at him, her expression some mix between sheepish and defeated. "Hey, sorry I had to bail. I…"

He crossed to her side of the car, only a little out of breath. "It's okay, I just…" He just what? Hated the idea of her going to see her father alone? "If you're going to see your dad, let me come with you."

Her eyebrows drew together, clearly perplexed. "Um, no. I'm sorry. Thanks for the offer, really, but I can handle this."

He reached out and took her arm, couldn't help

it. Couldn't help any of this. Maybe she was right and he did have some misguided superhero sense of duty, but how could he watch her go into a situation that could get her hurt?

His thumb brushed over where she'd had the gash on her arm that first night. "Maybe you can, but a little backup couldn't hurt." Because if she did come back scathed, how would he be able to live with having let her go?

"I know you think the cut thing was him hurting me on purpose, but it wasn't." She patted his hand that grasped her arm. "The glass broke and a shard got me. He didn't, like, come up and slash me."

"How did it break?"

She blinked then looked away. "Well…"

He had seen that look before. Almost always on a woman convinced she was at fault for another man's violence. "Well what?"

"He threw it."

"Where?"

"At me." She let out a gusty sigh and disentangled her arm from his grasp. "Look, I get it, really. I know what it looks like. But…he isn't a monster. It's not like he spent my whole life beating me. When he's bad off, he gets violent. Yes, occasionally I get the brunt of that, but I can take care of myself, Marc. I'm a cop, too."

"Tess—"

"I've done the bring a big-burly-guy-to-be-my-protector thing before. My boyfriend right out of high school was a bodybuilder. Bigger than you, Mr. Football Shoulders. All it did was agitate Dad from the start. He and James got in a brawl. Besides, he knows who you are. You're the cop he wasn't too pleased with the other day. So it would only escalate the situation."

"So don't go."

She shook her head, looking immeasurably sad. So much worse than his own lame-ass pity party a few minutes ago. "I can't let him kill himself or hurt other people. I have to fix this. I've been dealing with this my whole life. I know how to handle it."

"If it's been going on your whole life, why do you think you can fix it?" There had to be some way he could convince her not to go, to stay here, safe.

"I do sometimes fix it, thank you very much. I have gotten him help before, and things go okay for a while. But addiction isn't easy to break." She poked a finger into the center of his chest. "I appreciate what you've done for me so far, but I'm not about to let you think you can elbow your way into my life or my business. I can handle this."

"I'm not saying you can't."

"Oh, really."

"He hurt you. That isn't—"

"It is what it is. I can handle it. I have handled it. On my own, for thirty-some years. And here I stand before you, in one piece. So I highly suggest you back the eff off, Marc." She wrenched her door open, slid into the driver's seat. Before she could pull it closed, he grabbed it, earning him a glare. "Seriously, Marc, this is not okay."

He had to tell himself to uncurl his fingers from around her door. Had to force himself to take a step back. She didn't want his help; her father's disease was the most important thing to her.

That little thought worked to loosen his grip on the door. Unfortunately, it didn't evaporate the worry or the concern. This might be familiar, but that didn't mean he knew how to ignore it.

"Can you at least—" *oh, you pathetic sack of shit* "—text me when you get back?"

The anger melted off her face so quickly it was almost as though he'd imagined it. "Oh, damn it," she muttered, getting back out of the car, and before he could figure out what the hell was happening, she fisted her hands in his shirt and pressed her mouth to his.

Though his brain wasn't quite catching up, his body was doing okay on its own. His fingers tangled in her hair, moving her back a step as he kissed her in return.

She made a sound against his mouth and he was about to flick his tongue over that gorgeous top lip, but she released him and stepped away.

"Damn it, damn it, damn it," she muttered, pressing a palm to her heart. "I had to do that because you're such a sweet jerk face, but I'm not doing it again, okay?"

"O-okay."

"I'm not going to kiss you again. I'm not. Probably. No. Not." She shook her head and slid into the driver's seat. "Goodbye, Marc. I'll see you tomorrow. I'll be fine. Swear. I'll text you when I am safe and sound, but please, for the love of all that is holy and sane between us, do not wait up. Because I'm not sure I can bear it."

"What does that even mean?"

She didn't answer, just pulled the door closed and turned her key in the engine. He stepped away, for fear she might take him out in her rush to leave.

If she couldn't bear it, he should definitely do what she wanted, what she asked and go back to his apartment, go to sleep and pretend she didn't exist.

But the taste of her was still on his lips, the humming buzz of that kiss crackling over his skin. She thought his concern was sweet, even if she rejected it.

Yeah, not likely pretending anything tonight.

CHAPTER EIGHT

TESS PULLED HER car in front of her father's run-down apartment complex along the river. She didn't want to do this—at all—but she had to. His calls were getting more frantic and desperate. If she ignored him for much longer he'd get in some serious trouble she couldn't get him out of.

She stepped out of the car, making sure to lock it before resting her hand on the gun strapped to her hip. The whole reason she'd had to break off that kiss with Marc—she'd been afraid he'd notice she was carrying and be even more concerned.

Concerned. She felt mushy all over again. He was worried about her. It was such a…thing. She didn't want it to be. She really wanted to be offended or angered by his wanting to swoop in. But he'd stepped back when she'd told him to, and he'd wanted to know when she got home all right.

He was the worst possible thing for her. Because how could she ever resist someone wanting her to be safe? It was new. Intoxicating. Stupid making.

That kiss being a perfect example. But how could she not kiss him when he'd wanted her to text him when she got back? Maybe it was some misguided superhero complex, but at the same time…why would he exercise that if he didn't have some inkling of feeling for her?

A whistle interrupted her thoughts over Marc. Especially since the front of Dad's complex was poorly lit and she couldn't see the perpetrator of the whistle. Her hand rested on the butt of her gun.

"Hey, pretty thing."

She still couldn't make out who was talking, but she managed to locate a shadowy figure the voice was probably coming from. She made her voice low, authoritative. "Hey."

"You like to party, sweetheart?"

"Nope."

"I bet you'd like my kind of party."

Tess casually unsnapped the band on her holster, let her fingers curl around the handle. "Back off, buddy. I'm just here to see my dad."

"Oh, I bet I can make you call me Daddy."

She pulled the gun out of her holster since the voice was getting closer. "Vomit," she replied, doing her best to sound bored. She backed her way toward Dad's door.

"Don't run off, sweetheart," he said, and she could see him now. The same guy her dad had been arguing with the other day. The drug dealer–looking one. "Things are about to get exciting."

"Yeah, you got that right." She held up her gun so it glinted in the dim light, then trained on his chest. Steady. She'd held a gun on someone too many times for it to cause a tremor, even in the dark, even alone. Some skinny-ass piece of shit didn't intimidate her. "I'd really hate for you to make me shoot you, though."

"Cop," he spat. "Female cop. Even worse. Fucking dyke."

"Not the insult you want it to be, buddy. Now why don't you mosey on into the hole you crawled out of before things, shall we say, escalate."

The guy muttered a few more obscenities and nasty names, but he slunk to the corner apartment on the other side of the building. Once he disappeared behind his door, Tess pulled her phone out of her back pocket and dialed dispatch.

"Hey, Megs. This is Camden. Can you send one of the guys out to Meadowview Apartments? Apartment 1C. The guy's harassing people, might have drugs on him. If someone's in zone and can come shake him down a bit, I'd appreciate it."

"Sure thing, Tess. Want me to have them call you?"

"No, I'm good. Just send them over. Thanks." Tess hung up, then gingerly slid her father's key into the door. Sometimes it was best to be loud, announce her arrival so he didn't get paranoid.

But his message when Marc had been on the phone in his room had been weepy. The kind of distraught fear she'd never been able to talk herself out of running to.

She still remembered too clearly the time he'd tried to slit his wrists to ignore that kind of despair.

"Dad?" The overwhelming smells of cigarettes and piss greeted her. Mixed with the guilt already roiling in her stomach, it was quite a combo.

Obviously Dad had scared off the second cleaning lady she'd hired. Plates littered every available surface; ashes overflowed anything that could be used as an ashtray.

Nausea coated her stomach. Guilt lodged in her throat with fizzing tears. Guilt that she almost wished he'd get to that suicidal point again, so he'd have to be hospitalized, have to get help. The few months after that attempt had been steady. Healing. She'd thought they'd been on the path to normal.

Damn Marc and his voice in the back of her mind. *If it's been going on your whole life, why do you think you can fix it?*

Maybe she couldn't—a thought she didn't let infiltrate too often, because it was too damn depressing—but okay, maybe she couldn't fix a damn thing. It didn't mean she could give up trying. There was always the possibility she *could* fix it.

She stepped into the little hallway that led to the bedroom and stopped cold at his body sprawled across the floor. "Dad?"

She rushed to his side, sank to her knees, took his wrist in her hands. The shaking that had never manifested itself as she'd threatened the junkie outside took over now. So much she almost couldn't take a decent pulse.

But it was there. Steady. Probably just passed out from too much alcohol, based on the stench. She inspected his arms for signs of shooting up, his head for signs of hitting it if he'd passed out while upright.

But everything seemed to be fine. Breathing, pulse, no bumps, bruises or marks. She rocked back onto her heels in the same crouching position, trying to steady the shaking, the fear...

And ignore that little spurt of relief she'd felt when she saw him lying there. So wrong. So awful and wrong to hope something so awful, no matter how fleeting.

Once her heart rate slowed and the shaking stopped, she pushed to a standing position. Guilt and confusion and fear were par for the course with dear old Dad.

So she did what she always did when she came over and he was passed out. She searched his apartment. She found an empty bottle of Jack in the kitchen, then a half bottle of some cheap off-brand whiskey. She unscrewed the cap and poured it down the sink, scouring the rest of the apartment for other alcohol or signs of drugs.

She found a few minibottles in the bathroom, disgustingly enough, under the plunger. She emptied those, collected all the empty bottles in a bag. Then went through one more time because how were things getting worse if drugs weren't involved?

But there wasn't a drop of evidence that pointed at drug use. That was even more deflating than finding something. Because she didn't know how to fix this current slide if there wasn't extra reason for it.

She'd done everything she could to keep him away from alcohol—she never gave him money, only groceries and toiletries. He didn't have a job, a car. What else could she do that wasn't babysitting 24-7? Not a damn thing. She'd do a lot to fix him, but she wouldn't give up her career. It gave her everything.

What about what Marc's giving you?

She looked at her father, then the door. Marc—stoic, terse, sweet, good Marc. He gave her the feeling that she might matter, and that feeling was nonexistent outside of work.

Why did he have to be a cop? *But if no one knew...*

She turned her gaze from her father to the door. She could go back, get away from this...thing that was spiraling out of her control. She could find a life that didn't involve Dad.

It was a little fiction, really. She'd never escape Dad, guilt, wanting to fix him, but maybe she could live in this fiction for a night.

She crossed to Dad, rested a hand on his cheek, too hollow. He was too thin, too frail, too everything. Why couldn't she find a way to save him? Why couldn't she crack whatever code kept him going back for more of this misery?

"Bye, Dad. I'll check on you later." Inevitably, she

would, even if she didn't want to. Even if she had no answers. She'd keep coming back.

Because fiction or not, what other choice did she have? She picked up the bag of empty bottles and left, locking the door behind her with one eye on the door Junkie Boy had disappeared behind.

But the sound of an engine caught her attention and she glanced at her car. One of the Bluff City cruisers was parked next to it, Granger's form silhouetted in the dome light of his car.

She crossed to him, wishing someone else had taken the call.

He got out of his patrol car as she approached. "What's a pretty girl like you doing in a place like this so late at night?"

The fact he all but repeated the sentiment of the low-life junkie he was here to harass pissed her off more than she already was. "Screw off, Granger."

"Booty call, I take it."

"My father lives here. But congrats on being a disgusting pig." She wrenched open her passenger-side door and dropped the bag of empties in.

"Jeez, Camden, lay off the bitch pills."

"I've had one asshole in my face tonight. I don't need a second, and I'm not in uniform. Don't make me remember I don't have my badge with me."

He had the audacity to roll his eyes. God, she could punch the little fucker right in the nose. But Franks wouldn't just be giving her a stern talking-to over that one.

That was the only thing that saved him from getting his ass handed to him by a girl. "Apartment 1C."

"Hate to break it to you, but you don't get to give me orders right now."

Her fingers curled into fists, but she'd dealt with enough dickwads in her day to know the most infuriating thing you could do was act as if they were the inconsequential nothings they were. "Keep telling yourself that." She flashed a screw-you smile and slid into the driver's seat of her car.

She drove, fury at the male population flowing through her, but once she returned to her apartment, she felt empty, wrung out, numb. Sad, really, really sad. Because she hadn't found any evidence of drugs, which meant whatever was happening was just escalation for no reason.

Almost worse than drugs, because how did she fight something she couldn't find the cause of?

Never mind the prick run-ins, she had more important things to deal with. If only she had a clue as to what to do. For the first time maybe ever, she was on complete empty. With no reason for the furthering downward spiral, and no letting up, she had nothing to fight.

She trudged into the apartment complex and up the stairs. Maybe…maybe her fight had run out. She was getting older, and her life was her work. And her father. Was she ever going to have something for herself?

She wasn't a woman who'd had the luxury of

believing in signs or in fate or in anything good being dropped at her doorstep.

And yet, there, virtually on her doorstep, was a man. Waiting for her, worrying over her. No insults, no judgments on her character. He was a good man, and she knew so few of those. How…how could she keep resisting that? That someone cared. Enough to step back. Enough to worry.

"Hi," Marc said, very obviously self-conscious about his choice to sit in front of her door.

"Hi," she replied, watching him stand up with a smile.

"Everything go okay?"

Slowly, she walked to the door, pulling her keys out of her pocket. Marc stepped out of the way so she could unlock the dead bolt. No, things weren't exactly okay, but that was the story of her life. Not quite okay. Not quite normal. Not quite…hers.

Maybe it was time to change that.

"Tess?"

She pushed the door open, stepped in, then turned to him. "Come inside, Marc."

"Oh, I—"

She didn't wait for him to finish that thought. She grabbed his arm and pulled him inside, then closed the door behind him.

MARC HAD NO idea what was going to happen. He only knew how relieved he was that she was okay.

Of course, he was the idiot waiting around in the

hallway. If only the way she'd looked at him when she'd crested the stairs hadn't washed away all those idiotic feelings.

She'd been happy to see him. It had been obvious. How long had he wished someone would act happy to see him?

Now he was in her apartment, standing awkwardly by the door she'd shut, while she stared at him, some inner conflict all over her face.

"I said I'd text you," she said at length.

"I know."

"I said you shouldn't wait up."

"Yes, for all that was holy and sane, but I didn't have a clue what that meant and…look, I don't know what kind of guy you take me for, but the kind of guy who wouldn't worry about someone going into a dangerous situation is an ass."

"You are very much not an ass." She smiled up at him, stepping closer, her fingers grazing the faded logo on his shirt.

Um… "But you're safe, and we have to work tomorrow morning. So I should…" Get away from the woman whose life was ruled by a disease, just like everyone else he was close to.

But she kissed you when you expressed concern, offered help. This is different.

She got closer, fingers trailing up to his shoulders, resting there. "You should what?" She cocked her head, looking at him from beneath her lashes, her breasts brushing against his chest as she leaned closer.

He'd promised himself he hadn't been waiting for this. That this wasn't about her kissing him earlier. It wasn't about the erection he'd sadly, pathetically had to do something about once she'd left. That was sadly, pathetically making a reappearance.

He cleared his throat, only he didn't remember what she'd asked him. "What were we talking about?"

She laughed, her breath feathering against his neck. "I forget," she murmured, her mouth very, very close to his jaw, her fingers now cupping his neck, those gray eyes of hers focused on his mouth.

Then she closed the remaining distance between them, her lips warm and soft on his. Her body warm and soft against his. Everything about her like being enveloped by comfort.

There was no chance of him surviving any of this, so he gave up. He surrendered. To her, to them, to whatever thing leaped between them. He wrapped his arms around her. The heat of her mouth centered itself in his gut, in his dick.

She arched against his erection and he groaned, letting his head fall back with a thunk against the door. Her laughter echoed in his ears, making him feel way better than he had a right to.

"I thought you weren't going to do that again," he managed to croak out, trying to remind himself he wasn't going to, either. Utter failure on that.

She shrugged, grinning, her arms still around his neck, chest still pressed to his. He wanted to touch her, without the layer of clothes. Feel the skin of her abdomen, her breasts, know what she tasted like. Everywhere.

"I said probably. Guess the bad odds won out."

"Bad?"

"Well, ill-advised. Definitely not bad."

"Hmm." Since he was already giving up and giving in, he allowed himself to indulge the impulse. Pushing a stray strand of hair behind her ear, letting his fingertips graze her cheek, trace that top lip.

Her eyes never left his, but her breath caught. So he pressed his mouth to where his fingers had been—mouth, cheek, ear.

"I don't want to do something you might regret." He kissed her temple, brushed his fingers across her collarbone, emboldened by each hitch in her breath, each shaky exhale.

"Oh, it's almost guaranteed I'll regret it." When he pulled his hand away from her neck, she grabbed his wrist. "But I am very pro regretting this tomorrow and very anti having nothing to regret."

"Wait. I'm not sure I follow that."

She chuckled, pulling him deeper into her apartment. "I will regret having my wicked way with you, but it's better than not having my wicked way with you. For once in my life, I deserve a little…wicked."

"Can you give me some more information on what your wicked way entails?"

"See, I didn't expect you to be funny, always so

serious and stoic. But you are. It's a sneaky funny, but you are."

"Not something I hear too often."

She stopped pulling, put her hands back on his chest, resting her palm over his heart. "And good. Really, really…good."

"Let's not pump my tires too much." Which he said more because he wanted that way too much. Someone to think he was good. Worthy. That was all kinds of warped.

"No, you're not perfect, I just mean…you have a good heart." She hitched up her shirt, he thought to take it off, which he was all for, but then a gun holster on her hip came into view. She detached it from her belt and placed it on the table.

It stopped him in his tracks, that she'd be scared enough to take her weapon. "You took a gun?"

"Focus, Marc. Or I'm going to think you're more interested in saving me than in having sex with me."

His gaze immediately jerked from the gun to her face, and she grinned. He hadn't exactly let himself believe sex was a foregone conclusion.

But gun.

But sex.

"Don't superhero out on me."

"How does one superhero out?"

"They're too noble to take the very fine offer in front of them. I don't want noble. I want you."

"I just—"

"You." Then she did take off her shirt, and, well,

discussing taking the gun could probably wait. Until she wasn't standing in front of him in a bra. It wasn't a particularly sexy bra—just flesh colored and plain, but, you know, a much better view of her breasts than he'd been afforded prior.

"If you're so inclined to be available for having, you can meet me in the bedroom." She turned, took a few steps before pushing her jeans over her hips, letting them fall with each step. He was too busy staring at her ass in pink polka-dot panties to care if the pants removal wasn't exactly smooth seductress.

Because as that running spandex had proven without a doubt, Tess had a fantastic ass, and he wanted his hands on it.

Desperately.

So he followed. Despite every voice in his head that told him maybe they should discuss a few things first. Like everything. But when he stepped into her bedroom, she was sprawled out on her bed.

Gorgeous.

She lifted herself up on her elbows. "I see you decided to join me. Excellent. Now, please remove eighty-five percent of your clothing."

Funny. She was the funny, fun one. Anything he did to make her laugh was some weird offshoot of her humor and something about her. Being with her.

She wrinkled her nose. "Why are you looking at me like that?"

"Like what?"

"I don't know. Kind of..." She made a jerky

gesture with her hands. "Never mind, just take off your clothes."

"Are you sure you don't want to talk first?"

She dropped her elbows, laughing, which made her chest bounce. He'd had about all the bouncing he could take.

"Let's talk later." She patted the space on the bed next to her. "I would like to be doing other things with my mouth right now. Fun things. I would very much like some fun."

It was that little hint of sadness that had him reaching behind his head and pulling his shirt off. She probably did deserve some fun, and, really, what could be more fun than this?

It was a hell of a lot better than furniture shopping.

"You look good in a uniform, Marc, but hello, six-pack, you look even better out."

"I'm not sure I've ever been so shamelessly ogled before."

She sat up and smiled, the queen-of-the-world smile that had basically knocked him speechless the first time she'd flashed it his way. "What a waste. I'll make up for lost time. Drop the pants."

He did as she instructed, if only because she seemed to need that. Things to go her way—the way she wanted them—and who was he not to give her that? He was good at giving that and at least there was something in this for him.

She sighed, eyes roaming everywhere before they met his, full of fun and mischief. "A plus."

"I didn't realize I was being graded."

"Pop quiz. Now, here's the real test. Can you talk me out of my underwear?"

He knelt on the empty space next to her on her bed. She needed fun and distractions. Words might not be his forte, but he'd find a way to give her what she needed.

"Do I need to talk you out of them?" He traced the strap of her bra with one finger, gently nudging it off the curve of her shoulder then repeating the process on the other side. "I'm not so good with the talking. Doing, on the other hand…"

"Doing…works," she replied, her voice getting breathy as he traced his index finger along the edge of her bra. Her skin was warm, soft, and the flowery scent that had irritated him so much those first few days seemed to intensify without her clothes on.

He moved a hand up to cup her jaw, to make her look him in the eye rather than where he'd been touching her.

"Just so we're one hundred percent clear." He kept his focus on her eyes, his body from touching hers, even though it was hard. So. Damn. Hard. "Are you sure you want to do this?"

Her eyes widened a little, and she cleared her throat. "What, I'm going to say no, I'm not sure, and you're going to put your clothes on and leave?"

"I would."

She looked horrified for a second, though he couldn't figure out why. What was he going to do? Force himself on her? Surely, she didn't think…

Before he could finish that thought, she pushed him onto his back and straddled him. "You, Marc Santino, are a little too good to be true." She reached behind her back and unclasped her bra, letting it fall. "And for that, you are going to get yourself a reward." She leaned forward, her breasts brushing his chest before her mouth sank into his.

Well, he wouldn't say no to a little reward.

CHAPTER NINE

ANY TREPIDATION, ANY DOUBTS Tess had had disappeared. All he'd had to say was "I would" and all the rules and determinations she'd set for herself, for her life evaporated. Because no one, not one person she could think of, had ever been able to give up something they wanted for her.

Marc had said he would, so seriously, so earnestly, as though there wasn't even another choice. How could she not sleep with the guy? How could she not fall for the guy, regardless of how little she knew about him or how little time they'd known each other?

She didn't know about his family, the weird thing with his sister, why he'd come here. But she knew he cared. She knew he was a good man. Who liked biographies and sports and quiet.

She knew that the erection currently pressing against the juncture of her thighs needed to be inside her. With absolute certainty.

His big palms slid down her back, his fingers inching under the hem of her underwear until he cupped her butt. She moved against him and he groaned against her mouth.

"I should have, uh, brought this up sooner, but if you don't have condoms I'm going to need about twenty minutes to regain brainpower and run to the closest gas station."

"Lucky you, I am a prepared woman."

"Thank God."

"Be right back." She hopped off him and hurried to the bathroom, pushing around under the sink until she found the rarely used box of condoms. She took a quick peek at the expiration date, gratified that it wasn't until next year.

She all but skipped back to her bedroom, absolutely refusing to let any bad thoughts or regrets invade. Returning to find him on his back, arms folded behind his head, black boxer shorts riding up those impressive thighs, well, it helped.

"Please tell me you work out all the time to look like that."

The corner of his mouth quirked up. "Moving kind of put a dent in my schedule, but I'd be lying if I said I didn't spend a decent amount of time in the gym. I'm sure not as much as your bodybuilder."

She grinned at that. The fact he remembered that one random mention of James was weirdly sweet.

She tossed the condom on the bed next to him, then wiggled out of her panties. Enough weird sweetness. Enough him looking good enough to eat. Time to get to the main event.

"Christ, you're gorgeous."

She worked pretty hard to stay in shape, more for work and reputation than out of sheer vanity, but the tiny vain part of her was gratified to hear he thought so.

"Not so bad yourself. Please tell me you played football. I've been fantasizing about you in those tight pants."

"Sorry to disappoint. If it makes you feel better, that run the other day about killed me."

"Wimp."

"Not because of the distance. Because of you, in front of me, in spandex."

She laughed at that, couldn't help it. Imagining him being a little tortured during their run was a nice thought.

"You didn't even make a move."

"You didn't want me to."

When he said things like that, she was certain there was something hard and painful inside her chest, squeezing her heart. The feeling was so deep and real and new, and scary. Scary and exciting all wrapped up into this weird pain—hurty and nice at the same time.

She cleared her throat for who knew what time. "You didn't exactly act like you liked me those first few days."

"Kind of my default. I'm not very good with people. I tend to keep my distance. Easier that way."

She wondered what was easier, but maybe now—standing next to her bed naked, with him almost naked—wasn't the time for that conversation.

"Come here," he said as she hovered by the edge of the bed. "Please," he added, as if being polite was some sort of necessity in the bedroom.

She slid next to him, and his arms came around her, and why had she ever thought this could be something she could resist?

"I like you." He kissed her neck. "I respect you." Her shoulder.

"I…know." Why the hell was respect a turn-on? She had no idea. Maybe because she worked so hard for it. And he got that.

"I want you," he said, his voice lower, his hand gliding up her side, to her breast, cupping it and brushing his thumb across her nipple.

The warmth in her heart spread, centered at her core. He lowered his mouth to her nipple, tongue brushing across it just as his thumb had.

Yeah, this was definitely going to be okay. She slid her leg between his, enjoying the coarse friction, and then the hard length of him against her thigh. His hands roamed her back, her ass, her hips, his mouth exploring her chest.

She traveled his body with her hands, following the dips of muscle, the hard planes of his chest and abdomen. When his hands slid between her legs, she let hers slip under the waistband of his boxers.

She grasped his erection, squeezed lightly until he hissed out her name. She smiled, tugging at the boxers with her free hand until he got the hint and kicked them off.

Then there was nothing between them, and that was exactly what she wanted—what she needed tonight. She pawed around the bed for the condom packet she'd thrown on there. Enough exploration, enough teasing, she wanted more. She wanted to feel as if nothing, nothing separated them, even if it was a lie.

She finally found it, tore it open and produced the condom. "Ready?"

"Nah," he said, folding his arms behind his head again. "I could take it or leave it."

"Ha. Funny guy."

She liked the way he looked when she said he was funny. Baffled and pleased, one of those full-blown smiles that creased the skin around his eyes.

She liked even better when she rolled the condom onto his dick and the expression vanished. His gaze sharpening on her hands, his lips parting as she straddled him. His hands came to her hips, a grasp. Easy, light.

She liked that about him, how he could make her feel easy and light when nothing in life ever had been. Even relationships. Always shrouded by the things she tried to keep separate.

But Marc knew.

She didn't want to think about that now, so she lowered herself onto him, focused on sensation, body heat, being filled with him, enveloped by his arms.

"Hold on."

When she did, wrapping her arms around his neck, he very deftly rolled them so she was on her back, and he was on top, still inside her. "This okay?"

"Um, yes, I am not lodging any complaints." When he smiled, she smiled back. She could not recount a time when sex had ever been so smiley.

He brushed his lips against hers, slowly pushing deep, and it wasn't so smiley. It was more dreamy. Yummy. A delicious and much-deserved treat. Slow and languorous, he entered, withdrew, elbows bracketing her face, eyes never leaving hers except to occasionally glance at where they met.

She was about to hesitantly explain to him she could usually only orgasm if she was on top, but his hand drifted down her thigh, to her knee, lifting it, adjusting the angle and—oh, well—that could work.

"Better?" he murmured into her ear.

"Uh-huh." She arched to meet each thrust, the sparkling heated rise starting to fizzle, grow, explode. As she went over the edge, Marc's mouth crushed to hers, the first sign of any impatience, anything other than quietly restrained interest.

But that kiss, as the orgasm rocked through her,

was all pent-up desire. Lust. Lusty thoughts, and his thrusts went deeper, quicker, until he pushed one last time, pulsing his own release.

He collapsed on top of her, and it was strangely satisfying. Or was that just the orgasm? Nope—granted, some of it was the last dregs of pleasure—but some of it was the weight of him on top of her, pressing her into the mattress, making it feel as if this was where she wanted to be.

If only that were possible.

No. Not yet. For now this moment was all that mattered. The future could go screw itself.

MARC KNEW HE should go, or at least offer to go, but lounging in Tess's bed with her, still naked, was too damn great to willingly pry himself away from.

Tess sighed against his chest, the pattern she'd been drawing over and over on his abdomen with her fingers coming to a halt.

"Um, so that was great."

"It was that." He let his fingers trail through her hair, all loose down her back, but some of the lazy indulgence left her body, muscles getting tight, posture going rigid as she pushed up onto her elbow.

"You should…I know this sounds terrible, but you should probably go."

He met her apologetic smile and tried to make one in return. "No, I get it." And he did. He really did, but that didn't stop him from wishing things were a little different. He scooted off the bed and went in search of his clothes.

He'd spent a lot of his life wishing things were different, and it had never changed much of anything. So he got it better than she could possibly understand.

"I hope you do, Marc. Because I wish you could stay. You have no idea how badly, but my job, my reputation—it's everything to me. I need it. I need that department to look at me and see cop first, woman second. If it gets around that we—"

He stopped halfway through pulling his jeans back on, hurt that she'd even think— "I'm not going to go around bragging that we slept together, Tess."

"I know. I know." She crossed to him and framed his face with her hands, smiled. "I know."

That smile felt as if he'd won some kind of lottery. Or something bigger, better. Something he could do, just by being him. She saw when he made a gesture, an overture, when he tried to help. She noticed. She appreciated.

Even if some of his thoughts echoed all the things he was trying to escape or avoid, this was new, and he didn't want to forget what appreciation and notice felt like.

But it didn't change their reality, as evidenced by the way her smile went sad.

"I'm not sure how we're going to make this work," she said before exhaling loudly. "I know you wanted to talk about it before we…well, and maybe we should have. But I needed something for me, for once."

That resonated. Enough that he covered her hands with his, wishing he could find some way to keep them there.

"Any ideas on how to magically make this work for me? Because I'd be really good with that."

No, he didn't, though he'd be really good with it too. Sure, life and death didn't stand between them. He thought of Leah's reluctance to build a life with anyone due to her health issues. No, it wasn't something that big.

But complications did stand between him and Tess. Real complications that weren't easily dealt with, even if they weren't life or death.

He'd never presume to understand what it was like to be a woman on the force, but he doubted her reservations about her reputation were exaggerated. Especially after the way Granger had sort of disgustedly told him at the bar that night that she didn't fuck cops.

There were also down-the-road complications. As much as he hated to be the weirdo thinking that this would last, he was too much of a planner and a thinker not to recognize that even if they found a way to have a relationship, should things get serious enough for…serious things, one of them wouldn't be allowed to work at BCPD anymore.

What else did either of them have?

She pushed her thumb to the middle of his forehead. "From the pensive line right here, I'm guessing you don't have any answers for that conundrum, either."

"I...no."

"Bummer."

"Yeah."

"I guess it could be a one-night-stand thing." She stepped back, picking her bra up off the ground and putting it back on.

He didn't say anything to that, because the only thing he could think to say was *fuck, no.* And the only thing he could think to do was cross to her and take that bra right back off.

But...not what she wanted.

"I don't know how to get around it, you know?" She shrugged, stepping into her panties.

"I know." And he did. He was not the bulldozing kind of guy. He was a nice guy who did the right thing and took the high road and all that other bullshit that had gotten him nowhere.

Except here. Here was nice. More than nice, it was exactly, *exactly* where he wanted to be, more so than anywhere else he could remember being.

But he had to leave. He finished getting dressed, glanced at Tess, who was standing there in her underwear, chewing on her bottom lip.

The stirring in his dick was ridiculous and unwelcome. "It was...great."

She scratched her hands through her hair, making it even messier, even sexier. "Seems to be the consensus. I really am sor—"

"Tess."

She rolled her eyes. "Let me guess, friends don't say sorry any more than they say thank-you. I'll bring you brownies tomorrow. Or cannoli."

He should not get pleasure from her remembering that was his favorite, and he should not smile at her. But he did both. "I'll take it."

She crossed to him and he had to hold himself perfectly still to keep from indulging any of the things he wanted to do. Touch her. Hold her. Talk her back into bed, no matter how bad he was at talking.

She hesitated, then lifted on her toes and brushed a kiss against his mouth. "You're a little too amazing. I'm going to need you to develop some flaws so I can keep my hands off you."

"Well, if that's the case I'll continue to be perfect," he replied drily.

She let out another gusty sigh. "It seems silly to say it here, when there's a lot of really unfair things in life, but this blows."

"It does at that." He brushed some of the unruly hair behind her ear, then cursed himself for touching her, even in such an innocent way. Because he wanted so much damn more than that. "I do have flaws, you know."

"I know, but you hide them so admirably."

He didn't know what to say. All he knew was it

was uncomfortable having a positive characteristic attributed to him.

"Things are going to be weird now, aren't they?"

The chuckle escaped his lips, though he wasn't particularly amused. He felt, well, fuck if he knew. "We'll figure it out."

"Yeah? Okay, well, if you say so, Captain Quiet."

"Not allowed, Tess."

"You rocked this mortal's world."

"Leaving now."

"All right." She crossed her arms over her breasts, chewed on her lip a little more. "Enjoy your day off tomorrow. I won't be seeing you."

He let that sink in. "You know, you can. This doesn't negate the friends thing or the distraction thing. I'm not some creep who can't control his baser urges."

"No. You're not." She shook her head. "Too damn perfect."

"Not."

"You're going to have to give me some evidence of that." She pulled a T-shirt off the floor. It was crumpled and wrinkly, but when she put it on, it hit her midthigh, covering up the necessities. "But not tonight. I'm going to pretend the perfect guy gave me the perfect orgasm." She made a shooing motion toward the door. "You're going to have to vamoose if I'm going to accomplish that."

"Got it." Leaving was the absolute last thing he wanted to do, but he did what people wanted.

"Marc?"

He paused with his hand on her doorknob, debating whether he should look back or not. "Yeah."

"It did mean something. I don't want you to think I ignored all my rules for myself just because you're hot or I was super horny or something."

"Here I thought it was because I had X-ray vision."

She was beside him and poked his shoulder. "No. It's because you're exactly what I needed." She wrinkled her nose. "Corny, I know. But…true."

Corny, maybe, but it soothed his pathetically bruised ego. He gave her a nod, opened the door enough he could slip out without anyone looking in her door—not that he'd ever seen many people besides them in their hallway. "Night, Tess."

"Night."

She closed the door behind him, and Marc supposed that was…that.

CHAPTER TEN

TESS LOUNGED IN BED, afraid to leave her apartment. It seemed as if every time she did, poof, there was Marc, and as much as she wanted to see him, she knew she shouldn't.

The serious way he said, "I have flaws, you know," played over and over in her head. Because he did have those hidden hurts she'd been afraid he would, but she hadn't seen them. He'd seen all of hers. In all sorts of vivid detail, and the only bad thing she knew about him was he wasn't a talker.

Which, considering all his other talents, was not a bad thing. Not even a little bit. So the rest she knew about him was good and sweet, and she wasn't stupid enough to think he actually was perfect, but as she'd said last night, it was kind of nice pretending he was. He had been exactly what she'd needed.

As ill-advised as that need was.

She tried to imagine just doing it—going for it with Marc, screw what everyone at the department thought. But every time she did she saw Granger making blow job motions and Franks's opinion of her souring and...

She couldn't do it. Too much of her day was that job, too much of her life. The police academy, and then becoming a cop, had given her the kind of control she'd never had growing up, and as much as she liked Marc, as much as the sex was, well, fantastic, she couldn't trade that in for what kept her sane.

Determined, she got out of bed. She needed to run some errands, check on Dad, see if she could afford hiring another cleaning lady and, if not, do the job herself.

It was enough to keep her very, very busy.

But none of it's for you.

Well, she'd had her for-her thing last night and that was going to have to last for a while.

She pushed her feet into tennis shoes and laced them up, then stood staring at the door. There was no way she could run into Marc again. There wasn't.

But she hesitated until she realized what a wimp she was being. She'd been the one to initiate sleeping with him. She'd been the one to say it couldn't be more than that. So she could damn well stand to run into him in the hallway and not immediately remove all of her clothing.

And his.

God, he looked good naked.

"Focus." Maybe if she said it out loud she'd be able to. She took a glance out her peephole and hoped the hallway was as empty as it appeared.

Gingerly, she opened the door, and the hallway

was indeed empty. Feeling like an idiot, she tiptoed to the stairwell, then carefully walked down the two flights of stairs.

She made it to her car, no Marc in sight. She was relieved. Really. That heavy, sinking feeling in her chest was relief, not disappointment.

Or maybe it was dread. Dread over going to check on Dad. Yeah, she'd go with that one.

She drove the few miles to her father's apartment. In the daylight she didn't feel that carrying was as necessary, and if she was going to run errands afterward, she hated toting her gun around.

That didn't mean she didn't watch apartment 1C with a close eye as she crossed the patchy, poorly kept yard in front of the poorly kept, sunken-in, sagging apartment complex.

It was all she could afford for him and keep them living separately, and that was one of the few things they agreed on—not sharing a place.

She knocked, hoping she had really rid his apartment of all the liquor last night. Or that he'd just be waking up, unable to start looking for a drink yet.

When Dad didn't answer, fear and dread and guilt lodged in her throat. Oh, hell, when didn't it when she was on either side of this door?

She pulled out her keys and unlocked the door. "Dad?"

The kitchen and living room looked the same as they had last night. Nothing seemed to have moved.

Oh, God, what if she'd missed something last night? What if he really had been hurt and she'd missed—

A groan emerged from the hallway and she hurried to it, but Dad wasn't sprawled out on the ground. He was in either his bedroom or bathroom and she wished for some relief.

It didn't appear.

"Dad?"

He stumbled out of the bathroom, grizzled and unsteady. He pointed a shaking hand at her. "You took it."

She recognized that look. Too well these days. Anger. Blame. Violence. She didn't always want to fight back. In fact, usually it made her sad. Like that little girl trying to figure out why it was her fault Mom had left.

She didn't feel sad now. She felt downright furious because she'd spent her entire life trying to fix him, help him, make it up to him—even if she knew there was nothing to make up.

And he couldn't give an inch. Give her one break. One year, one month, one fucking week where she got to worry about her own life and her own problems and just plain old her. One morning where she'd come and he'd be sober or with it enough to be… normal.

Normal had gotten increasingly sporadic, and she hadn't even realized it until now. Months and months of things getting worse. A gradual escalation.

She was at her breaking point. "Yup. Took them. Dumped them out. And I'll keep doing it."

He lunged toward her, hand raised as if he was going to slap. Normally she sidestepped attempts at a blow, but today she didn't have it in her to be the passive avoider. She grabbed his wrist, twisting his arm behind his back like she'd do to any lowlife who tried to attack her when she was on duty.

"You're sick, but you're pushing me too far." Tears stung her eyes, regret loosening her grip. She stepped back, releasing his arm. "I can't do much more of this, Dad."

He sank to the floor and started to sob. Loud, messy sobs that eroded the last dregs of anger in her heart.

"Why can't you help me, Tessie? Why won't you make me better? Everything could be better if you'd just find a way…" The rest of the words were unintelligible.

"Go to a hospital, Dad. A treatment facility. It's the only way. You're not well, and I can't make you better."

"No wonder she left." He looked over his shoulder at her, then spat on her shoe. "You're terrible, Tessie. So fucking terrible. You're supposed to help me. You."

It shouldn't hurt. The lies, the words of a sick, pathetic man should not cut right through her.

But they did. They hurt. Hurt enough that there

was nothing else to do but leave. Because she couldn't help him. She couldn't fix him.

And she was tired of trying.

THE LAST THING Marc wanted to do today was go to lunch with Leah, but it was probably the best thing he could do with himself. If he stayed in the apartment, well, his reputation as perfect was about to be seriously tarnished.

He was used to ignoring what he really wanted for the sake of the greater good. In fact, he was so used to it he didn't even realize he was doing it half the time. Also, because he'd gotten so used to it, he'd all but stopped letting himself want things.

But regardless of the past or the present, he wanted Tess. Badly. That usual ease he had with denying himself was sorely absent.

So he grabbed his phone and wallet and keys and walked out to his truck intent on having lunch with his sister, whom he had no idea what to talk to about.

Yippee.

He glanced at Tess's door as he stepped into the hallway. It wasn't as if he actually expected to see her. Despite that that seemed to happen to them frequently enough.

He wasn't at all disappointed that he made it to his car without a glimpse of her. Not a bit. In fact, he was relieved that her car wasn't in the lot. She was out enjoying her day off, and he would be doing the same.

Good for the both of them.

He drove down to Main Street and the place Leah had suggested for lunch. She was already there, sitting at a table and fiddling with the menu.

"Hey," he greeted, taking the chair opposite her. He didn't know if he should be comforted or disappointed she looked about as awkward as he felt.

"Hey. How's it going?"

"Good. Good."

"Good."

It was ridiculous that they were siblings and yet awkward silence was the most common thing between them. But, hell, if he didn't know what to do about it after years, when was he going to start?

They made some strained small talk, ordered, then each looked around the restaurant as they waited for their food. Marc racked his brain for something to say, but the harder he tried, the blanker he got.

The food finally came, and they each began to eat. It was painful. Why had he agreed to this?

Because you're trying not to be a dick of an older brother.

Right.

"So." Leah popped a fry into her mouth. "Um, scttling in at work?"

"Yeah, it's good." But he didn't want to talk about work because work involved Tess and, yeah, no. He took a big bite of his hamburger instead.

Another silence with Leah tapping and fidgeting. "Any action with the boss lady?"

He choked on the bite of food but managed to swallow. "You're not seriously asking me that." The fact that his face was getting hot with embarrassment made it worse.

She chuckled. "I don't know what to ask you, and that's about all I know about your life. So, until you're willing to spill more details..." She lifted her palms to the air then dropped them. "I got nothin' else."

"How's Jacob?"

She groaned. "Please, I love the guy, but I already have to have this conversation with Mom all the time. Next thing you know you'll be asking if we've been engagement-ring shopping yet or giving me tips on how to get Jacob to propose."

"She thinks you're waiting till they move so she can be part of wedding preparations."

"Ugh. Jacob is lucky he's worth putting up with her for."

"It's because she cares." It didn't make sense. Mom's antics toward Leah were ridiculous and over-the-top, but when Leah criticized her, even rightfully, he always felt the need to defend. And he felt like a tool.

Was being here really better than trying to keep his hands off Tess?

"I know she cares. But it doesn't make it less annoying. You're older, why can't she be trying to marry you off?"

Because she doesn't care about me. But he didn't

say that. He focused on eating and finding a subject that would have nothing to do with their mother.

"Did you watch the Wild game the other night? Where Rominski got his nose bashed in?" Hockey was the safest topic he could come up with. So he hit it hard even though he knew Leah preferred base-ball.

Anything was better than the three topics they'd already covered: Tess, Mom, caring.

They awkwardly made it through the rest of lunch, and it wasn't terrible. After the not-so-great start, it had gotten easier, more comfortable. No matter how little they knew about each other's lives, no matter how many issues in their relationship, she was his sister, and he wanted to try.

"Um, you know, if you want to make some friends, I'd really like it if you came to one of our MC outings. I think you and Kyle would get along pretty well. And Henry. You're all the silent broody type. You can sit around glowering at each other."

He managed a chuckle. "Sounds like a blast."

She reached across the table and awkwardly pat-ted his arm, which was about as good as a hug from Leah. "It'd be good. To meet some people. Henry's girlfriend is having us do some potluck dinner–type thing to welcome spring or whatever. You should come."

"Am I going to be the only single person there?"

"You could bring your boss lady."

"No. Coworker. Period."

"Sure."

"I should get going. But…I'll think about it." He stood as she did and then they managed an awkward side hug. "This was good."

She smiled up at him. "Yes. It was. Hopefully it'll get better."

"Guess we'll have to keep at it."

"Guess so." She released him. "I'm glad you're here. I'll even be glad when Mom and Dad are here. Please remind me I feel that way when I'm tearing out my hair."

"Deal." They said their goodbyes and walked to separate cars, and Marc did actually feel a little good about how lunch had gone. He didn't imagine that staying in place once Mom and Dad moved to Bluff City for good, surrounding him with their constant Leah worship, but for the interim, he'd call it a success.

He occupied himself for the rest of the afternoon by trying to find a gym with a decent rate and decent equipment and then grocery shopping for the week. He was quite proud of himself. He'd had a productive day that didn't involve ruminating over the Tess situation…too much. Maybe he'd tossed a box of condoms into his cart at the store, but they were just…to have on hand. Not in case Tess changed her mind about the one-night-stand thing.

Suuuure.

He pulled into the parking lot of his apartment complex and refused to scan the lot for Tess's car.

If she was here, great. If not, that was great, too. Not something he needed to concern himself with at present.

He managed to finagle all the bags into his grasp and walked up the flights of stairs to his apartment.

And there was Tess. On his doorstep. Looking sheepish. And beautiful. How the hell was he supposed to make the right choice here?

CHAPTER ELEVEN

"GROCERY SHOPPING. I did that, too," Tess greeted lamely.

"Um. Oh." He stood there at the top of the stairs, blinking at her, holding what looked like an uncomfortable number of bags.

"Can I help?"

He blinked again, then seemed to resign himself to the fact she was here, butting into his life again.

Because, damn it, she wanted something good in her life and he was the best available option.

He stepped toward his door, keys already in hand. "Are you sure you want to do that?"

She pushed to a standing position so he could get to his door and unlock it. "Yes," she said, sounding like a breathy idiot. "I'm sure."

He did his nod thing and then pushed the door open, inclining his head in a signal for her to go first.

While he held on to a lot of heavy-looking grocery bags, biceps straining at the weight. *Hi, biceps, we missed you.*

Jeez.

He pushed the door closed with his foot and then

strode to the kitchen. Without saying anything, he began to unpack his groceries. It was annoyingly all healthy stuff, too. Like fruits and vegetables and tuna fish. Protein powder and yogurt.

Not a damn bag of gummy worms in sight. She could really use some gummy worms. Bears would do in a pinch.

Because she'd never done anything like this. Like last night. She didn't ignore reason and what had to be done for what she wanted. Never. In all her life.

But that's what she was going to do, damn it. Yes, that's what she was going to do. "I have a proposition for you."

He looked up from his mushrooms. He'd seriously bought mushrooms?

"Proposition?" he said at length, and though he kept his expression frustratingly blank in that way he had when they'd first worked together, she noticed his hand had tightened on the package of mushrooms. Considerably.

"I...yes. A proposition. One you're free to say no to."

He turned to the refrigerator, shoving the mushrooms inside with more force than necessary. Followed by a bag of baby carrots, a package of broccoli.

Seriously, where was the junk food? The secret cake stash. The cookies, damn it.

"You think I'll say no to any proposition you're going to offer me?" he asked, his back still turned.

"Well, it's kind of insulting."

His posture changed and the noise that came out of his mouth, something like a harsh laugh, wasn't exactly nice.

Hidden hurts.

She took a deep breath. He knew her hurts, she could know his. And they could have something. If they were careful.

Something for her. For once.

"I thought maybe... Well, the thing is... You know, this would be easier to do if you could turn around and look at me."

He didn't do it right away. Stood straighter, then after a few humming seconds closed the refrigerator door, slowly turning around, eyes meeting hers.

She opened her mouth but no sound came out, because, jeez. He was looking at her all broody and intense like last night and, um, what was she thinking/saying/doing?

"Go on."

"Right. Right." She took a step forward, wringing her hands. She couldn't remember a time she'd felt this nervous, this vulnerable, because she'd learned a long time ago not to ask for things she wanted. She'd learned to go out and get things herself or to do without.

She should do without, but what an exhausting way to live. And Marc was right here and—

"Tess."

"I thought we could sleep together again," she blurted, hating herself a little even as excitement sparked in her blood. "Maybe date, but it'd all have to be done secretly—that's the insulting part."

He didn't move. Didn't speak. Didn't react. It was so Marc. She wished she could do that as well as he did. Study. Assess. Think, all without giving away a thing.

"You can say no," she said again, not quite as flippantly or steadily as she would have preferred.

"Why would you risk this thing that's so important to you? I don't mean that dismissively. I understand why it's so important to you, Tess. I do. So, why?"

She had no doubt he did understand, and she had no doubt if he kept being so sweet and understanding she'd choke to death on the lump in her throat, because, damn it, she was not crying in front of him again. No way.

She swallowed, cleared her throat, trying to dislodge that lump. "My whole life right now, and for a very long time, is and has been two things. Work and my dad. I love my work. I don't know what I'd do without it, but the fact of the matter is I help people all day, or try to help people all day, and then I either come home and hide out from helping my father, or I go help him. I don't get a whole lot of thanks from any of these people I'm helping, you know?"

"I do."

He said it so emphatically, it made her think about all those little hints that he had something going on under the surface. Those hidden hurts she wanted to know more about. She wanted to see him. Understand him.

She stepped forward, purposefully dropping her hands to her sides so she'd stop wringing them together. "Nothing is for me. Every once in a while I scrimp enough money together to buy a leather jacket or a nice phone instead of the cheapest version. Every once in a while I sit down for an evening and binge on a TV show. But, like, ninety-five percent of my life is not… It's doing things for other people, and as much as I like that or don't have a choice in that, I'm at a breaking point, I guess. A pre-midlife crisis. I want something for me."

"And that's…"

She put her palm to his chest. "That's you." She forced herself to look into those intense brown eyes, the color of some sweet liqueur. "I like you. I like how I feel with you. Maybe I can't really have you, but if we could pretend for a little bit, on the down low, I could really, really use that."

He opened his mouth to speak, but she wasn't ready for that, so she put her hand over his mouth. Which was silly, but she liked touching him. She liked being this close. And she liked that he let her do it.

"I don't mean, like, I need you to swoop in and save me."

"I'm getting tired of the superhero thing," he grumbled against her palm.

Which made her smile. She liked his grumble. That he didn't take everything she dished out.

"I just mean to say, I'm not some helpless, desperate creature, no matter how much this week has tried to prove otherwise. I will survive if you say no. You should only do it if—"

His hand grasping her wrist and tugging it away from his mouth was enough of a surprise. Then his mouth was on hers and, oh, hell, who cared? They were done talking.

His arms banded around her, holding her close, nearly immobile. Desire and frustration simmering in the way his mouth crushed to hers. Which was somehow so freaking hot, that combo.

He pulled back, but only about an inch, and his arms around her didn't loosen, the warm coil of desire not cooling a degree. "Are you busy right now?" he asked.

She blinked up at him, trying to make sense of words that weren't *take off your clothes right now.* "N-no. Not busy."

"Did you want to discuss the details of this arrangement first?"

"Oh, God, no."

"Good." His mouth crushed to hers again and she was being propelled back to the couch and she shouldn't be this giddy and excited over something that could be such a giant mistake.

But she was, and hell, might as well enjoy it.

BUYING THOSE CONDOMS had come in really handy. He was pretty sure he'd never had floor sex before. Which was a shame. There was a lot to be said for floor sex.

There was a lot to be said for Tess. Period.

And a lot to be said for how damn complicated this was, but Tess was curled up against him, head on his shoulder, and the thing she wanted— something for her—echoed something he wanted. She deserved it way more than he did, probably, but it didn't change the fact he understood what it was like to ignore or push away your own wants for the sake of someone else.

That he wanted something for himself. Wanted to live for himself. Now was as good a time as any.

Except it's secret. And you're still coming in second.

Well, so be it. Let it be the biggest secret he'd ever kept. It being secret—just theirs—made it even better. More theirs. Untouchable by anything else.

And if she refused his help sometimes, well, he could deal with it. He was good at dealing with that kind of thing.

At least she appreciated the offer.

"This rug is uncomfortable," Tess murmured into his neck before pressing a kiss to his jaw and getting to her feet. She scratched a hand through her unruly hair as she looked around the room, presumably for her clothes, which were quite impressively strewn about, if he did say so himself.

Even more impressive, the sight of Tess, naked, standing above him. Very impressive. Perfect, really.

She grinned down at him, nudged his leg with her foot. "I like you smug."

"I didn't know that was an admirable trait." He clasped his hand around her ankle, moving his thumb over the curve of bone.

"It looks good on you on occasion." She bent over and picked up her panties, stepping her free foot into one opening and then trying to pull her ankle from his grasp.

Because she was here, not tossing him out or scurrying away, because this was so much better than being alone, than just about anything right now, he released her leg but got to his knees.

"As much as I hate to see you cover up, let me help." He slowly edged the hem of the underwear up her legs, gliding across the smooth skin of her calves, thighs, hips, until they were all the way up. He pressed a kiss to one hip bone, then the other, desire stirring yet again.

Her hand smoothed over the top of his head, and she gazed down at him with heavy-lidded eyes. "Wow, ready for round two?"

He opened his mouth to respond, to keep the easy, fun banter going, but his phone rang.

Tess cocked her head. "Caller ID says *Mom*."

"I'll call her back later." He got to his feet, reached over to the end table where his phone was and clicked the ringer off.

"You can take it. Or call her back right now, if you want."

"Tess, you really want me to talk to my mother with the start of a hard-on while you're standing there almost completely naked?"

Her lips quirked a little, but she looked back at the phone, an odd pained look on her face. "Is she terrible?"

"Nope, she's great."

Her eyes finally returned to his face. "You don't seem convinced."

"I don't?" He handed her her bra, because if she really wanted to talk about his mother, he was not going to do it while she was naked.

She slipped it over her arms and he rooted around for his boxers and pants, purposefully not meeting her gaze.

"No. You say it like it's something you're supposed to feel, not something you actually mean."

"But I do mean it. She's great. Dad's great. Love them both."

"Yeah, still not very convincing."

He pulled his shirt over his head, noticing she'd done the same. "I don't know what you want me to say, Tess. I'm not lying."

She was quiet for a few moments, studying him carefully, as if she could see through it all, which was silly. The whole thing was silly. Her thinking he didn't mean it. The guilt coating his stomach. The fact that one phone call he hadn't even taken from his mother had interrupted something that had been pretty damn great.

Tess touched her fingertips to his cheek. "Tell me something I don't know about you."

He arched an eyebrow at her, but she only smiled. A smile that could do a hell of a lot of damage to the male population, he was convinced. Or maybe just a whole lot of damage to him.

"One thing. You know everything about me."

"No, I don't."

She rolled her eyes. "All the big stuff. Tell me something big."

"Well, I'm invincible, being a superhero and all."

She poked him in the chest. "There's that sense of humor, but it won't deflect me, sir. I am trained in the art of interrogation."

"And I am trained in the art of not giving anything away."

Her eyebrows drew together and she smoothed the finger digging into his chest to press her palm to his heart. "One thing. Please?"

He supposed he could give her something. Why he had become a police officer. What it was like growing up with a gravely ill sibling, and all the weird stuff that remained because of that. But it seemed so lame in comparison to what she'd been through, and if this whole...arrangement was for her, something just for her, maybe he could be what she needed and not worry about himself. He was good at that.

He at least deserved to keep some piece of himself hidden away, some piece of himself that wouldn't be hurt when this didn't work out.

"You know last night when you kissed me and then left?"

"I do recall."

"I came back here and jerked off in the shower."

She pouted, but it curved at the ends. "That's not very big."

"You'd be surprised."

She clapped a hand over her mouth as she laughed. "Awful. Dirty, dirty." Then she wrapped her arms around his neck and squeezed. "Love it, you secret perv."

He allowed himself to wrap his arms around her waist, enjoy the feel of her pressed up against him. He even allowed a little sliver of seriousness to intrude. "I'm very boring. I have led a very uninteresting, safe, pleasant life."

She pulled back just enough so their eyes could meet. "You don't seem pleased by your uninteresting, safe, pleasant life."

She wasn't going to give up, and maybe he wasn't willing to give her something big—not when hers was all so much bigger, not when sharing everything would be…too much—but maybe he could find some sliver to give her.

"You know, I find myself doing a lot for other people, pushing what I want to the background. I don't have nearly as good a reason for it as you do. But I understand wanting something for yourself."

Her lips curved, and it struck him how pretty she was, the heavy top lip, the slight dusting of freckles on her nose and those eyes. She was gorgeous, inside and out. "Do you have any idea how beautiful you are?"

She visibly swallowed. "You know, if you weren't so good at that serious face, I'd tell you that was one cheesy line."

"I mean it, though."

"I know you do." She brushed her mouth across his. "You want to make it to bed this time? I have some creative ideas for pillows before I turn into a pumpkin and have to get back to my place."

"You could stay."

She pulled her bottom lip between her teeth. "Um, actually, I think it's best if we're sort of careful about the time we leave each other's apartments. No late nights. No early mornings. Never at the same time."

He wouldn't let that hurt because she'd been upfront from the beginning. She couldn't let this thing between them threaten her career. She wouldn't let him help with her father. He wouldn't let it hurt, because he understood how important a job could be. How family obligations could tangle up your life.

So he smiled and gestured toward his bedroom. "Lead the way."

CHAPTER TWELVE

WORK WAS WEIRD. There was no getting around it. Tess was hyperaware of every movement of her body, how it might be construed, as if anyone could see right through her. Even after a week of lots of sex with Marc but no sleepovers, and acting like nothing but coworkers at the station, she couldn't get comfortable.

She wished his two weeks of riding shotgun weren't over. If she was behind the wheel she could focus on driving, focus on anything other than *did I just stare at his butt? Did someone notice me staring at his butt?* But since her job for the next two-ish months was observing him, she couldn't stop second-guessing every look, every order, every compliment.

This whole arrangement they had was turning out to be a pain in the butt, until she remembered all the sex.

Good sex. Also, Marc cooked for her. He'd watched the first few episodes of *Friends* with her even though for some terrible reason he didn't find it funny. But he tried. Good food. Good company. Great sex. It was kind of worth eight hours of tor-

ture four to six days a week. Eight hours of them
responding to calls together, in his car, with him
behind the wheel, being his unchatty, überhot self.

Luckily, Dad had been calling all morning after
an almost weeklong silence, which at least took her
attention off Marc every once in a while. She could
instead feel miserable over the way they'd left things,
over her determination not to go over there or talk
to him for a while.

So when the phone vibrated in her pocket, she ignored it. Marc hadn't said anything, but she knew
the insistent buzzing that had caused her to turn off
the ringer completely wasn't fooling him.

But he didn't say anything. He had to have some
kind of dark, horrifying secret past, because the guy
was too damn good at giving her what she wanted.
How was she supposed to combat that? Not make
it obvious at work that she was falling for him? Not
be desperate to spend the night with him instead of
trudging back to her place or sending him on his
way to his?

But it was her life. So she was taking what she
wanted. He was too good to be true, so she was taking him. Even while she waited for the other shoe to
drop. For some nasty past to come to the forefront.

Was it realism or paranoia that kept her looking
for something bad? Something off? Even as she
spent as much time with him as she could logically
excuse. Even when he made her laugh.

Perfect did not exist, but aside from not liking

small talk and not keeping a supply of gummy anything, the guy was damn near perfect. She was almost kind of desperate to find a flaw. Just to believe
he was real and not, say, some serial killer.

She really needed to get it together. "We should
probably head back to the station for roll call."

Marc nodded wordlessly, changing course. God,
this was painful. But in the most incomprehensible
way, it was kind of...exciting pain. All this awkward silence and overcautiousness with each other
would melt away as soon as they got home. It would
be shed as quickly as their clothes and, yes, it was
weird and warped, but totally worth it.

At least during roll call they could sit separately,
although Tess would rather sit next to Marc and pretend that he was repulsive than listen to Granger
whisper-complain about some bitch who rejected
him last night while Captain talked about a situation down on the docks that the night shift needed
to be looking into.

Tess managed to focus on that, mentally noting
some stuff to discuss with one of the night shift
guys tomorrow morning. Police work. She was a
policewoman and she could and would think about
things other than a hot guy taking care of her every
yummy need.

Shh, brain.

Evening shift guys dispersed to get in their cars,
some of the day shifters took their time to start head-

ing out, but Tess and Marc waited them out until they were the only two in the room.

"Ready?" He didn't smile, but that serious cop face was relaxed somewhat, anticipation sparking in his eyes.

He was much better at the not-smiling thing, because she couldn't help herself. She grinned up at him, with only the sights and smells of a job that was everything to her as a reminder she had to keep her hands in her pockets.

"Camden?" Franks's voice barked.

Tess jumped, which she knew only made her look guilty. Which she kind of was, but not... *Get it together.* "Captain?"

"Who did this report?" He held up some papers. "Two nights ago. Attempted robbery over on Shirley Lane."

"Um, well, Santino did, sir." She hated to throw Marc under the bus, but he had done the report. "I read over it, of course, before we sent it into the system, but—"

"Relax, Camden. First report I haven't had to send back in ages, aside from yours. Good job, Santino. And, Tess, you're definitely proving yourself as the best damn FTO I've ever had here."

"Th-thank you."

Franks nodded then left, and Tess wanted to sink into a chair. She wanted to disappear. Turn back time. Because, shit, shit, shit, she was risking Franks's good opinion of her for...

She glanced at Marc and he smiled ruefully.

"Bit of a scare, huh?"

Tess nodded. The scare hadn't even completely worn off, and yet…against everything she would have ever expected herself to do, she reached out and squeezed his hand. Quickly. "Worth it," she said on little more than a whisper. Because it was worth the scare, and the tiptoeing and the fear they'd get found out.

Because this was for her, and something just for her felt too good not to be worth it. Marc felt too good not to be worth it.

He blinked once, the surprise in his features so palpable she wondered if anyone had ever seen what she saw when she looked at him. Someone completely, utterly worth it.

Watch it.

She needed to. Calm it down. Back off. Keep her eye on what was important. But…but…

She didn't want to.

WHEN MARC AND Tess arrived at their building, they did what they'd been doing the past few workday afternoons. She made a big production of saying goodbye at the patrol car, dawdled around a bit while he entered his apartment. He left the door unlocked, which went against every ounce of safety he believed in.

But about thirty minutes after, she'd slip into his

apartment, having changed into plainclothes, and always start with the same greeting.

"I'm starving."

And the unlocked door for thirty minutes was worth it. How they'd created a routine in such a short period of time, a routine he hated to break, was beyond him. Everything to do with her was beyond him.

He was freakishly enjoying this. So having to interrupt the routine blew. Hard. "I, uh, have to have dinner with my family tonight." He'd been meaning to tell her that all week, but it kept...not being said. Possibly because he was dreading the visit, so he really didn't want to talk about it. Or have her ask more questions about his family. Have her want to know anything.

Things were good. He didn't need her to find out about his lame issues and think less of him. She thought he was worth it. Worth risking something she'd once said was everything to her.

He was important to someone, and he was going to make sure he kept that up. Give her everything she wanted, make her believe he was that guy without any flaws.

"In Minnesota?"

"No."

She poked his shoulder. "Joking." Then she frowned at the bowl he'd put together for her. "But that's food."

"I made it for you."

She looked at him in wonder. "You didn't have to do that."

"You eat crap, and it's just leftovers from last night."

She shook her head, pulling the bowl toward her. "And you think *I'm* a mother hen." She took a bite, moaned in a way that was not fair when he had to leave soon to make it to Leah's for dinner with his parents.

"You can eat here if you want." *Wait for me.* But he didn't say that, because it wouldn't be fair to ask.

"If things were different…" She got that soft look that had become the expression he associated with *time to go.*

He pushed a strand of hair behind her ear, because she always smiled when he did, because these nights seemed to be the only time she didn't have her hair pulled back and he liked the feel of it between his fingers.

"That if-things-were-different list is getting long, isn't it?" she asked, putting the bowl down and stepping so they were close enough for her to lean against him.

"Yes, and quickly."

Tess sighed. "I just don't know…"

"I know."

She let out an exasperated sigh. "I envy how you always say that with absolute certainty."

"I don't—"

Her phone buzzed. He knew she'd turned it off

this morning, but apparently she'd turned it back on. And, based on her pinched face and wince, he could guess who it was.

She looked up at him sheepishly. "I'm ignoring it."

Something twisted in his gut—an old familiar feeling. That there would never really be even ground because she'd always have this thing, buzzing in her pocket, interrupting.

Being more important.

"Ignoring it for how long?"

She looked surprised for a moment, and she stepped away. He'd crossed this weird line they had nonverbally agreed on. The line of her father.

Because it's none of your business. Because you're worth some things, but not others.

"I should get going," he said before she could answer his question. A question she didn't want him to ask so he wouldn't demand an answer. Because he was a good guy who did the right thing.

And what's that done for you so far?

Well, he was here, wasn't he? Finally with someone who saw what he did for them as meaningful. That was a pretty fantastic place to be, regardless of all the little niggling voices in his head sometimes. "Stay as long as you like. Just make sure to lock up afterward if you leave before I get back."

She studied him for a long time, and though her expression wasn't blank, it was something he couldn't read. Some emotion foreign to him.

"I'll be here when you get back," she said at last, with no hint as to why she'd studied him so hard.

"Then I'll be happy to see you."

She shook her head. "I have no idea what to do with you when you say shit like that."

"Like what?"

"Sweet, perfect, romantic shit. No idea what to do with it."

"I'll start keeping it to myself."

She fisted her hand in his shirt. "Don't you dare." She pressed a kiss to his mouth, one he wanted to deepen until he forgot about everything, but...

"Your family dinner."

"Yes. That. Bad to cancel, I guess."

"It would be. A family dinner is a nice thing to be able to have."

He should think that. He absolutely should, but the sentiment was hard to muster.

TESS SAT ON Marc's couch trying to find something on TV. It was weird being in his apartment by herself, but she hadn't made the move to go home.

Mostly because she'd said she'd be here when he got back, but even more so because he said he'd be glad.

Tess found herself smiling like an idiot. She had never felt this way before. Not so quickly, so eagerly. Maybe it had something to do with the timing—being a little fed up with her current life, but more, she thought it was Marc. Just him. Them. They clicked, seemed to give each other something, if not important, at least nice.

She had a feeling it was both. But she couldn't think about the future because that meant thinking about, well, the future. At some point she'd have to choose: Marc or reputation.

That smile-killing thought was exactly why she didn't let her mind go there.

Her phone buzzed for the umpteenth time. She'd considered hiding it in her apartment, but on the off chance Marc called she wanted it with her. As it was going, Dad hadn't left any messages, so it was just an uncomfortable reminder for a few seconds every twenty minutes or so.

You're terrible, Tessie. So fucking terrible.

No. She wasn't. He should treat her like a damn saint for all she put up with, for all she tried to do for him. He should bow at her feet every damn day.

But he didn't. He blamed. He cursed. He did everything he could to push her far away. He didn't really want help, or he'd take it.

Maybe it was time to tell him that. Stand up for herself. Live for herself.

He'd left a message this time. She would listen to it, determine his mood, and then if he was rational enough she would tell him to stop calling. She would tell him she was bowing out. No more of this. She didn't deserve it, and if he straight up refused to get better, she was too old to keep believing she could change him.

This was it. She was going to cut the ties. For good. A line in the sand. The determination made her feel some weird mix of giddy and fearful, excited and disgusted. She wanted things to change and she was done waiting. Done hoping.

It was time for an ultimatum. Doubts threatened, but the excitement over having a life that was her own was too big, too great to entertain the negative thoughts.

She called her voice mail, forcefully keying in her password. Maybe he'd be good enough she could go over there and they could sit down and have a real—

"You evil bitch."

Well, so much for that.

"You're just like your mother. Abandon me when I need you. Don't bother coming back, you worthless—"

She shakily hit the number for Delete before the message could finish. She knew what came next. Words worse than *bitch*. Threats. And she didn't want to hear them. She wouldn't.

Just like your mother.

He was right. Terribly, horrifyingly right. She was thinking about abandoning him. Walking away because it was too hard. Even though he was sick.

He's sick.

Grandma had always said that. It was the only thing Tess really remembered about her grandmother. That she'd occasionally show up, clean up wherever they were living and pat her on the head. "It's okay, Tess. He's just sick. Someday he'll get better."

But it wasn't okay, and he continued to not get better. She didn't want to believe better was a lie, but, well, she was a cop. She didn't ignore evidence.

Just like your mother.

The thought was so deeply unsettling, so awful, she immediately picked up her phone and dialed Dad's number. She was not her mother. She wouldn't give up. On anyone.

He didn't answer. She should go over there. She had to. *Don't bother coming back.* No, going over there right now would be too dangerous. He was angry. He would be violent. She wasn't going to abandon him, but she couldn't put herself in danger, either.

Was that what Mom had done? Escaped from danger? Escaped from a man who'd maybe always been this way, even though Tess had always believed this was a symptom of her mother leaving?

Maybe it wasn't. Maybe this was him. Just a sick bastard.

But if that were the case, why had her mother left Tess with him?

Tess curled up into a ball, giving in to the tears. Marc wasn't here, even though she pathetically wished he was. But he wasn't, so she let herself cry into his couch. Let herself wallow in the damn futility of the situation.

Because she would never allow herself to be her mother, so there was no way her life would ever be her own.

CHAPTER THIRTEEN

MARC LOOKED AT the cannoli on his plate and tried to force some cheer. Because Tess's words had stuck with him. A family dinner is a nice thing to be able to have.

Because she didn't have one.

"What do you think, Marc?"

Marc looked at his mother, tried to remember what they'd all been talking about before he'd zoned out.

"Are you feeling all right?" Mom reached across Leah's table and put a palm to his forehead. "You haven't been yourself. Not coming down with something, are you?"

"No, Mom, I'm fine." The concern was nice, though.

"Good. We can't forget how careful we need to be around Leah, even with just colds."

So much for concern.

"Mom, I'm around the general public all the time. Haven't keeled over yet."

Marc glanced at Leah. Jacob had his arm around her, a gesture of comfort in the face of Mom's overworrying.

Again Marc's thoughts drifted to Tess. She made him feel worthwhile, not just a bearer of germs that might incapacitate Leah. A person. A person who could give her what she wanted and needed.

Except help with her dad.

Yeah, except for that.

"Marc Paul Santino! You haven't been paying attention at all this evening."

Marc forced a contrite look. "Sorry."

"How's work?" Dad asked.

"Fine."

"Problems with the boss lady?" Leah asked, her feigned innocence fooling Mom, but not him. He glowered.

"No."

"So, then, one could construe that things are going well with the boss lady?"

He wanted to glower again, but the weirdest thing, Leah teasing him about Tess actually made him almost, *almost* laugh. A kind of sibling teasing they had never participated in much. Usually because he didn't have a teasing sense of humor.

"Who is this boss lady you're talking about? What is going on?" Mom demanded.

"Nothing is going on. Leah's just talking about my field training officer."

"A woman?"

"Yes."

"How old is she?"

"Mother."

"What? I'm just curious." Mom made a big production of wiping the sides of her mouth off with her napkin even though she'd yet to take a bite of her cannoli. "Can't I be interested in your work?"

If she had ever been, maybe. But...Mom's interests were 1. Leah. 2. Leah getting married. 3. The possibility of Leah having children. 4. Dad. Maybe Marc's marriage possibilities came in at number five. Maybe.

But, hey, five was something, right? Better than what Tess's father did to her. He needed to keep reminding himself of that.

"You're not interested in his work. You're interested in his marriage prospects."

"I most certainly am not!" Mom swatted Leah's arm playfully, a smile playing at her lips.

Though part of him was irritated at the whole conversation, at the whole dynamic of everything, he couldn't ignore the fact that Leah and Mom mending fences seemed to have made them both happier, and that was good.

Even if it only served to shove him even farther out of the fold, it was better than always trying to help bring them back together, better than comforting Mom when years ago Leah had rebuffed any involvement in her life. Better than hoping to be noticed. Because now he knew he wouldn't be.

So this was better, even if it hurt. Because there were a lot worse things than being ignored or unvalued.

"Leah, your father wanted to look at your truck.

He thought your brakes sounded squeaky this morning."

"Well, okay. My keys are hanging by the—"

"In my pocket," Jacob finished for her. "Because I found them lying next to your shoes."

"Oh. Right." She took the keys Jacob handed her and then passed them to Dad.

"Why don't you go with him," Mom said, giving her a nudge. "He'll need you to back out and—"

"I can do it," Jacob offered, but Mom waved him away.

"Nonsense. Leah and her father can spend a little time together."

"She's up to something," Leah muttered, but she patted Jacob on the shoulder and then followed Dad out of the dining room.

Mom craned her neck until she was happy with how far away they were, then she got up and hurried to her purse that had been sitting on the couch. She brought it over to the table, a ball of fluttering, nervous energy.

What the hell was going on?

Mom pulled a box out of her purse. A ring box.

Why did it look vaguely familiar?

"Now, Jacob, I'm not pressuring you at all, I just wanted to offer you an opportunity."

Jacob smiled, but Marc recognized the wide-eyed look of fear underneath it. Leah had that look a lot, only she wasn't quite as polite in trying to cover it up.

"This is an engagement ring, or a wedding ring. However you would want to use it. Of course I won't tell Leah you have it, and you can use it whenever works for you, but we thought it might be an option. Unless you had a family ring you wanted to use, of course."

If it had been any other ring, Marc might have felt bad enough for Jacob to jump in and say something. Mom could be a little inappropriate when she got fixated on an idea, and while he hated to be the one to rein her in, he'd always stood up when it got really bad in the past.

He couldn't stand up. He couldn't move. That was…that ring was… "That's Grandma's ring. That's…" His. It was his. Grandpa had given it to him after Grandma's funeral. So it could be passed down. A Santino heirloom. For *him*.

"Well, you left it with us. I didn't think you'd mind." Mom barely even glanced at him, she was so fixated on Jacob.

Which was good, because the shock and hurt had to be written all over his face. He hadn't left it with Mom and Dad. They'd put it in a safe-deposit box with other valuable things because he'd been fucking twelve when Grandpa had given it to him. "I have to go to the bathroom," Marc said, hoping Mom was too busy fawning all over Jacob to hear the hoarseness in his voice, feel the palpable…

Hurt. Christ, this hurt. He was used to Mom's

inattention hurting, but not like this. Not so deep, so visceral.

He walked stiffly to Leah's cramped half bath, but, nope, he couldn't do this. Regardless of Jacob's answer, he could not spend the rest of the evening here without...without saying something. Without letting the anger and the hurt seep out.

And he didn't want to do that.

Actually, he did. He really did. That's what scared him enough to know he needed to leave. He stepped out of the bathroom, patted his pockets down to make sure he had everything, and then—without making any goodbyes that might come out a little too rough—he slipped out the front door.

He shoved his hands into his pockets, not sure what else to do with them. He'd had to park a few houses down because the person across from Leah was having a party, and every step was heavy, stiff, as if his legs were lead.

He'd given up a lot of things for Leah, for the greater good of the Santino family, and he'd even accepted that Leah's heart transplant as a teen necessitated it, or made it okay, or something.

But this was not okay. Grandpa had given that ring to him, and now Mom was giving it to fucking Jacob. A man who was, by all accounts, very nice, and Leah loved him and all that other bullshit, but he did not have the last name Santino.

"Marc!"

Marc paused. He didn't want to have a conversation with Leah about leaving, didn't want to have to lie. Or explain why this hurt. Especially to her. Or anyone. Ever. He kept walking.

But Leah's footsteps followed. "She's so out of line."

"Jeez, Jacob told you already. Impressive."

"She's… Doing that wasn't right, for a lot of reasons, but that ring is yours." She hurried in front of him, and only because she was breathing a little heavy did he stop. Because the last thing he needed to do was cause her to have an asthma attack.

Yes, keeping Leah safe was ingrained in his being even though they'd spent most of the past ten years completely apart.

"She's right, though," Marc forced out. "No one special in my life. Might as well be yours." Because why would he make a big deal about this? He had no one to give that ring to.

"I'm not even engaged! Jacob is not proposing. When or if he does or whatever, it's not going to be with that ring."

"Why not?" He didn't look at her—he was afraid of what might pop out if he did. So he just stared at his truck beyond her shoulder. "It's a family heirloom. You're a Santino. Use it."

"It's yours. Grandpa gave it to you. I know I was sick then, but I wasn't totally absent. I remember Grandpa giving you that ring after Grandma died."

"Come on. I was, like, twelve. It was nothing."

"Why are you pretending?" she demanded, standing between him and his truck, hands fisted on her hips, looking as if she was ready to fight him if he tried to take another step.

So he did his best to look bored. "What do you mean?"

"It has to mean something to you. Why are you pretending it doesn't? I'd never take that ring, you know. Because I know it's not mine and it'd never feel right. So she can give it to Jacob all she wants, but he won't be giving it to me when—if—oh, fuck, when we get there."

"I don't know why you're getting so worked up about this." Didn't know why he should give up his pretending. It was the only thing he had.

"I don't know why you're *not* getting worked up." She threw her arms in the air. "Get worked up, Marc. Get angry. You have the right."

"Thanks for your permission, but I'm going home. I'll see you later." He stepped around her, and though he expected her to try and stop him, she didn't.

"It would not kill you to show an emotion. To voice a controversial opinion. It would not be the end of the world."

Marc didn't respond, kept walking to his truck. It might not kill him, but he'd long ago learned his emotions and his opinions didn't matter. So why fucking bother?

TESS JOLTED AWAKE when something banged. She sat upright trying to figure out what the hell was happening. She was on Marc's couch and…

"Oh, Christ, I didn't know you were still here." Marc rubbed a hand over his head. "Sorry, Tess."

Tess blinked trying to get her brain to engage. He looked…she wasn't sure. Angry, contrite and something deeper she didn't think she'd ever understand since he kept it so well hidden away. "Why'd you slam the door?"

"I…accident."

"So completely unconvincing, Santino." His expression darkened. Jeez, his family dinner must not've gone well at all. She wondered what made him say his parents were great and he loved them when obviously there was some kind of tension in the relationship.

She looked around the room until her eyes landed on the microwave clock visible from her vantage point. "Nearly ten. That was some family dinner, huh?"

"I…" His eyebrows drew together and then he turned abruptly, flipping the dead bolt on his door, then locking the chain, which, she realized, he must have added because her apartment certainly didn't have one.

It was that and the way he walked to the kitchen without saying anything, and maybe the dregs from her emotional upheaval earlier that made her wonder if…jeez, did she know him at all?

"I can go. I should, really." She got off the couch. If she hadn't fallen asleep she probably would have left. Ten was late. It wasn't a good idea to stay. But she'd wanted some kind of comfort, even if Marc didn't know what he was comforting. He was good at comfort.

She didn't think he'd be too good at it tonight, judging from his demeanor. But maybe that meant she owed him some.

He stood in the kitchen, palms flat on his counter, staring hard at it. "I'm in a foul mood."

Yes, he definitely needed some comfort. "Let me help." She crossed to the kitchen, kneaded her fingers into his shoulders, attempting to dislodge the tight knot of muscles.

But his shoulders only tensed more, going from hard rock to impenetrable metal. "Marc." This wasn't the ease and distraction he'd been offering. The nice guy who always knew what to say. This was some stranger, and that sank the earlier sadness even deeper. "Give me an inch here, huh?"

He turned so her hands had to slide off his shoulders, and the weird look on his face was what she determined must have been some kind of fake forced smile.

"You're terrible at putting on a happy face. Try the blank one. You're better at that."

Only then did his mouth actually curve with any kind of humor behind it. Not a lot, but at least something.

His hands rested on her shoulders, curling around them, a strong, comforting grip. She couldn't remember anyone ever putting their hands on her, looking at her the way Marc did, actually making her believe things could be okay. But that was exactly the effect Marc had.

"It was a weird night. In the end, it's nothing. Not in comparison to what you have to deal with."

Ouch. That kind of…hurt. She wasn't sure why. It was probably true. There were definitely things out there worse than she had to deal with, but hers was still pretty shitty. Even so, why should that mean he didn't tell her what was going on? "So?"

"So. It'll blow over. It's nothing." He released her shoulders, walked out of the small square of a kitchen. "You didn't watch the next episode without me, did you?"

But she barely heard that stupid question, that stupid change of topic. She was not being distracted from…

What? Wanting to get to know him better? So she could fall even deeper into this thing that really didn't have much of a future that wasn't really damn complicated?

Well, yeah. Damn it.

"Just because…" It was his superhero complex again, only it didn't seem nearly so admirable or sweet in this context. It seemed distancing. Her problems were worse, so she'd just never get to know his?

That wasn't right.

"Just because my family issues might be more complex than yours doesn't mean you should feel like you can't talk about them."

He grabbed the remote to his TV. "I don't want to." He flipped the TV on, such a dismissive gesture, irritation started to lean toward anger.

She marched over to him and grabbed the remote, clicking off the TV, getting even angrier when he gave her a condescending *really, that's all you got?* look.

"Well, I want to hear about it."

"Too bad."

"No, it's not too bad. You know every nasty detail of the stuff that goes on in my family. You can at least give me some piece of you."

His eyes narrowed, mouth twisting into some kind of sneer. There was no blankness, no trying to pretend anything. This was anger. A kind of furious anger that made her stomach jump uncomfortably.

"Oh, I know every detail?" he said, stepping toward her, and though it was a threatening step, she didn't move backward. She didn't wince. He might be angry, she might feel as though she didn't really know him, but she didn't believe he'd actually hurt her.

She had enough blows thrown her way to know the difference between unrestrained violent anger and fury that would never turn into an attack.

"What happened the night you decided that after all the no-cops stuff you were going to sleep with me? Or the next night when you showed up at my doorstep wanting more, after saying we couldn't? What does he say when he calls you? Why do you keep thinking he might get better?"

The questions hurt. Not physical blows, but little cuts against her heart, because he was right. There was plenty she kept under wraps, plenty she wanted to keep that way. But he at least knew something—she didn't know anything. "Marc."

"Don't go pushing me like I know everything. Do you know how many times I shut my mouth because I know you don't want me to ask?"

"Yes." And she did. He got the same blank look every time she evaded a question as he did every time she figured he kept a question to himself. "I...know."

"Well, then."

"Marc." She had to say something, but her emotions were such a confusing whirl of conflicting things. "I..." She swallowed. "Believe it or not, you're not...I actually don't want you to be perfect, because it makes me feel pretty stupid. So, if you could offer a flaw or two, I'd appreciate it."

"Tess..."

"Just a little hint you aren't the perfect guy."

"That little outburst not enough?"

"Nope. Everyone gets angry. Everyone lashes out. Tell me what happened. You don't have to tell me anything else. You don't even have to explain. Give me a sliver." And that felt...kind of gross, really. Her whole life spent begging people for little slivers of what she needed.

When was it her turn to get the whole thing?

He was silent for a long time, but his gaze was on her face, as if he could read all the hurt and sadness she was trying to ignore. As if he sensed it all and was going to swoop in and be Mr. Perfect and solve it.

Except it never seemed to actually get solved.

"When I was twelve, my grandmother died and my grandpa gave me her wedding ring. You know, to keep the tradition alive or whatever when I got old enough."

Her stomach did a weird jittery thing at the word *wedding*. "O…kay."

"Tonight my mother gave it to my sister's boyfriend. So he could use it, when he proposes to Leah. Which isn't even a foregone conclusion, except, okay, it probably is. But…"

"It's your ring."

"Yes."

"How could she give your ring away?"

"I don't—" She got the feeling he was going to say something big, important. But then he thought better of it and said, "Know. It's stupid. Just a ring. Pathetic to get all worked up over. Leah has just as much right to it as I do. She's a lot closer to marriage than I am. So I shouldn't be upset."

"But you are." She slid her arms around his neck, gingerly at first, then strengthening her hold when he didn't push her away and didn't reciprocate. Just stood there stiff and unmoving. "There's nothing wrong with feeling something, even if it isn't… You don't have to be perfect or good all the time."

"You'd be surprised." But he lowered his chin to his shoulder, a smidgen of that tension releasing.

So she held him, because she didn't have the words to convince him otherwise. But maybe she could find them. She'd make it a priority to find them.

CHAPTER FOURTEEN

MARC DIDN'T THINK anything could make him less twitchy about not being in charge of his workday, but watching Tess work did ease the frustration of being an observer half the time.

He noticed things he sadly would not have noticed if he wasn't involved with her. As he watched her take the statement of an angry shop owner over his broken storefront window, Marc was filled with discomfort over the fact that despite ten years in law enforcement and working with other women, he'd never given them much credit for having to do more.

It had been obvious the man had initially dismissed Tess as inconsequential when they'd walked up. Which only made her insist on taking his statement and handling this call. In a million subtle ways, she finally had the guy treating her like a police officer.

Had Marc taken the call, he never would have had to handle it in any special way.

Tess nodded at the man, tucked her notebook into her breast pocket and then strode toward him. Shoulders back, eyes cool, the perfect picture of a calm, unflappable police officer.

But when she met him on the sidewalk she let out a frustrated breath. "I hope that guy knows I could have him on the ground with his hands behind his back in ten seconds flat."

"You could demonstrate. I wouldn't tell anyone," he offered. Even joking about it went against his normal character, his normal instinct, but he seriously would not mind watching Tess kick that jerk's ass.

Tess snorted out a laugh as they walked up the hill toward his patrol car. "Thanks for the offer. Maybe next time."

"You're very good at your job."

She wrinkled her nose at him. "Oookay."

"I just mean, I watched you turn him from thinking you were not worthy of taking his statement to him taking your card and believing that you'd write up a report. You're good at that."

She shrugged. "Had to be."

"So you won't take a compliment."

She pressed her lips together, but her mouth began to curve. "Not from the guy I'm…" She looked around, then gestured toward his crotch, then hers and made a goofy face.

He didn't want to laugh. The secrecy thing wasn't funny.

But his mouth twitched, and he knew she caught it when she grinned at him. She stopped in front of an abandoned storefront, a few feet away from their cruiser.

She let out a wistful sigh. "I wish somebody would buy this poor old place. I used to love it when I was a kid."

"What did it used to be?"

She smiled sheepishly at him, but her gaze returned to the dusty window with a faded For Sale sign in the corner. "It was a fancy restaurant. Like, seriously fancy—way too fancy for Bluff City. I used to walk by on my way home from the library or the Y and people would be in there in suits and dresses. They always had these big bouquets on the table—not fake, either. Real flowers. Candles. A million forks and spoons for who knows what."

Her finger traced what was left of some etching that had been scraped away. "I had this idea that I'd get older and belong there, or feel like I could. Like it was age and not money that got you in the door." She blew out a breath. "Silly. This girl does not lead a fancy-restaurant kind of life, and I absolutely live in the wrong town for it, anyway. Just a little girl fantasy."

But…it wasn't silly. Not really. He thought of what her childhood must have been like, with an alcoholic, abusive father, even if she tried to make him believe there had been times when her father wasn't like that.

She'd grown up in an unstable world with no mother. His childhood had been a challenge, and it had had its own air of instability, but he'd had two people who were there, who kept him fed and sheltered and comfortable. Tess hadn't even had one.

She'd been on her own, and she'd dreamed about a fancy restaurant in a little Iowa river town. Such a small thing, and that's what made it so big.

He almost put his arm around her before the bulk of his uniform reminded him of where they were and what they were doing.

No touches. No *caring*. They were two officers working side by side. Something he'd never imagined could be complicated, constricting.

Tess moved for the car, skirting the front halfway before stopping and slapping a palm to her forehead. "Keep forgetting. Your car. You drive. And the next two calls are yours, since I took that one. I just couldn't let that guy think he could treat me like—"

"I know."

She backtracked to the passenger side.

He stood on the curb, struck by the sudden thought that this wouldn't be a permanent thing. When they'd first met, he'd been counting down the days till his training ended so he could go back to feeling like a real cop. Feeling like he was actually working, not being babysat. And now… "You know, it'll be weird when you're not with me on the job."

It was her turn to make the faintest of reaching movements before dropping her hand, remembering as he had that they couldn't be, well, anything here. Except coworkers.

"Yeah." She scrunched her forehead and slid into the car. He followed her lead, taking the driver's seat.

Her phone buzzed, as it so often did. As she so often did, she ignored it, her gaze steady on the abandoned building she'd just been admiring. Nothing showed on her face, no pain, no regret, no hurt. Even her posture hadn't changed.

How long had she been dealing with this? All of this? He'd seen her cry; he knew she hurt. Deeply. But on the job, she could turn it off, and it was huge, really. Bigger the more he knew her and understood about her.

An overwhelming need to do something overtook him. He only knew he needed to act, give her something. He couldn't fix her problem, even if she'd let him.

So he'd have to do the next best thing.

Instead of moving the car into Drive, he pulled his phone out of his pocket. Maybe he was being paranoid, but he didn't want to take the chance that he could be heard over the mic. So he typed a text message and showed her the screen. He didn't want to send the message to her phone, since it made her tense every time it went off.

Tonight: give me two hours, then come over. In a dress.

She bowed over his phone as she read and then typed before handing it back to him.

A dress? Are you up to something kinky, Officer Santino?

He rolled his eyes, pushing the car into Drive and keeping his eyes focused on the road. "Just do it, Officer Camden," he muttered, gratified when she laughed. More gratified when she very carefully and quickly brushed her hand against his thigh.

He could give her something, and Tess, being Tess, would appreciate it. It would mean something. Maybe this whole thing between them had started out as a way to help her or give her a distraction or whatever it had been, but it didn't have to stay this way.

He could mean something. Something big. Not just the silent, steady distraction or foundation who could be counted on to do what was necessary but wasn't given much in return. Not just a shoulder to cry on or lean on for support, but an actual meaningful, important piece of her life. Whom she appreciated.

This could be the start of something he'd never had, and he'd do whatever it took to get it.

TESS STOOD IN front of the mirror in her bathroom, trying to decide if Marc would notice the dress she had on was old and faded, a little ill fitting. But it did pretty nice things for her butt, so he probably wouldn't.

She had to bite her lip to keep from grinning, and

her cheeks already hurt from all the grinning she'd been doing since she'd started getting ready.

Whatever he was up to, whatever he was planning, even if it was something simple and regular, that he would plan at all was so irregular in her world, it made her stomach lurch in a mix of nerves and delight.

He was going to do something sweet for her, and she hoped to God she could keep her shit together enough so she didn't cry. There had been enough tears and breakdowns. She was ready for happy.

When her phone rang, she swallowed. Like a pin to a balloon, all her giddy excitement deflated.

Never going to be free of this, Tessie.

She took a deep breath and grabbed the phone off the bathroom counter. The fact of the matter was she still had an hour before she was supposed to go over to Marc's apartment, and maybe if she spoke with Dad he wouldn't bother her this evening and ruin everything.

"Dad?"

"Hi, Tessie."

"Is everything okay?" The fact that he hadn't greeted her with threats or tears, just a simple, ordinary hi was…weird. She didn't trust it.

"I was hoping you could come over."

He sounded so lucid, so calm. So different from the past few weeks. Hope sprang, so quickly it was painful. She knew better than to trust it, but that hope always grew over whatever she knew, every experience that came before. "Why?"

"We should talk, Tessie. Don't you think?"

She chewed her lip and glanced at the clock. She *did* have an hour, and with the exception of lipstick, she was ready. "Now?"

"I'm sober, Tessie. I haven't…had a drink all day. Please come over. I need you."

How would she ever be able to say no to that? To a please. To being needed—especially if he was sober, and while he lied plenty about the state of his alcoholism or the amount of alcohol consumed or hidden in his apartment, he very rarely claimed to be sober when he wasn't.

"All right. I'll be over in ten, but I…I have to leave by six at the latest. I don't want you getting upset. I have plans. Plans I can't break."

"That's okay, Tessie. That's okay. It's good you have plans. Just come over for a little bit so we can talk."

"O…okay." She hung up the phone and looked at herself in the mirror one last time. She took a deep breath and then set the timer on her phone. She would not be late for whatever Marc was planning. She was going to find balance here. Not abandon her father, not give up the good things in her life.

She slipped her lipstick into her purse. She rarely took a purse to her father's after she'd figured out he stole money out of it when she wasn't looking, but he was sober. Surely she could give him the benefit of the doubt here. She grabbed her cute pair of heels and slid her feet into some shlumpy boots—that way she wouldn't need to stop at her apartment on the way back. She could go straight to Marc.

Nerves tightened in her stomach as she moved down the hall. She should tell Marc where she was going, assure him she wouldn't be late, but...

She didn't. She still had an hour. And she didn't want him to know how weak she could be. She didn't want him to cancel whatever he was planning. No, she needed that, as much as she needed to reach out to her father when he was sober.

Maybe, just maybe, she could talk him into a treatment facility and her life could really, really, *really* be on track for the first time in a long time.

She drove to Dad's apartment, doing her best to breathe deeply and evenly. She would not get her hopes up, she would not let her guard down. This was a quick visit to talk, and that was it. She'd visit, bring up treatment if it seemed like a good time, and then be back to Marc in time for whatever he was planning.

She parked and walked slowly across the yard, clutching her purse to her stomach. She was nervous, plain and simple. Nervous because he was sober, because there was hope.

She didn't want to analyze that, how bad things had gotten. She slipped her key in the lock, announcing her presence, startled to find her father sitting at the tiny kitchen table. Which was clear of debris.

He'd cleaned. Well, just the kitchen. The couch and living room right off the kitchen were still cluttered with crap, but *still*.

Dad blinked at her outfit, squinted. "I'm not ruining your plans, am I?"

"No. I just have to leave when my alarm goes off."

But he stared. Hard. That squinting, strange look never leaving his face. She couldn't read it. Whatever he thought about her dress and her plans was hidden under a layer of sobriety she hadn't seen from him in months.

Maybe years.

She barely remembered what it was like to deal with him sober, and that hit her harder than it should. The realization things had slipped so far without her noticing, with her still thinking she had it all under some kind of control.

"Could you make me some soup, Tessie?"

"Sure." She swallowed at the lump in her throat at how weak and resigned he seemed, and went to work to heat him up some canned soup.

Dad sat at the table while she stood over the stove. Occasionally she'd peek at him as she stirred. He looked more old than sick, although he couldn't hide the tremors in his hands, the wistful looks toward his fridge though she'd done a check to make sure there wasn't any beer. Sometimes he tried to tell her beer didn't count, but he wasn't doing that tonight.

He was being so...so...normal, and the hope that had bubbled into being when he'd called was full-on balloon-level bursting. Maybe they were getting somewhere. Maybe this was the start of a new phase. He'd just needed to get really bad off again to get better.

She ladled soup into a bowl and set it in front of him. Then she sat at the table, as well.

"You should have some. We haven't had dinner together in forever." He attempted a smile, but she had to wonder if he'd forgotten how.

"I…I have dinner plans, Dad. I'd be happy to make dinner plans with you some other night." *If you'll promise to stay sober. If this is the start of something good.*

He stirred his soup with shaking hands, quiet, somber. It was almost worse than him yelling, worse than him being drunk, because she didn't know what to do with this.

He ate a few bites of soup, and she sat with her hands clutched together wishing she knew how to make this count. How to bring up treatment and help without everything going wrong.

"Did you want to talk about something in particular?" she asked as gently as she could. It had been so long since she'd dealt with calm and sober Dad, she was half-afraid to broach any subject for fear it would evaporate. For fear she would ruin all this hope.

"I just wanted to see you."

She couldn't breathe for a second. She couldn't

remember the last time he'd said something heartfelt to her that was loving. Something a father should say to a daughter.

"I'm not…" She took a deep breath and let it out, reaching across the table to rest her fingers on the top of his hand. "Even when I keep my distance, I'm not abandoning you. I won't. I know things can get better. I know they can. But when you're…in a bad way, I can't risk my safety."

"I'd never hurt you, Tessie."

The blatant lie caused her to pull her hand away, lean back in her chair. Should she point out all the ways he had? Should she remind him he routinely threatened physical harm and on occasion delivered on it?

"You do hurt me, Dad."

He didn't say anything to that, or meet her gaze. He ate the rest of his soup in oppressive silence, a silence she didn't have the wherewithal to break.

Her alarm went off, and she remembered Marc, and hope. A life for her. A good one, even if it wasn't perfect. Marc gave her something and she deserved that something.

She wasn't always sure she didn't deserve this, but she deserved some good, too. "Dad, I have to g—"

"Maybe…maybe you could show me one of those treatment centers again. Maybe…maybe that's what I need. So I'm not hurting you."

She couldn't get a breath at first. He was saying... She blinked at her stinging eyes and swiped the alarm off.

He hadn't asked about or let her speak of treatment centers without threats and anger in years. *Years*. And now he was bringing them up?

The hope was in overdrive again, wishing for an answer, a fix, change. Finally, finally. He was asking to hear about them, so this could actually be it. Her turning point.

Don't get your hopes up.

But the voice of reason was no match for the bright shining light of possibility. A future where her father *was* a father, and she could trust him enough to truly have a life of her own without worry or fear or sacrifice.

"Sure." She brought up her internet browser on her phone and typed in the treatment center she'd committed to memory.

Too expensive. Too faraway. Too everything, but she would do and sacrifice anything if it meant fixing this. Really solving his problem. So that they could *both* have lives free of this disease that had eaten up too much of both of them.

"I think this one would be a good option." She slid the phone over to him. He didn't take it, but he peered at the tiny screen looking only moderately disgusted.

"I know it's not exactly a vacation, but think how much better you'll feel."

Dad snorted. He wasn't scrolling, his face was

just looking more and more…angry. "I haven't had a drink all day and I don't feel better," he grumbled.

Her stomach sank, but maybe if she pressed a little… After all, if he was sober, he wouldn't get all irrational. "Nothing is ever going to get better if—"

"This is all lies," Dad muttered. His hands shook harder, his cheeks mottled red, and there was the father who was familiar to her. The one she'd never be free from. Because he had moments of sobriety when he wanted to change.

"Lies and bullshit." He pushed away from the table, began to pace restlessly. "Fucking bullshit."

The balloon of hope didn't pop or deflate, but it filled her chest so much it hurt. She had to calm him down, get him back to being receptive. "Dad."

"Why did I let you talk me into this?" His hand was eerily steady as he wiped it over his thinning hair. "Those people with their smiles and their nice clothes, and it's all shit. I've been there. It doesn't look like that. It doesn't fix anything."

"You have to want to be fixed," she said. In her head it was a fierce declaration, but it came out weak. A plea.

Dad slammed his fist on the table, sending her phone flying and the empty bowl of soup rattling. Tess flinched and hated herself for it, because, really, wasn't she used to this? The sudden anger.

The complete disregard for his own role in making things better.

"I have to want to not drink and you drive me to drink. You with all your bullshit and lies and it's your fault. *Yours*."

It was over. The hope vanished. The excitement gone.

He was never going to change. She couldn't abandon him, but he was never, ever going to want to get better. Their lives were always going to be... this.

She slid off her chair and picked up her phone. "Never mind. I'm sorry." Sick with herself for saying those words, words he didn't deserve, love and hope he didn't deserve.

But she said them, and as she left, she couldn't even muster the determination not to come back. Couldn't believe that hope was lost.

Why couldn't she believe that?

She drove back to the apartment complex, refusing to cry by sheer force of will. She pulled into her space, got out. She was late. In this ridiculous dress with stupid lipstick in her purse and heels in her car. Why...why had she thought she could have something for herself? When she couldn't resist the pull of everything that wasn't.

She trudged upstairs, briefly thought about canceling outright. But she thought of the way Marc had typed that text on his phone.

If she couldn't resist the pull of her father, then

why the hell should she resist the pull of something good?

She reached Marc's door, turned the knob and swore.

It was locked.

She'd missed her chance.

She thunked her forehead to the door. Before she could pull away, she heard a chain being moved, the click of a lock being released, and then the door opened.

Marc appeared, a blank, unreadable expression on his face. "A little late."

"I…" She swallowed down all the words, all the apologies, because if she started she was afraid the words and tears would never stop.

"Your dad?"

She squeezed her eyes shut and nodded. He was wearing nice clothes, though the button-up shirt was slightly askew and unbuttoned at the top. If he'd been wearing a tie it was long gone.

As she stepped into the apartment, it smelled delicious, like always, but there was a big vase of flowers on the counter, an array of silverware on the table. Candles

Oh, *God*, he'd put together her fancy-restaurant fantasy and she'd missed it. And for *what*? For *what*? Tears pricked in her eyes and she wanted to blink them back, be stronger, more resilient, but this hurt. It cut and ached.

Someone was finally giving her…a gift. Care and attention and damn sweetness and she had *missed* it.

"I'm so sorry. I…"

His fingers curled around her shoulders and gently, so much more gently than she deserved, he pulled her to his chest.

"He…looked at treatment centers," she mumbled into the solid wall of him. "I couldn't…"

"You don't have to explain." He was holding her, *hugging* her, and she should believe him. He was doing and saying all the right things, but there was this nagging feeling something was wrong. She'd messed up.

All of it, and she had no idea how to make that right.

Marc let Tess sniffle into his shoulder, rubbing his palm up and down her back in an effort to comfort her. She'd looked wrecked when she'd put two and two together about what he'd been preparing.

But how could he not offer comfort? It was just a stupid gesture, after all. She had more important things on her plate than him.

It was comical, really, that he'd thought this would be different. That he could be what someone wanted enough to put him first.

He didn't feel anger that she was almost an hour late. He didn't feel his normal frustration, as though he were beating his head against his parents' concrete wall of Leah.

He felt cold. And resigned. It didn't feel wrong—it felt undeniable. Maybe this kind of thing was all he was good for. To be the second round of something. The foundation. The stoic comforter.

Maybe this was all he had to give. After all, he'd had relationships with women who did not rush to someone else's aid at his expense, but he'd never loved them.

Not that he loved Tess. It was too...soon for that. Too...much. So, no. Not love. But he did care. Very much.

So this must just be where he stood. There was no more. Not from his family. Not from Tess. It was, and he had to accept it. Be what they needed, ignore any foolish want of his own.

More was not in the cards, and he was very good at ignoring that need for more.

CHAPTER FIFTEEN

MARC WOKE UP in his bed with a woman beside him. It had been a long time since that had happened.

He wished it could feel good, that he could enjoy it, but he knew what it was. An apology. She'd been sorry for missing his surprise, so she'd stayed over.

Well, you should be appreciative of an apology. You don't usually get that. Yes. True. He should be appreciative of Tess. So what if she put her father first? Hell, at least she admitted it and felt bad about it.

She yawned, stretched out and into him. Then blinked her eyes open, and he was determined to ignore the selfish voice in his brain that wanted more from her.

She crawled on top of him, curling fingers around his neck and then dropping a kiss to his lips. He smoothed his hands down her sides, rested them at her hips.

She grinned, kissing him on the nose, but her eyes drifted to his clock on the nightstand next to the bed. "Oh, crap, we so don't have time for morning sex."

"I bet I could—"

But she slapped him away before he had a chance to finish that thought or the gesture that went with it. She scurried off the bed. "You sorely underestimate the time it takes me to get cop ready in the morning."

"What exactly does cop ready entail?"

She shook her head. "I'm pretty sure if I explained it to that anal, organized mind of yours, your ears would bleed and your eyes would explode."

"Wow. Gory."

She grinned, hopping as she pulled up her jeans then buttoning them. "I was going to go with the face-melting scene in Indiana Jones, but thought that might be a bit of an exaggeration."

"Just a little."

"All right. I'm going to sneak on out. Meet me at the patrol car."

"Coffee?"

"Yes, please." She ran fingers through her hair, he supposed to make it look more manageable, but she didn't accomplish it. She looked tousled. A very excellent look for her.

She turned to him, head cocked. "Can I ask you something?"

"When people say that, they're asking something they know the other person doesn't want to answer." He didn't move from the bed, but found a place beyond her shoulder on the wall to focus on.

"Okay, I'll just ask. When your mother gave the ring to your sister's boyfriend, what did you do?"

"What do you mean what did I do?"

"I mean, did you say something or did you pull a Marc?"

His gaze flicked to her because he didn't know what that could mean. Okay, he had an idea of what it could mean. "Pull a Marc?"

"Don't play dumb. You know exactly what I mean." She pointed a finger at him, much like a scolding parent might. "Where you pretend like it doesn't matter, nothing matters, you're a perfect fortress of blankness."

"That happened days ago. I thought you said you had to hurry to get cop ready." He gestured toward the door.

She didn't move for it. She folded her arms across her chest. "Yes, fortress of blankness, just like that."

"Tess." Frustrated with this whole line of conversation, and the fact she was pushing when she didn't have a right to push—not after last night—he shoved back the covers and swung his legs over the edge of the bed.

"So, I'm going to go out on a limb and say you pulled a Marc and pretended you didn't care, and I want to know why."

"Why do you want to know why?" He rummaged through his drawer even though everything was folded neatly and he knew where what he needed was.

"Because I want to know you." She sighed. "I…it

wasn't a line when I said you were worth it. I don't take us lightly."

It should be a soothing thing, not something that strained at the last threads of patience he had, but it wasn't comforting. It was fucking irritating. "Okay, you don't take us lightly. How exactly is this going to go, then?" He pointed at his uniform hanging on the back of his bedroom door. "At some point I believe this becomes a bit of an issue."

It wasn't what he was really pissed about, and it was a dick move to pretend it was, but…well, he didn't know how to give her that part of himself. Not when he knew she'd crush it.

She blinked at the uniform, then back at him. "I…"

"Exactly. Look, getting to know all my stupid family stuff is pointless."

"First of all, and I keep telling you, just because your family crap isn't as terrible as mine doesn't mean you aren't allowed to be upset with it." She fisted her hands on her hips, and it irritated him that she was angry. Why was she mad? She didn't have a right to be mad. Not today.

Instead, she stepped toward him, hands still on her hips. "Why are you so bound and determined to be tight-lipped about everything? To make everyone think you're fine when you're not?"

He forced every word of the sentence that came out of his mouth to be clear, strong and convincing. "I am fine."

"You're a shitty liar, and someone with your deep, abiding moral code shouldn't lie."

"Sorry my moral code offends you so damn much. Now, why don't you—"

"Don't be a dick when I spent the night with you."

"I thought that's what you wanted. Me to show you a flaw. Here you go, Tess."

"You know what? Forget it." She turned and walked to the door.

"I thought so." Because, yes, no matter what she seemed to think she wanted, his temper was selfish and ugly and no one wanted that. No one wanted him to want to be important, they wanted him to stand by and keep his feelings and wants to himself.

"You're not making the point you think you're making." She wrenched the door open then hesitated and closed it again.

After a second or two of silence, she turned to face him. "I care about you," she said fiercely. As if it was an important, irrefutable fact she wouldn't let him deny. And that froze him, froze his anger, made everything seize up inside him.

What was he supposed to say to that? Who had ever turned to him when he was being a dick and said they cared? Hell, how many said that to him when he *wasn't* being a dick?

"Maybe I don't know how that's supposed to go. Maybe I'll never figure it out, but it doesn't change that I do. Ass face."

He felt shaken, flipped over. So he clung to the least important part of her message. "Ass face, huh?"

"I am nothing if not creative in my pet names."

They stood at opposite ends of the room. Her eyebrows were drawn together, lips pursed, everything about her tense and irritated. But…also concerned. About him. About what he felt.

She thought he mattered. *Last night does not prove that.* But he knew how to deal with last night–type things, didn't he? Hadn't that been what he'd been telling himself? He was used to that. He could keep…being used to it.

"I care about you, too. For the record," he managed to say.

"I know, but I think it's more important you know. You don't have to hide your feelings away from me because you think I won't like them. A disagreement, an argument, it doesn't negate the feelings we have for each other. Any more than not knowing how we're going to manage a future does."

He wasn't convinced of that, any of it, but the fact she was trying to convince herself of it was… something. She was something and he'd be an idiot to push it away.

A fucking moron.

"We really should get ready for work, but maybe tonight…tonight we can talk."

Her lips curved, not a full-blown smile, but enough to know she was cheered, encouraged. That smile should serve as a reminder that this was a mistake, knowing it couldn't end the way he wanted it to. If he wanted to keep his heart intact, returning that smile would be disastrous.

Well, maybe he'd already screwed that up.

TESS DROPPED HER utility belt on the kitchen table, locked her gun in the safe and then stood in the middle of her apartment.

Anger coursed through her, but something deeper lingered after her father's latest message.

A hurt she didn't know how to ignore, a hurt that made her want to give up. Quit BCPD, give Marc the brush-off and just accept the fact she was her father's keeper.

I found some things of your mother's. Burning them if you don't come get them today.

She was being manipulated. She *knew* that, she *felt* that.

She shouldn't care. She should not give one second's thought to something of her mother's, the woman who had abandoned them both before Tess could even remember. Why should she care about that woman's things?

But she did care. She had never seen anything of her mother's, never had anything. Once she thought she found a picture, of a woman who she'd seen a resemblance to, but Dad had claimed it was of some cousin and thrown it in the trash.

She trudged to her room, shedding her uniform shirt and adding it into the pile on the floor. Followed by her pants. Then she stood in front of her closet and tried to figure out what on earth she was going to do.

She had to go. She couldn't focus on having a *talk* with Marc if she had this hanging over her head, and, damn it, just as she deserved Marc, she deserved something of her mother's, even if *she* ended up burning it. That would be her choice, and maybe she could find some clue…some piece of the puzzle of why her mother would abandon her with Dad.

She dragged on some jeans, stripped off her undershirt and replaced it with a T-shirt. She was going to get what was hers.

Damn straight.

She glanced at her watch. If she really hurried, and Dad didn't pitch a fit, she could get back without being too far off her and Marc's usual schedule. So she shoved her feet into tennis shoes and hurried.

Of course, when she arrived at her father's apartment complex, her heart all but stopped. Two BCPD police cruisers were parked in front of the building, a crowd and a few of the evening officers in the yard.

Tess hurried out of her car, heart hammering in her ears. "What are you—" She stopped herself as it finally sank in that they weren't near her father's apartment—it was 1C, where the sketchy guy from the other side of the building lived.

"What's…going on?" she asked the first officer she saw, grimacing when she realized it was Granger.

"Busted that guy for distribution," he replied, gesturing toward the door. "Starting to be a little suspicious you're always around, Camden."

"If you recall, my father lives here."

"Tell your father to get better accommodations. This place is a shit hole."

She wanted to tell him to fuck off, but what did that serve? Besides, it *was* a shit hole. But it was the only shit hole she could afford and her father agreed to live in. So, really, Granger could fuck off, but telling him did nothing.

So she bit her tongue and turned to her father's apartment. She had to remember she was hurrying. She had one purpose and one purpose only. Get her mother's things and get home to Marc.

"You know, just because the captain thinks rainbows shoot out your ass doesn't mean everyone thinks that."

It took a great feat of will to keep walking, not to turn around and let her temper loose. But once again, pricks like Granger only fed off response. Got off on thinking they were important.

And he wasn't. Of course, as she slipped her key into her father's lock, she wasn't so sure she was dealing with important here, either.

He's your father.

Who had put that voice there?

Feeling immeasurably tired, Tess announced her arrival. Her dad stepped out of the shadows of the hallway looking halfway decent. As if he'd showered and shaved and dressed this morning.

"Hey, Dad."

"Tess." He scratched a hand through his thinning hair. God, he was getting old. Looking old.

She swallowed at the lump in her throat. "I want Mom's things."

He shuffled into the kitchen. "All right." He started pawing through cupboards, not making any eye contact or addressing all that stood between them.

"Where are they? What did you find?"

He shrugged. "I…was lying." He stopped his puttering, although he kept his back to her. "I'm sorry, Tessie. It's been a bad few days. I always miss her a little more in the spring."

Which wasn't true. Not exactly. He used that excuse a lot. *I miss her a little more in the*—seasons, months, days of the week sometimes finished the sentence. He was always missing her a little more.

Almost thirty years later. It didn't seem right. How could you still miss someone so much after thirty years that you threw your life away to wallow in your misery? She had no reason to believe otherwise, but she had to believe, for her own sanity and hope for the future, that love didn't mean ruin.

And if it did, maybe she'd find a way to stay far, far away.

All of it made her vaguely uncomfortable, so she started edging backward toward the door.

"Abandoning me again?"

"I'm not abandoning you. You won't help your-self so—"

"If you've come here to scold and yell and try to ship me off to a treatment center, I suggest you turn around and leave. That doesn't help me."

She meant to say she'd come for something of her mother's, that he'd manipulated her here, but that didn't come out. "What would help you?" Tears burned her eyes; the pleading note in her voice was desperate. Because she felt so damn desperate. "What would help? I'd do anything, Dad. Please. Please."

"I've had enough of you berating me." He opened the refrigerator, stuck his head deep inside. "Next time you get groceries, I want bagels."

It was dismissal. It was...so many things she didn't know what to do with. Why had he got her to come? Just so he could treat her like shit?

She needed to be stronger than this, so she did what she'd been doing for so many damn years it was just sad. "All right." And turned to the door.

"You were supposed to save me, Tessie. I don't know why you can't."

It's not my fault. It is not my fault. She wanted to say the words aloud, but she couldn't force them out. They stuck in her throat, in her mind, and she wished she could get them to stick in her heart.

She stepped outside, pulling the door closed be-hind her. She had things to do tonight that did not involve guilt trips she didn't deserve. She had someone waiting for her. Someone who cared. Who didn't blame her or hurt her.

That was the kind of relationship she needed to be reaching out for, pouring her effort into. She wouldn't abandon her father. Couldn't. But she didn't need to be his crutch, either, running to him every time he beckoned with his lies and manipulation. And he didn't need to be some bizarre crutch in assuaging her misplaced guilt.

No more manipulations. No more...

Who're you kidding?

She trudged toward her car, any strength or anger or determination completely and utterly erased. How did he always manage to break her?

"Quick visit."

Tess startled, whirled around to where Granger was lurking in the shadows. She'd never gotten a threatening vibe from him, just harmless dick behavior, but something about the way he was staring at her right now made the hair on the back of her neck stand on end.

"What do you want, Granger?"

"Nothing. Just can't help but think you're acting a bit shady, Camden. Maybe I should be watching you closer."

She rolled her eyes, doing her best to loosen the tension in her shoulders. "I don't know what your deal is lately, but I'd work it out in a different way than picking on someone who's your superior."

"I'd watch the superior act. It can be taken down a notch."

If he wasn't a fellow cop, a coworker, some kid she'd trained out of the academy, she'd have her hand on the butt of her weapon. As it was, she kept her hands loose and ready, but at her sides. "Try and threaten me again, kiddo. See what happens."

She took a deep breath and turned toward her car, listening intently for sounds that he was following her. Though her gut remained coiled with tension and fear, she made it to her car, slid inside, all without Granger making a move.

But he was watching her, his gaze cold. She wouldn't give him the satisfaction of seeing her shiver, so she casually pushed her car into Reverse.

And breathed a sigh of relief once she was driving down the road. Until a few minutes later she noticed a BCPD police cruiser behind her—346. Granger.

What the hell was this guy's problem all of a sudden? Okay, it wasn't exactly sudden. He'd always had a little problem with her being a woman, but she thought she'd gotten him over it. Sure, he might think she got special treatment, but he'd gotten over some of that antagonism.

Not so much anymore, apparently.

She turned off two streets earlier than she normally would, and Granger didn't follow. *You are being ridiculous.* But everything in her gut—that little intangible thing she almost always believed— told her that something about that kid wasn't right.

CHAPTER SIXTEEN

MARC STARED AT the clock and tried not to grind his teeth. An old bad habit he'd kicked a long time ago. Or thought he'd kicked. But with Tess fifteen minutes late, after last night, and the impending doom of actually having to talk about himself or his feelings, he felt the need to grind something.

When a knock sounded on the front door, Marc frowned at it. Tess didn't knock. She slid right in. Who could this be? Maybe he could ignore it and it would go away.

Okay, no, he could never ignore a door knock. He looked through the peephole and panic froze him.

His parents. With Tess due any minute. *Sound the alarm.*

Trying to feign as much cheer as he could muster, Marc opened the door. "Mom. Dad. Hi. I didn't know you were coming over."

Mom moved in without waiting for an invitation or without him even moving out of the doorway. She pushed until she was inside, eyes assessing every inch.

"This place…is…something." Mom wrinkled her

nose, then sniffed the air. "You're cooking." Before he'd even closed the door behind Dad, Mom was in the kitchen smelling and tasting and making noises about his garlic use.

"Not much of a kitchen. And the outside of this place. My goodness. Why didn't you buy a house like your sister? I'm sure Jacob could have pointed you in the right—"

"I don't need a house," Marc said as equitably as he could manage. "I wanted somewhere small." Possibly somewhere not totally permanent. Just in case.

In case of what, he had no idea, but it hadn't felt smart to buy. Not here.

Mom started adding random spices to the sauce he'd been simmering and Marc tried to find some way to get her out. Get them out. Tess and his parents…that was a thing he didn't want mixing. It was bad enough he'd agreed to *talk*.

The door creaked open and Tess slid through, her back to the three of them as she closed and locked the door behind her. "You would not believe what just happened to me. Something is up with Gra—" The moment she turned around, looked up, gaze landing on his parents, she stopped speaking, mouth hanging open. Since he wasn't beyond wide-eyed terror himself, no words came out of his mouth, either.

Mom was the first to break the silence. "Whoops. We barged right in and didn't even give Marc a chance to tell us he…had plans. Don't mind us, we'll be right on our way."

"No. No, you don't have to leave on my account," Tess squeaked. "Please, I'd feel terrible if you left." Her gaze flicked to his briefly. "You must be Marc's parents."

"Yes, and you must be…"

"Boss lady," Dad said with a sly smile.

"Oh." Mom drew out the syllable.

"No *oh*s. This is my neighbor Tess."

"I see. So not who Leah was talking about?" Mom's mouth curved downward into a pout. But as quick as it occurred, it disappeared and she clapped her hands together. "Either way, it's so good to make friends with the neighbors. Marc isn't always good at the friend making. You must have really charmed him."

"Mother."

Mom waved a dismissive hand in his general direction. "Well, now, you know it's true." She smiled at Tess. "I take it you were the recipient of dinner, so we will just skedaddle."

"But you're visiting. You should—"

"Nonsense." Mom grabbed Dad's hand and started moving toward the door. "You two have your evening. We'll see Marc tomorrow." Mom got Dad to the door. "It was nice to meet you."

Then they were gone. Marc stared hard at the closed door. He couldn't imagine Mom "skedaddling" if this had been Leah. But, because it was him, it was only a mild curiosity and a "let's get out of the way."

He should be relieved and thankful they were getting the hell out of here instead of harassing Tess.

But it was just plain hard to accept that, knowing the reason behind their departure was that his life wasn't half as important to them as Leah's.

"A surprise visit, I take it," Tess said, looking at him with a cocked head.

"Yup." He turned to the food he was making, trying to make his expression, his feelings, everything as neutral as possible. "Not even sure why they came."

"I'm sure they came because they wanted to see you."

"Right," he muttered. Before he could tell her dinner was ready and make it clear that he wasn't going to be doing any of that talking he'd promised, Tess wrapped her arms around his waist from behind.

"They seem nice."

"Nice. Yeah. They are."

She squeezed. "You're so unconvincing." She rested her cheek against his back, and even though he knew she wanted him to explain himself, even though he knew she had to have been late because she'd visited her father, he relaxed.

It felt good to have someone wrap their arms around him. Good to be comforted, period.

But he wasn't at all sure about Tess seeing that

weakness, offering support, even if it felt good. So he pulled away.

"Grab a bowl. Dinner's ready."

"It smells amazing. You didn't sneak something healthy in there, did you?" She sniffed at the casserole dish of spaghetti squash, but he stepped in front of it and took the bowl from her hands.

He scooped the shredded pieces of squash, covering it with the sauce he'd made, then handed it to her and nodded toward the little table he'd bought on his last day off. With her help. "Sit down and eat. Then tell me what you were going to tell me when you barged in."

She let out a huff and slid into one of the chairs. She poked her fork into the bowl. "You did hide healthy stuff in here."

"Try it," he instructed, making up his own bowl. He set it on the table, then went about getting them something to drink.

He slid across from her and glared. "Take a bite, Camden."

She poked her fork at him. "What if it has something in it I'm deathly allergic to?"

"What are you deathly allergic to?"

"Beside the point."

He chuckled, feeling overwhelmed by the warmth of affection squeezing around his chest. Like something more than affection, deeper than care. Something that took the breath out of his lungs because it was all…too much.

When things were too much, he ignored them. "What were you talking about when you came in? Something I wouldn't believe?"

She pursed her lips, then finally took a bite of the squash. She wrinkled her nose as she chewed, but instead of telling him his health food was gross, she poked around for another bite.

"Tess."

"What do you think of Granger?" she asked, eyes focused on her bowl.

"What does that have to do with anything?"

She looked up, eyebrows drawn together, expression perplexed and unsure. "Just humor me for a second."

Marc didn't see much reason to lie. "I think he's a prick."

"I… He's been…" Tess fidgeted in her seat. "Weird lately. Like, I kind of knew he was a jerk when I was training him, but I thought I'd swayed him toward the path of least dickishness."

"Okay, so what happened?"

"He's been… I get the feeling he's vaguely kind of threatening me."

Very carefully, Marc set down his fork. The way he might at any stop with an asshole spouting off at the mouth, he let the anger settle deep in his gut while keeping a complete appearance of outward calm. "How is he threatening you?"

"I don't mean it in a physical way. I mean, more

like he seems to think I've done something wrong. And he's going to find out what it is. I don't know if it's because my father lives so close to that drug dealer guy or what, but he's… Something is weird about how he's been treating me."

"I see." The anger he usually kept so well locked away until he could punch it out at the gym or run it out around the block boiled. It bubbled. He stood.

"What are you doing?"

"I think I'll go have a talk with him."

"Oh, please." Then she seemed to understand that he was serious. "Don't you even… Are you kidding me right now? I can handle Granger."

"Yeah, so can I." Handle his face into a brick wall. Because Tess had enough shit on her plate— she didn't need some asshole who thought he was important because he had a badge screwing with her, too.

"I trained the guy. You have no tools at your disposal that I don't have except a slightly larger build."

"Yeah, slightly."

She pointed her fork at him, and the I'll-kick-your-ass hardening to her features was nothing to be trifled with. "The fact of the matter is, when it comes to work, I'm currently your superior. And his. So you'll sit down, and calm down, and I'll handle it."

She was right. He knew she was right. He hated that she was right, but that didn't change anything.

Stiff with anger and frustration, Marc sat back down. Underneath the table he clenched and unclenched his hand. He had to let it go. She didn't want his help, she didn't need his help, so he would keep it to himself until she did.

That didn't need to make him feel like nothing. It didn't. Even if it did, she didn't have to know. That's how things worked best. When no one had a clue as to what he was really feeling.

Why was it so much harder with Tess? No amount of clenching or unclenching, no amount of telling himself it didn't matter, could keep the question from spilling out. "Are you ever going to let me help with anything?"

She looked like a deer caught in headlights, wide-eyed and frozen. "I'm fine."

"And I can help. I'm not sure our ability to do either is righter or wronger than the other."

"I can't let you undermine me at work. Things with my father are a delicate balance. You… Believe it or not, this helps. Having dinner with you. Talking to you. Feeling like there's some little piece of my life that's mine, it helps."

"Good." And it was. He just needed to know he was helping, and he could relax. If this helped, he'd keep doing the hell out of it.

It didn't matter if that put him in second place. He was good at second place, wasn't he?

"Now, you," she said simply.

"Me, what?"

"Tell me about your family."

"If this whole…thing we have going on distracts you from all your shit, let's leave my family out of it. Have our nice dinners, our nice evenings, and forget—"

Abruptly she got out of her chair, and he thought she was going walk right out, but she didn't. She crossed to him, grabbed his face between her hands and pulled so he had to look up at her.

"I want to know you," she said, forcefully. "I want to know that this stupid feeling I should not allow myself to have—but I don't even care because it's that awesome—I want to know what I feel for you is something real. So, I want to know you. Tell me. Something. Anything. Do not give me blank faces and brush-offs."

Marc stared at her, the grayish eyes and the top-heavy mouth and every inch of her gorgeous face. Her palms were warm against his cheek and jaw. She smelled like her floral perfume, and this… It was so much a thing he wanted to keep.

But did he want that more than all those feelings he denied himself? Could he really let that go after years of keeping it in? Keeping it in was how he kept going, how he dealt.

Could he knowingly walk into a situation that was achingly similar to his family life? Taking the backseat. Never being important enough to make a difference.

"Marc." Her fingertips traced his cheekbones.

"Please." Though he could fight a lot of things, pretend not to feel a lot of things, her simple *please* was his undoing.

TESS'S HEART WAS beating so hard and so loud in her ears, she could barely hear. She needed something from him. Some hint as to the weirdness between him and his parents, some idea of what resided underneath all those layers of quiet brooding.

She needed to know this deep, uncomfortable feeling of possibly being in love with a guy she couldn't be in love with after such a short period of time was, well, was going to be worth the inevitable pain.

"My…sister was born with a heart defect."

She had no idea where this was going, but it was the first he was talking about his sister, his family without it being vague. So she nodded, hoping it would encourage him to go on.

"You know, you joked about me not playing with her when I was a kid because I was too macho or whatever, but honestly it was because she was sick and I wasn't allowed."

"Oh." Oh. Well.

"It's a weird situation, I guess is what I'm trying to say. My whole life has kind of revolved around her health, or lack thereof. Which isn't wrong or bad or something horrible my parents did, it just…is."

"But, she's okay now, right? Or did you move because—"

"She's fine. She had a hcart transplant years ago, and aside from a few…things, she's mostly healthy and fine."

Heart transplant. Jeez. It wasn't dark or complicated like her family issues, but it was heavy. Big. Life and the threat of death. "So why were you so tense with your parents? Why the comments about them not wanting to see you?"

"Because…" Gently, so gently she wanted to squeeze him, he took her hands and removed them from his face. Then he stood and turned his back to her, the tenseness in his shoulders so sharp she wished she could do something to relax them.

"Leah's health made her the center of their life, and I…" Hc didn't move, she wasn't sure he even breathed, his shoulders were so still. "I don't quite make the cut, I suppose. They cared for me. I ncver wanted for any necessities. They are good parents."

"But you don't think they love you?" She swallowed down a longing so familiar it was like a part of her. The question of parental love had always been more question than reality for her. If one could even call Mom leaving a question of love. She pretty much had the answer on that one.

"Of course they love me. In that kind of way you love all your family members. But Leah's the center of their life. Everything they work toward. I'm more of a rock or foundation-type thing. There. Supportive. But not something anyone pays much attention to."

He turned to face her, jaw set, eyes determined. If she wasn't looking for it, she'd probably miss it, but underneath that determination was hurt. Sadness. She moved to hug him, but he kept talking.

"See? It's really all very stupid. Pointless. Nothing. It's nothing like what you've had to deal with."

Some of the sympathy that had welled inside of her faded away. "You don't always have to be comparing."

"I only mean it's nothing."

"You tell yourself that a lot about a lot of things, don't you?" She could see that pattern. He convinced himself his feelings didn't matter. He made himself blank. Pushed it all down. She'd seen that without totally understanding, but now that she knew this...

She understood. She understood him. Maybe his family issues kind of paled in severity to hers, but it didn't take away the fact he'd dealt with something difficult. Something painful, and probably scary and hard.

More, he didn't think he deserved to have it mean something. That his feelings didn't matter because they weren't as big as hers.

"Well, all that's utter bullshit, darling."

"That's what I'm trying to tell you."

"No. The feelings aren't bullshit, you thinking they aren't important or valid is. We all have crap, Marc. Deep, twisted crap. Some of it's worse than others but it hardly negates the crap of feeling..." She took a deep breath, uncomfortable with offering even more of herself than she already had. Especially when this was so…screwy.

But she couldn't help herself. She just couldn't. "It's hard feeling like you don't matter. Period."

He remained very still. Very blank. "I've tried very hard to be…" He trailed off, his forehead getting scrunched, his jaw clenching then unclenching.

"To be what?"

"Someone they'd appreciate," he said through clenched teeth. "Everything they asked, everything they expected, I did it. I know how pathetic this sounds, but I've just wanted them to acknowledge that. But they don't. Because Leah's all that matters."

She pressed her palms to his heart, because she felt an echoing pain in hers. She'd never felt as though she didn't matter. In fact, it was the opposite. She mattered too much. She was responsible for too much.

But she wanted to be acknowledged for that, too. She wanted it to matter, and it never had. "You matter," she said, possibly more fiercely than the situation warranted.

He rested his hand over hers. He didn't say anything, and she didn't know what she wanted him to say. Well, she had an idea, but it was such a foolish thing to want, she pushed it out of her mind.

"I think you should tell them how you feel. Just…" She spread her fingers wide so he could lace his with hers. "The fact they're here and they were all interested in who I was means they care, Marc. Maybe they don't see, but they care. You can't blame them for not being able to see through this unaffected aura you give off."

"You do."

I love him. It hit her on a deep, visceral level. This man, so desperate to do right and help and not be hurt—she was totally in love with him. Because of things like that. Because he could make her feel important and capable and *her.* Just by being honest.

And she didn't have a snowball's chance in hell of figuring out what she was going to do about that.

CHAPTER SEVENTEEN

MARC HAD NEVER felt so raw and exposed before. In fact, the feelings were so foreign, he was having a hard time figuring out how to deal with them aside from standing like a statue with his hand linked with Tess's over his heart.

Where more foreign, complicated feelings knotted together, making it hard to breathe or move or think or talk. Statue Marc was his go-to, and he was there. But so was Tess, and she wanted more from him. To know him.

"I think it's easier to go on as things are," he finally managed to get out. "I've actually kind of liked the way things are going as of late." Because if she saw too deep, understood too well, she'd know that every time she asked him to step back—it killed him to do so.

Her mouth curved and she stepped closer. "Me, too." She said it emphatically, her eyes a little shiny.

Strange.

"But I still think you should, well—" Her free hand slid up his chest, his neck, the back of his head, her palm grazing the short bristles of his hair. Then over his forehead, down his nose, covering his eyes, and when she got to his mouth, she smiled. "Tell them. How you feel. Maybe they don't know they're hurting you."

"They're not hurting me," he said into her palm. More because he wanted it to be true than because he was under any illusion it was.

Her hand moved back down his chest, covered his hand that was covering her other one. All on top of his heart. "It's not wrong to feel hurt." She paused, looking at their joined hands before tentatively raising her gaze to his eyes. "You should be able to tell people how you feel."

He had a hard time getting his breath in or out. That last sentence, the way she so carefully said the words, the way her eyes met his, their hands entwined. It all seemed to mean something bigger. Less about his parents, about her father, about the things that made everything between them complicated.

More about them in this moment and feelings he wasn't sure he knew how to deal with in the context of reality. But in the context of this evening, of this apartment...

"Tess." He didn't know what else to say. Hell, he barely got her name past his lips. He could hardly breathe properly because right here in this moment he felt so much, so deeply, that he didn't know what the fuck to do.

Welcome to the past few weeks with Tess. All

sorts of things he didn't know what the fuck to do with.

But when she put her fingertips to his mouth, he pressed a kiss to them. Then to her palm, and her wrist. He didn't have the words to express the chest-shrinking, jittery thing going on in his general heart area, but maybe he could still find a way to give her some insight.

He cradled her arm with one hand, pressing another kiss to the inside of her elbow, the rise of her muscle, then he nudged the collar of her shirt off her shoulder so he could kiss her there, then her collarbone, the side of her neck.

Her breath fluttered across his cheek, but otherwise she didn't move. She let him explore with his mouth, light brushes of his lips against the soft hollows and expanses of her skin. From one shoulder to the other, then down her opposite arm, wrist, fingers.

"My turn," she said, curling her fingers around his wrist and pulling his hand to her mouth. She did the same thing to him—soft lips against all the same places on his arms, his neck. But she stopped there, her tongue flicking out and grazing his shoulder, then licking up the side of his neck until she reached his jaw, where she nipped at him.

"Kiss me?" she asked.

As if she had to ask. As if he'd ever say no. He lowered his mouth to hers, gently, lightly. He'd almost call the kiss tentative, but that wasn't it. Testing. Teasing. Until she sighed against his mouth and linked her arms around his neck. With her body pressed against his, the pressure of the kiss intensified. He tangled his fingers in her hair, cupping her scalp, letting his tongue explore the texture of her mouth, her lips.

When she pulled away, they were both breathing heavily, both had each other in a tight grip. He couldn't remember a time he'd been this desperate to hold on to someone.

"Come with me." He took her hand and led her to the bedroom. It seemed imperative to lie next to her, be entwined with her.

She went with him. He could have sworn they'd gotten all the nervous and random awkward pauses out of their sexual encounters, but nerves jangled in his gut. A hollow, twisting feeling. It wasn't as if this were suddenly more important. She'd always been important. The crackle of attraction had been instantaneous, and getting to know her had only made that attraction sharpen into care.

So, nothing he felt was new. But it felt that way. Or maybe it just felt more important. Bigger.

Christ. It was too much. All this feeling and not saying it and not understanding what was curling inside him, making everything this weighty.

"Marc?"

He blinked down at her, irritated with himself for losing focus. Irritated with himself for all of this and his lack of handle on it.

Her mouth was still open, but no other words came out, just a stilted exhaled breath. "I…"

He almost thought she was going to say it. The crazy thought going around and around in his head that he kept trying to ignore.

He was…in love with her. Part of him didn't believe it was possible, but it was one of those things that once he'd thought it, that word he didn't know what to do with, he couldn't unthink it or change his mind or miraculously know how to say it.

"I want you to make love to me," she said very seriously.

"I'm planning on it."

Her mouth curved. "And then I'm going to spend the night."

"Good. I enjoy that." Too much. This was all such a dangerous pretense. Never in his life had he had trouble resisting danger, but now…

He couldn't resist it even if there was some part of him that wanted to.

She audibly swallowed and he did the same. Nerves kept him from making the next move. Christ, nerves with a woman he'd had plenty of sex with.

Tonight had made everything so much more.

He should tell her. Force the words out. She wanted him to express his feelings, so he should damn well express them.

And if you're reading the situation all wrong? It's been a few weeks. What sane person falls in love after a few weeks? Desperate people do that. Not sane people.

The thought made his heart sink. He knew he was pathetic when it came to his family situation, but he'd never considered himself desperate. Maybe all this was just desperation to find some kind of love.

But why now? When he'd never felt it before? No matter how much he would've liked to. It wasn't desperation.

It was Tess.

"I love you," he blurted. Awkwardly. Horribly. "I think." Even worse.

She pressed her lips together, but it didn't last as they curved into a smile, and then a little laugh. "Oh, thank God, because I'm pretty sure I love you, too, and that is just crazy."

The relief was so huge, so palpable, he wished he could sit down. "Fucking nuts."

She laughed again, something more like a giggle. "What are we going to do?" Her smile sobered, and she leaned against him, grasping his shirt at his sides.

"No clue," he replied, wrapping his arms around her.

"Maybe we put that part aside for tonight. And deal with it later."

She sounded so hopeful—even though the practical part of his brain knew that wouldn't change anything, certainly wouldn't fix anything, he couldn't deny her that. He couldn't deny them this one night of feelings before they had to complicate it with reality.

"Yes. Let's do that."

She grinned, grasped the bottom of her shirt as if to pull it off, but he stepped in before she could complete the action.

"No. Let me." He took the edge of the shirt out of her grasp, and then slowly lifted the fabric over her head.

"Oh, man, I wish I'd worn nicer underwear."

He took the strap of her plain, nondescript bra between his index finger and his thumb. "You look beautiful."

"Flatterer." But she said it on a happy sigh.

So he took the other strap between his fingers the same way, slowly sliding them down her shoulders, the backs of his fingers trailing against her arms. He gave the straps a tug until the bra moved down.

He kissed her chest, the space between her breasts, brushing fingertips lightly over the tops of each, then across her nipples. She let out a shaky breath and unsnapped the bra bunched around her waist, letting it fall.

He sank to his knees in front of her, pressed a kiss to her stomach, smoothed his hands over her hips.

"Um."

He traced his fingertip along the waist of her jeans, watching intently as tiny goose bumps popped up along her skin. He toyed with the button of her pants. "May I?"

She watched him, wide-eyed, and then nodded. He unsnapped the button of her jeans, then lowered the zipper.

She cleared her throat and he looked up at her, surprised to find uncertainty on her face. "Everything okay?"

"Yeah, I just… If you're after doing what I think you're doing… I know it's kind of weird, but no one's ever, um, done that for me before. If that's what you were planning. If not, it's no big de—"

He shut her up by pressing a kiss to her belly button, which caused her to squeak instead of finish her sentence. He tugged at her jeans, goal in place now.

"Allow me to be the first."

TESS THOUGHT SHE might squeak again as Marc starting pulling her pants down her legs. Once he got them to her ankles, she stepped out of them.

But he didn't get up off his knees.

Surely it had to be odd that a woman in her thirties had never been on the receiving end of oral sex, but it had just never happened. She hadn't had a lot of serious, long-term relationships where she'd felt a lot of the trust and love and future-type feelings she would have needed to be comfortable enough to do this.

And she—he—they were going to do this. After saying *I love you*s. Terrible, wonderful *I love you*s.

She was afraid she was going to cry.

Marc traced the waistband of her panties with his

fingertips, much the way he had when her jeans had still been on. Only this time they traveled all the way to her back, and then his palms slid over her butt.

Cry. Die of lust and desperation. One of the two.

He pulled at the sides of her panties, slowly pulling them down. Excruciatingly slowly for a man who'd seen her naked quite frequently over the past two weeks.

"You can tell me if you don't like something."

"Oh, right, okay, yeah." Nice sentiment. One that was hard to wrap her mind around when her underwear was now on the floor and she was completely naked in front of his completely clothed, kneeling body.

He paused, his hands resting on either thigh. "And I don't have to do it if you don't want me to."

She blinked down at him. "N-no. No, I want you to."

"You're kind of stuttery."

"No, it's just weird doing something I haven't done before. I want to. God, I want to. But, you know, I'm used to being a little bit more in control."

He considered her very carefully, one of those guarded studies she wished she could understand a little better.

"It's certainly not something to do if you feel uncomfortable. I want to, but I'd never want you to allow something just because I want to."

Funny, those two little sentences clarified his careful looks. He was trying to figure out what she wanted so he could give it to her. He was concerned she was doing this because he wanted to, because that's what he would do if the situation was reversed.

"I've confessed my love for a guy, which throws all sorts of wrenches into the career I love, and now I'm about to have oral sex for the first time. I'm a little overwhelmed." She smiled and drew a finger across his mouth. "I don't think you ever have to worry you're pushing me into something I don't want to do. You're very careful about that, if you haven't noticed. Now, I'm kind of naked here, so if we could get the show on the road."

He chuckled, whatever concerns he had seeming to dissipate. "Have a seat. Take a load off." He patted the bed behind her, a big grin on his face.

She liked that grin. No, she loved that grin. Rare. For her. Because of her, she liked to think. So before she sat where he had instructed, she planted a kiss on his mouth, which made his grin grow, and sat, pleased she was the cause for his happiness. Pleased he loved her. Pleased with every damn little thing. All the worries and concerns niggling at the corner of her brain went completely silent when Marc's hands grasped her knees and slowly pushed them apart.

He kissed each knee, hands slowly sliding toward inner thigh territory, mouth following. Teasing, exploring, driving her to the brink of pleasure with just his mouth.

She clutched his shoulders, needing something to anchor her as the orgasm spiraled through her.

Then she flopped back on the bed because she couldn't maintain an upright sitting position anymore.

He chuckled and got up on the bed, covering her body with his. "I'll take that as a job well done."

"Mmm" was all the response she could muster. Wow. Wow. She managed to grin up at his too-smug face, but smug was nice on him.

She traced his hairline with her index finger. "Give me a second to get my strength back and it'll be your turn."

"First time should be all about you. No reciprocating." He kissed behind her ear, then down her neck, and when she whimpered he stayed right there, using his mouth once again to make desire begin to coil.

"You can't make everything about me, you know," she said, leaning her neck in the opposite direction to give him more access. "At some point, you have to want things, too. You have to get things, too."

"Believe it or not, I consider the next part something I very much want." He reached across the bed to his little nightstand where he kept the condoms.

"I am serious, though. Don't just give me what I want because I want it."

He looked down at her, very seriously, any hint at humor gone. "Maybe you deserve that."

Deserve. She'd never spent too much time lingering on thoughts of what she deserved. Dangerous business, that. "No, I think we both deserve to try and get what we want. Sometimes we will and sometimes we won't, because hello, life. But I don't want you pretending with me, got it? If this love thing is going to work, we need to be on equal footing. I think we could both use a little equal."

"I hate to bring this up right now—"

She clapped a hand over his mouth, because of course responsible, practical Marc would latch onto the *if this love thing is going to work* part. "Nope, we're not thinking about that part tonight."

"All right," he said against her palm. "But you are the one who brought it up."

"Well, I'm changing the subject." She took the condom, pulled it out of its package and rolled it over him.

"Good change." He smiled down at her, and against everything she knew was sensible and smart, safe and self-preserving, she smiled back.

"I love you," she murmured, because she didn't know how long she'd be able to say it without the complications and the reality setting in.

"I love you, too," he returned, and all the dumb or irrational paled in comparison to that moment. She couldn't regret this. No matter what happened in the future, she'd never be able to wish this hadn't happened.

CHAPTER EIGHTEEN

MARC WOKE WITH a jolt to the sound of a phone buzzing. Tess was moving groggily in bed next to him, but he was pretty sure it was her phone, not his.

"In my pants," she mumbled, pawing around on the bed.

"They're on the floor."

She said something else, or maybe it was just grunts and incoherent mumbles. He really couldn't be sure, but the buzzing stopped.

Tess stumbled off the bed and he glanced at the clock. Two in the morning. Those kinds of phone calls were rarely good.

This time her phone chimed. "Message," she murmured, holding the phone up to her ear and crawling back into bed.

She rested her head on his shoulder, and he could hear a man's voice coming from the earpiece of her phone. He couldn't make out words, but it sounded like...weeping.

Tess went completely still, completely tense. She threw back the covers, dropping the phone.

"I have to go."

"What is it? Your father?"

"Yes, he's..." He switched on his bedside lamp and she winced against the light, but it only slowed her down for a second. She pulled her pants on, then threw on a T-shirt that turned out to be his.

"Shit," she muttered.

"It's okay. Wear it, but tell me what's going on."

"He..." She raked fingers through her unruly hair. "He said he's going to kill himself if I don't come over."

Marc was out of bed in a flash.

"No. Please. Don't. This...I've dealt with this before. Not often, but I know how to handle it. Get back in bed. Go back to sleep. I'll be back in a few hours, tops."

"We're supposed to wake up for work in a few hours."

"I know. I know. But I have to go. I can't argue with you right now, Marc."

"I'm not arguing. I'm going with you."

"I already told you why I can't let you do that."

"I'll drive you, and I won't even get out of the car. I'll sit there and wait."

"For hours? So someone can call the cops on you? No, honey, I have to do this." She turned and left the room without allowing him to argue further, but he wasn't done.

He couldn't possibly let her go. Alone. In the middle of the night. To that shit hole and a man threatening suicide.

She was pushing her feet into her shoes. "You cannot go alone. At least call someone at the department. Call Stumpf. He's a good guy."

"Dad'll get hysterical if they show up."

"Good. They'll involuntarily commit him and you can be done with this bullshit."

She paused for a second, as if she was considering it. He held his breath, hoping to God she would.

But she shook her head. "No. I can't run the risk he goes through with it. Look, once I get there and calm him down and make sure he can't hurt himself, I'll work on seeing about the involuntary thing. I do have his voice on message saying he's going to kill himself. So…just let me do this on my own. Okay?"

"No. I can't. I cannot stay here while you go to a dangerous place and a dangerous situation."

"I'll have my gun. I can take care of myself."

He wanted to argue with her. Two was better than one—when it came to people and having protective weaponry.

But he also wanted to be able to give her what she wanted. He wanted to be able to trust her. She always handled it, had for however long before he'd gotten involved in her life. What did he get out of forcing his way on this?

"Call me when you get there. When you know what's going on. When you're on your way. Text. Call. Please don't make me wait here thinking you've been hurt."

She reached for the door, hesitated. Then turned

around and wrapped her arms around him and squeezed. "I won't get hurt. And I'll keep you updated. And…" Her grasp loosened, fell. "I love you."

"I love you, too." Which he had to say between gritted teeth, because how did you love someone and let them do this alone?

"Tess, I will step back. I will wait here because I know that's what you want, but if I think for a second that you're in danger, I am coming after you." Even he had his limits.

She turned in the open doorway, expression conflicted and hurt. "I won't get hurt."

That had to be true, because if she did get hurt, he didn't know how he was going to live with this. He wanted to tell her to be careful. Tell her again not to go. Call the department behind her back and have someone there.

But it wasn't what she wanted. She wanted to handle this on her own. Deal with it her own way. Without him. So he had to live with it.

"Come back here when you're done."

"You should get some sleep."

"Don't be stupid, Tess." The hurt on her face sharpened, but he was barely holding it together. He couldn't be nice *and* give her what she wanted.

"All right, all right." She stepped into the hall, and he wished he could think of something reassuring to say. Her father was threatening to kill himself, and all he could do was lash out. Barely contain his anger at her not letting him go with.

But she was gone and he forced himself to close the door and not do anything but wait for her to call. He'd time it. If she went twenty minutes without contacting him, he'd get in his car and go.

That had to be fair. A compromise. Maybe not what she wanted, but he could only give her so much of that.

But he would. He would.

Such a good night. Even if it was complicated. Even if it was nuts. Loving her, her loving him back. All interrupted by someone else's disease.

The hallmark of his life that he couldn't escape.

Tess hated that she was crying before she even got to Dad's. Hated that she was torn up about things more than just the fact he was threatening to kill himself.

That should be the worst, but the worst had been refusing Marc's help. Because she wanted it. She wanted it so badly, someone to stand behind her and help her deal with this mess.

But she was too embarrassed, too afraid it would ruin anything she might be able to accomplish with Dad.

So she was alone, and she felt alone and scared and so damn tired.

But what choice did she have? The tears, the suicide talk, that wasn't manipulation. Not when he'd attempted it before. No, that was real, and she could not ignore that.

She pushed the car into Park and hurried out. She unlocked the door and stepped inside. "Dad?"

It was dark. Quiet. Eerie. The tears didn't stop. They intensified. "Dad?" He had to be okay. How could she ever live with herself if he wasn't okay?

Terrible, Tessie. Just like your mother.

"Dad?" Her voice wavered, and she was afraid to take another step inside, but she did. Just one shaky one.

You have to do this. No one else can. She took a deep breath, let it out, then took another step, and there he was.

"So you *can* come when I need you." She couldn't see him. Like the junkie next door the other night, he was a shadowy figure. The same fear worked through her, only she couldn't bring herself to put her hand on her weapon. Not with her own father.

"Why don't I turn on the light, huh?"

"Don't fucking move, Tess."

There had been a handful of times in her life Dad had really scared her. Down to the bone. The one time he'd been on drugs, once when she'd been very young—eight or nine—and she hadn't been able to wake him up. Then the suicide attempt. And now, tonight.

She couldn't remember him ever, *ever* calling her Tess. Even in his lucid moments. She was always Tessie.

But he'd said Tess. Cold. Calm. It was like something out of a horror movie. Where the bad guy had no conscience, was just evil.

But this was her dad. He wasn't evil. Just sick. *He's sick.* "Dad, you're scaring me." Even though she wanted to shrink away, *run* away, she stepped toward him.

No response. No warning. Then suddenly something hard bashing into her cheek. So hard she fell to the ground, dizzy and out of sorts, her keys flying out of her hand and smashing into something that sounded as if it broke. Pain radiated from her jaw all the way up her skull. She couldn't hear anything over the weird ringing in her ears; her vision was dim.

She tried to speak but nothing came out. She had to struggle to get a breath in. To try and think what to do next. Things were kind of blurry, but she was pretty sure that was blood dripping into her eye.

Blood.

He'd hit her with something. Viciously. Violently. Premeditated.

"I'm so sorry, Tessie." Suddenly she realized he was crying, and even in the dark she could make out his shadow coming toward her. "I don't know why…why do you make me do these things? Why?"

He kept moving toward her and she scooted away, shaking so hard she could barely accomplish it, but she had to get away from him. She had to get—

She stopped and pulled her gun out. She left the

safety on until she could get her shaking under control, but she held it toward him.

"D-don't get any c-closer."

"Tessie. It was a mistake. I was just so angry. You made me so angry with all that treatment bullshit. Everything is so bad and it wouldn't be if she was here. If you'd never been born. Why'd you ruin it all, Tessie?"

"Please. Please stop. Stay away." She edged around him. She needed to get out of here. She needed to call Marc.

Oh, God, Marc. He… She couldn't think about that right now. She scooted herself to the door, managed to wobble to her feet.

"Don't go, Tessie. I need you. I'm sorry. I didn't mean it."

The anger was as vicious as the pain in her face, because he'd done this. Maliciously. He'd done this to hurt and punish her. So he *had* meant it, and she'd never talk herself out of that simple fact. "Go to hell, Dad."

She wrenched the door open and managed to get outside. Her legs weren't steady, and she was dizzy, but she managed to propel herself to the side of the building, behind a bush, where she could hide from any unwanted attention until she could figure out what to do without her keys.

At least she had her phone.

Oh, Marc was… He was not going to take this

well, but in the battle of lesser evils—Marc or the department coming—she'd go with Marc.

He might be angry. He might even tell her he'd told her so. But at least it wouldn't ruin the rest of her career. She'd certainly lose a good portion of the respect she'd earned in the department if they saw what she allowed to happen.

Once she could get her shaky fingers to cooperate, she dialed his number. He answered before the first ring was even done.

"Everything okay?"

"Um…" No, not even a little bit, and there was no way she could hide it from him. Not after the blow Dad had inflicted. She didn't even know what he'd hit her with, but it had been big. And hard.

"Tess, are you hurt?"

She squeezed her eyes shut, which hurt so damn bad it caused even more tears. "N-no," she whispered.

"Tess. Please."

"Okay, I—I may be a little hurt."

He made some noise, but it was too far away from the receiver for her to make out what it was. "I'm on my way. I'm calling Stumpf."

"No—"

"It's already done. Stay safe. I'm on my way. Stay safe, please, for the love of God, just keep yourself out of his way. Christ. Tell me you're okay."

"I'm okay. I am. I really am. I'm out. Please don't worry."

Another noise away from the receiver. Possibly cursing or yelling. Something he didn't want her to hear, which made her want to cry harder.

"I love you. I'm going to call the department and then I'm going to call you right back. Okay?"

"Okay."

"And you're safe."

"I'm safe. I'm okay. And I'm sor—"

"Not on your life, Camden. Don't say that to me right now."

"I love you."

"That works. Now give me a few minutes, that's it, and then I'm calling right back."

Tess leaned against the aging, smelly concrete of the side of the building, one hand resting on her gun, the other clutching the phone. Her face ached and burned. If nothing was broken she'd be lucky.

Unfortunately, it wasn't just bones she was worried about being broken.

MARC HAD ONLY ever driven this fast when running code in his patrol car. Never in his own vehicle. But how could he not break every law to get to her as soon as humanly possible?

Luckily Bluff City at three in the morning wasn't that difficult to speed through, and he pulled into her father's apartment complex not too long after he'd hung up with her the second time.

Long enough. Damn it, where was Stumpf? Or

someone from BCPD. Damn it. Damn it. Damn it. Where was Tess?

He hopped out of his truck. "Tess?" He didn't see her anywhere. If she'd gone back in there… If her father had…

"Tess?" he shouted. He didn't give a rat's ass that people were sleeping, he needed to—

"Marc. I'm right here." She stepped around a bush, just a shadow. A tentative shadow.

He rushed over to her. "Where are you hurt? What did he do?"

She walked carefully, but she wasn't limping or holding her arm or anything to indicate she might be hurt. He pulled out the flashlight he'd had the foresight to grab from his glove compartment.

She winced against the light, and there was blood. "Tess." He gently turned her face and— "Jesus Christ." There was blood. Something had scratched up her face, and her cheek was swollen, as was a spot by her temple.

His eyes burned as he tried to think of what to do. "We have to get you to the hospital." He didn't know what to do. Where was Stumpf? He should let Stumpf take care of it, but fuck that. "I'm taking you to the hospital. Stumpf can talk to you there. I'll call him once we get you inside."

"Marc."

He gingerly moved his arm around her shoulders and began leading her toward the car.

"I don't want to go to the hospital."

"I know. I know, honey, but you have to." Everything inside him felt like gelatin. He was having a hard time finding the strength to walk, let alone hold her up. Her face looked terrible. Awful.

And he'd let her… And she'd made him…

He forced himself to take a breath, to find some center of calm and steady. He needed to be her calm and steady.

Finally, Marc heard sirens in the distance.

"I don't want to talk to him." She stumbled, but Marc managed to keep her upright.

"You have to press charges."

She glanced back at the building.

"Tess. This is not a choice. Have you seen your face? Do you see what he did to you?"

"I know. I know. It was wrong." But she was still looking at the apartment, not at him, taking slow, painful steps away. "He's my father," she said weakly.

"Tess, look at me, please."

She did. Her eyes were kind of glazed and she wasn't steady. She was definitely more hurt than she let on. It was hard to get the next words out with a ball of emotion lodged so deeply in his throat, but he had to say it.

"You cannot let this continue. You know you can't." Gently, just the lightest of touches, he put his palm to the cheek that hadn't been pulverized. "Tess, please tell me you understand that. You have to see this kind of thing too much not to see what he's doing."

She leaned into him. "I just want to go home."

"I know, baby. I know." He held her as tightly as he could without hurting her cheek. The cruiser pulled up, and if he hadn't spent the entire drive over here all but screaming obscenities, he might have been tempted to let a few more loose.

Because when Stumpf stepped out of the cruiser, he wasn't alone. He was with Granger.

CHAPTER NINETEEN

TESS COULD TELL by the way Marc stiffened that something was wrong. She wasn't sure she had it in her for any more wrong. She wasn't sure she had it in her for…anything.

Marc was right. She'd had to pull a gun on her father to feel safe. He'd attacked her, completely on purpose, no matter how apologetic he'd been afterward.

She absolutely needed to press charges. But…

Why was that *but* in her brain? What was wrong with her? What was wrong with her that deep in the recesses of her brain—or her heart, maybe—she felt as though she was to blame?

"Santino."

Tess tensed too at the sound of Granger's voice. Marc was holding her. It was the middle of the night. And oh, shit.

She needed to pull away. To get it all together. To be Officer Camden. It wasn't as though she'd never had someone try and attack her before. A few incidents during arrests. Men who'd taken swings at her—a few times they'd even connected. This was not new. This wasn't something she couldn't handle, because she'd handled it before.

Strong. Alone. No big shoulders to lean on, no comforting arms to hold her.

But those were arrests. Strangers. Criminals. Not her father.

"I can't do this," she whispered into Marc's chest. She didn't know if he heard her or if it mattered. She didn't know…

God, she just wanted to sleep. She wanted to do anything but face her coworkers with her own failings. All of them. Dad. Marc. All the ways she'd tried to be strong, and now she was the weak victim crying on a man's shoulder. Letting him make her feel safe.

"Isn't this cozy."

That pissed her off enough to pull away from Marc, to make sure Granger could see the blood on her cheek. "Yeah, my face feels really fucking cozy."

Granger had the good sense to look shamed, to look away. To keep his big asshole mouth shut.

"What happened, Camden?"

"She needs a hospital." Marc's arm remained around her shoulder and he started ushering her toward his truck.

Stumpf nodded, and while his gaze between her and Marc was considering, he didn't say anything.

Wow, she must really look bad.

She hated this feeling of three men dictating what she was doing, but her brain still felt rattled.

Everything felt wrong, and regardless of whether they were men or aliens, it felt good to have someone else deal with the consequences for once.

Stumpf cleared his throat. "We should probably drive her, Santino. That way I can take her statement in the car and—"

"Tess?"

She didn't look at Marc, partially because her face was throbbing and she didn't want to move it, but more because she didn't want to see his face. Or anyone's.

"I don't care." And she didn't. She didn't care about anything, because what the hell was left? She'd failed Dad so spectacularly, and he'd failed her to the point she didn't know how she'd ever go back.

And Stumpf and Granger weren't morons. They were putting two and two together. Her and Marc.

What the fuck was left?

"I just want to go home. If something was broken, I'd notice by now." Finally she forced herself to look up at Marc, because she wasn't going to look at Granger, and she was afraid Stumpf would look at her with pity.

She wasn't 100 percent sure what she'd find on Marc's face, but it wasn't Granger's bullshit and she highly doubted it'd be pity. "Please take me home."

He swallowed visibly, the conflicting emotions and the sheen to his eyes evident now that they were under the weak parking-lot lights. He touched her good cheek. "You could need stitches."

Marc cared. Really cared, not because she was a woman or a victim. He cared about *her*, and, well, if situations were reversed, she'd be doing the same thing.

She'd want him to be okay and safe and cared for. So she wanted to go home, and she wanted Marc to take her there.

She flicked a glance at Stumpf, who was looking elsewhere. Good man. She didn't dare look to see what Granger was doing. "I really don't think I need a hospital. It's some bruising and a few scratches. It'll heal. Stumpf, I'll give you a statement and then I'm going home before you go in there. Everyone understand?"

If she weren't exhausted and in a hell of a lot of pain, she'd be disgusted Stumpf looked at Marc. As though Marc got to make the decision. Just because he was a man.

But he was a man who cared about her, and for tonight, she was going to let that be something. She needed something.

"Let's get this shit over with, huh?" She motioned to Stumpf. "Get out your notebook. I don't want to stand around here all night."

Slowly, with another look at Marc, Stumpf pulled out his notebook and began to write.

MARC GLANCED AT Tess in the passenger seat. Her eyes were closed and she held an ice pack from his first-aid kit to her face. She hadn't said anything since Stumpf had told her he didn't need any other information and she'd offered a thank-you before climbing in his truck.

She'd wanted to leave before they arrested her father. So he'd driven her away. Marc felt as if he was wading through a big pile of doing it all wrong. He should have gone with her. He should have made her go to the hospital. He should have done a million things.

Instead, she was slumped in his passenger seat, as defeated as he'd ever seen her. When he pulled to a stop in the parking lot, her eyes blinked open. Her sigh filled the interior.

"Do you think you could have a concussion?" he asked, tentatively, because he didn't know what questions he had a right to ask. Which questions wouldn't hurt her even more. The last thing he wanted to do was add more hurt to the pile weighing her down.

She pulled the handle and pushed the door open. "No. I'm fine."

He had to grind his teeth to keep from asking her what her father had hit her with. Stumpf had already been over it and she said she didn't know because it had been dark. And he'd already asked her, twice, if she'd lost consciousness.

No and no. He knew he needed to back off. He could see it in the careful way she held herself so he wouldn't offer an arm, a shoulder. She didn't want to lean on him. She wanted to stand on her own two feet.

It was killing him.

But this wasn't about him, so he needed to find a way to breathe through all the tension and helplessness coiling around his lungs.

She leaned heavily on the railing as they walked up the stairs. He stayed behind her, just to make sure...

Hell if he knew. Hell if he knew anything anymore.

They reached their flight and she reached into her pocket. "Shit. I forgot. My keys...they're back at my...at his place."

"Do you need anything from your apartment?"

She shook her head. "I guess not."

He wordlessly unlocked his door, stepped inside, and she followed. He bolted the locks behind her and then they both stood there.

"You must be exhausted."

She nodded, then winced. He swallowed down the urge to insist she go to the hospital. In reality, she was right. She'd be in a lot more pain if she'd broken something, and with her face cleaned up and the ice pack doing its work, the scratches looked minimal. But it was still awful. Just downright horrific.

"I'll go get you some ibuprofen. And some new ice. I'll—"

"You don't need to nurse me. It's more of a shock than anything else."

She obviously hadn't looked at herself in the mirror yet. She obviously didn't understand how much damage had been done. He had to resist the urge to shake that weary acceptance out of her, to get it through to her that nothing that had happened was okay. Not one second of it. "It's more than that, Tess."

She swallowed. "I can't process it all right now. It's too much. Can we not talk about it?"

"Go lie down. I'll be right in." She needed some new ice. Some painkillers. She needed…everything, and he was going to do his best to give it to her.

She didn't move at first, instead watched him march to the kitchen. But as he started getting things together, she finally disappeared into the hall.

He took a minute to breathe. Breathe through all the emotions making that normal instinct hard. He couldn't remember the last time he'd been so close to tears. Maybe after Leah's transplant. He'd only been fifteen, but the relief she'd come out on the other side okay…he'd cried in his bed that night.

Alone. Because he hadn't wanted to cry in front of his parents at the hospital, even though they had been crying. He'd wanted to be strong.

He needed to find that same strength here. Be the strength she needed. He was good at that. Coming in second and cleaning up the messes. She was worth it. She needed it. He had to be that for her.

But it didn't feel second nature right now. It felt hard-won. He filled a glass with water, pulled out a bottle of ibuprofen and a pack of frozen vegetables from the freezer. He took a deep breath, and he walked to his bedroom determined to be every last inch of what she needed.

As though his whole life had been practice for this moment, and if that was the case, maybe it was worth it.

Tess had lain down on the bed, though not under the covers. Her shoes were still on and she lay on her side, the unharmed side of her face buried in one of his pillows.

"All right. New ice pack. Some ibuprofen. Anything else you want?"

"Will you lie with me?" she asked, her voice muffled by the pillow.

"That's never something you have to ask," he managed to say, though his voice was rough. "Never."

He placed his supplies on the nightstand and crawled into bed, lying next to her on his side. She reached out and linked her fingers with his. He removed the watery ice pack from her cheek and replaced it with the bag of frozen food. She'd need some bandages for those scratches, but trying to reduce the swelling seemed more important.

Her lips curved on one side—the good side. "Thank you for not saying *I told you so*. I'm not sure I could have dealt with that tonight."

He didn't know what to say to that. He didn't want to tell her that. He hadn't told her anything.

He'd failed by stepping back, stepping away. Path of least resistance. No *I told you so*s.

Her index finger trailed across the back of his hand. "It's okay that you wanted to."

"I don't want to. I want to go back in time and not listen to you is what I want to do, but I can't do that."

"No, you can't." She looked at their linked hands. "If there was time travel available, I'd go back a little farther than that."

"How far?"

She reached out with her free hand, ran her index finger down the length of his nose. "You can come with." Her face scrunched up and she adjusted the bag on her cheek.

Trying to keep the frustration out of his voice, Marc grabbed the bottle of ibuprofen and shook a few out. "Take these. I can't stand watching you wince every five seconds. Hopefully they'll help."

She sat up and took the pills, washed them down with the glass of water he handed her. Then, as if the energy to sit up was too much, she wilted back into the pillow. "Thank you."

"What are you thanking me for?"

"I've never had someone take care of me before. At least that I remember. I guess when I was a baby. But, mostly, it's just been me. I know you don't want my gratitude, but I want you to know that it means something to me." She cleared her throat. "So I'm going to lean a bit, because I need it, but don't think I'm weak."

"Tess, I could never think you're weak."

"I didn't want them to arrest him." She closed her eyes. "I knew they had to. I knew I should want it, but I didn't. Not really." A tear slipped down her cheek, and he reached out to brush it away, his own emotion clogging his throat.

But he had to be strong. So he was. "You can't blame yourself. Anything that he's done, ever, you can't blame yourself for that."

"I *know* that." She blinked her eyes open, staring at the ceiling, eyebrows drawn together. "I don't always feel that, unfortunately. I'm so afraid that's weak."

He shifted, gingerly slipping his arm under her neck, drawing her near. She rested her good cheek on his shoulder, and he leaned his cheek against her head.

"I love you, Tess."

She expelled a breath against his neck. "I know. You have no idea how glad I am that you do."

It released at least a fraction of the tension he felt inside. He hadn't been able to keep her safe, and he couldn't fix this, but he could give her something. That would have to be enough.

TESS COULDN'T SLEEP. She stared at the dark ceiling above her, counted the rise and fall of Marc's breathing, but she couldn't drift off.

Her cheek ached and burned and her ice pack of

vegetables had long gone limp. But she didn't want to wake up Marc. She didn't want to move.

Her body felt like a lead weight. Like everything that had ever happened to her was holding her down on the bed. Or maybe it was just the comfort of lying next to someone, knowing he cared, knowing he loved her. She didn't want to get up. She didn't want to leave the warmth and comfort of someone who would give her ice packs and bring her painkillers and sleep next to her.

But her father was in jail. She had put him there. No matter what comfort Marc gave, she couldn't get over that. She couldn't pretend that it didn't matter. She couldn't pretend that she didn't feel at fault. Because even if it was pathetic, the blame stifled any attempt at getting angry.

She wanted to feel angry. She wanted to be able to rage against the man who had hit her in the face in the dark. She wanted to be the kind of person who knew it was wrong, who knew without a shadow of a doubt that she had nothing to blame herself for.

But she wasn't that person. She felt guilt and blame and shame and none of the anger or righteousness that should accompany a vicious, violent and premeditated attack.

Disgusted with herself and her thoughts, Tess got out of bed. She walked quietly to the bathroom in Marc's hallway. She flipped on the light, winced at the change in brightness, and then winced again because the first wince hurt her face.

She caught sight of herself in mirror for the first time. She hadn't wanted to look. The pain lingering despite the ice pack and ibuprofen was enough evidence to know it was bad. But it was even worse than she had expected.

Almost the entire side of her face was swollen and covered in already purpling bruises. There were scratches across her cheek, although none of them were too deep.

One blow. One simple strike against her cheek had done a spectacular amount of damage. Inflicted by her father. It shouldn't be a surprise. Things had been escalating this way for months, years, maybe her whole life? Maybe this was the inevitable conclusion of a daughter certain she could fix her father despite all evidence to the contrary.

Tess forced herself to keep looking at the injuries on her face. She needed to memorize them. She needed to commit each scratch, each bruise, each swelling bump to the forefront of her mind so that she would never forget.

In fact… She tiptoed out of the bedroom, grabbed her phone from the nightstand, then tiptoed back. She pulled up the camera, took a picture. Maybe it could act as some kind of reminder.

She couldn't help him. She'd never helped him. Nothing was ever going to change. This was the end. She could not allow herself to ever go back. This had to be it.

So she stood in front of the mirror willing herself to be angry, hurt, devastated. She willed herself to feel everything so deeply, so painfully that she would never believe his bullshit, or her own, again.

CHAPTER TWENTY

IT WAS STRANGE, driving his Bluff City police cruiser to work without Tess by his side. A few weeks wasn't all that long in the grand scheme of things, but every day he'd worked at BCPD, Tess and her flowery perfume had been right there.

Instead she was on his couch watching some DVDs and hopefully enjoying at least a few seconds of her day.

Okay, probably not enjoying.

He wished he could stay with her. Wished he could be with her for at least today, and if things were different he might have taken the day off. But he did not expect Granger to have kept his mouth shut last night. No, he expected Granger to have all sorts of stories spread around the department by now.

While *he* didn't care, because they could all go fuck themselves, he knew Tess would care. Did care. That was the last thing she needed to come back to whenever she was able to come back.

Marc parked his cruiser in the department parking lot. He wasn't sure if he was going to be allowed to go alone today or if someone would be taking Tess's place as field training officer, but either way he did not foresee it being a very fun eight hours.

Marc decided to go straight to Franks's office. It would be easier than trying to track down someone who might already be on duty. However, before he got to Franks's office, Granger appeared.

"Santino."

"Granger." He gave a polite nod and tried to step around him, but the idiot stood there in his plain-clothes looking way too smug.

"Guess you took my 'she doesn't fuck cops' as a personal challenge."

It took everything in his power not to slam his fist into the guy's mouth. "Why the hell do you keep showing up, Granger?"

"Work here, remember?"

"Yeah, and you're on evening shift. Yet somehow you were on midnight shift last night. And now it's morning and you're still here."

"Wanted to catch the captain." The little smirk he gave sent Marc's teeth on edge.

He should walk away. He should absolutely ignore this guy and move on, but…but… "Make you feel important to tattle?"

"I'm looking out for the good of the department. The fact of the matter is, Tess's pussy already has every guy here by the balls and I don't think—"

Marc grabbed a handful of Granger's T-shirt and shoved him into the wall. Hard. He'd never rammed someone against a wall in anger before. Occasionally out of necessity, if a criminal got a little out of control, but never because he was angry.

He was angry now. Violently so. His free fingers curled into a fist and he could imagine, he could picture with absolute clarity his fist bashing into Granger's nose.

"Santino."

Marc closed his eyes, just for a second. Captain Franks. He dropped Granger's shirt, had to force his gaze away from the asshole's smirking face.

"Captain."

"My office."

"Yes, sir."

"Enjoy," Granger muttered once Captain was out of earshot. "And if you were thinking you'd be able to keep it on the down low for precious fucking Tess, well, it's too damn late for that. Captain knows she's a useless slut. He's probably fucked her a few times him—"

Even knowing it had every possibility of getting him fired, Marc cocked his fist and rammed it right into Granger's jaw.

Granger stumbled backward, but he didn't fall. He righted himself then charged Marc. It was easy to shove him away, but Granger kept coming. Until Captain called their names, jerking his door open so hard it banged against the wall.

"Santino. I said my office. Now. Granger, go get yourself cleaned up and then wait."

"Captain, he—"

"Do it," Captain barked. "Inside. Now," he said to Marc.

Marc nodded, trying to find a way to even his breathing, to get rid of some of the unsteady anger still pumping through him.

He should have been above it. Should have waved off Granger's words as the whining of a pathetic piece of shit. Instead, he'd jeopardized his job. All for one satisfying punch to the face.

Although it had been pretty satisfying.

"Sit."

Marc did as Franks instructed. He sank into an uncomfortable chair against the wall next to the door. Franks stood in front of his desk, expression grave.

"Santino, I don't know how they did things back in your old department. I don't know what the hell is going on here, but this kind of behavior—"

"Unacceptable. I know, sir." Marc sat in one of the chairs, ramrod straight, staring at the wall in front of him. "I apologize. I lost my temper, and it's inexcusable."

Franks's frown went deeper into a scowl. "We don't know each other that well, Santino. I know Granger can have a bit of a mouth, and this incident last night…" The captain looked incredibly uncomfortable. He turned away from Marc, then back again. "I'd like to hear your rundown of events."

"Sir?"

"I've seen Stumpf's report. Granger's been on and on about…things. I want to hear what your role was. Then we'll discuss your altercation with him."

"I—" Marc cleared his throat, trying to remember his role. Even *if* Granger had been an asshole telling everyone he and Tess were sleeping together, it didn't mean Marc had to give everyone that impression.

It was none of anyone's business.

"Camden has been having a few run-ins with her father. She received a call that he was threatening to commit suicide, and so she went to check on him. She'd dealt with similar situations with him before and was concerned about getting anyone involved for fear he'd go through with it."

"You know all this because?"

"She told me." At Franks's raised eyebrow, Marc had to force himself to unclench his jaw. "I was with her at the time."

"At…" Franks looked at some papers on his desk. "Three in the morning?"

"Yes."

Franks sighed. "Do you know the rules about this sort of thing?"

He almost went the *what sort of thing* route, but he really doubted Franks would appreciate that. Besides, there wasn't any denying what was going on. "As far as I know the only rules against people… having relationships is if it goes as far as marriage."

"And you understand why?"

"I guess I've never thought about it." Sure, he'd thought about one of them having to leave if things got that far, but never the reason behind it.

"We can't, as a department, police who you choose to spend your time with, but when it comes to lawfully combining your lives, we can't send you both into dangerous situations. It becomes an issue of family, and safety. We can't in good conscience sacrifice that since we're here to protect the safety of Bluff City."

Marc didn't know what to say to that. Any of this.

"Now, you've only been here a few weeks, so maybe this is all overkill, but I have worked with Tess for ten years and I feel like I know her well enough."

"Not enough to know what was happening with her father." He immediately regretted saying it when Franks's mouth firmed into a thin, almost invisible, line.

"The point is, I'm choosing to trust you and Camden. Your personal lives are your personal lives, as long as that does not affect your work. Should things take a turn for the legally binding side, we'll need to discuss this further. But as long as it remains a separate issue, I want nothing to do with it."

That was…very diplomatic, and while he knew it'd be a relief to Tess, there was still a whole department of side eyes and whispers to deal with.

"As for Granger, I'll have a talk with him. Stay out of each other's way, and no more altercations.

As it is, I'm going to have to formally write you up. It'll go in your file, and as long as there are no other incidents, it'll be expunged after a year. That being said, two write-ups during field training will lead to termination. Clear?"

"Yes, sir."

"Good. You're going to be riding with Gordon until Camden gets back."

"Yes, sir."

"You can go now."

Marc nodded, got out of his chair and stiffly walked toward the door. He wasn't fired. He was barely in trouble. He didn't have the energy reserves to process all that.

"Oh, and, Santino?"

Marc paused in the doorway, waiting for some kind of snide comment about his relationship with Tess, or a warning about getting in fights in the precinct.

"Give Tess my regards. She's one of my best officers." He looked at a picture on his desk. "Reminds me of my daughter, actually. Shameful thing, being hurt by your flesh and blood. I hope she recuperates soon."

Marc gave a curt nod, chose his next words carefully. "I won't try to defend hitting Granger. Wrong place. Wrong time. Maybe just wrong, period, but he's out to make Tess's life a little harder, and I won't let him do that right now."

"I won't argue with that, but I can't keep you on

if you hit him again." Franks took a seat at his desk. "On duty."

"I understand, sir." For the first time since he'd moved here, he felt good about getting the job with BCPD, aside from anything to do with Tess. Captain Franks was a good guy, and aside from Granger, it was a good department.

Maybe he'd moved here for Mom and Dad, in the hopes they'd notice, but he was starting to feel as if he was staying for himself.

TESS WAS PRETTY sure she was going completely stir-crazy. Even she could only watch TV and nap for so long. Eight hours straight was a stretch. She couldn't remember the last time she'd had eight hours to herself that didn't include doing something for Dad, doing errands of her own or work.

She'd dreamed of having a day to herself, just to lounge. Now she had it, and it sucked. Although possibly because her face felt as if it had been...well, smacked with something really, really hard.

She blew out a breath, once again talking herself out of calling the jail to check on Dad. He was the reason she was in this whole damn mess. It didn't matter how or what he was doing. He'd cut that tenuous thread of her support.

Sure, he did.

She pushed off the couch. She had to do something, but had no car and no keys to her apartment. She was practically a prisoner herself.

It was almost three. She could make Marc take her somewhere, but she knew what she looked like. What it would look like if she tried to hide the injuries and go out with Marc.

She sank back onto the couch and groaned. This was excruciating. She looked at her phone one more time. There were a handful of texts from a few of the dispatchers, some of the midnight shift guys, letting her know if she needed anything they were available.

It had been a surprise to wake up to. The support. Sure, she'd supported them in their own times of need, but she'd somehow never expected to need it back.

If she spent one more second thinking about the past twenty-four hours, she was going to jump out the window. It was almost three, Marc should be home soon, and while it was a little early for dinner, she was going to make some anyway.

"Suzy Homemaker, here I come," she muttered, marching resolutely to the kitchen. She poked around the fridge and cupboards. Though she was more than used to making her own meals, what Marc kept on hand was so different from what she did, it was hard to figure out what to make. He didn't have the little blue box of macaroni and cheese, one of those premade salad kits, lunch meat. He had all this fresh crap.

She found a bag of some weird-looking pasta.

Easy enough. He didn't have canned spaghetti sauce on hand, but she could probably make some herself.

So much better than thinking about Dad or the pain in her face.

Keys jangled in the lock, then the knob turned. Marc stepped inside and frowned. "I told you to lock the chain."

"That's a terrible greeting."

"Tess."

"Marc."

He sighed then gave her a puzzled look. "What are you doing?"

She looked at the pot she'd gotten out. "I'm making dinner."

His lips curved, just a hint, and then without taking off his boots or his utility belt—which she was pretty sure was sacrilege in his crazy clean and tidy world—he walked right over to her and kissed her.

Gently. So gently. She almost wanted to cry, but they'd had more than enough of that. Probably had more than enough ahead of them.

"That hurt?" he asked, his voice a whisper against her mouth, his fingers brushing over her shoulder as if she was delicate. Fragile.

She wasn't supposed to want that. It went against everything she stood for as a strong, capable woman. But Marc made it feel like love, not some diminishment of her strength.

"No, it didn't hurt."

"Good." He looked at her empty pot and grinned. "You're good to come home to."

"Well, I'm losing my marbles from being *home* all day, but that wasn't a bad way to be greeted, I have to say."

"Stumpf is going to get your keys tonight. He's going to call me once he gets them and we can go get your car. Or I can. Up to you."

"Thanks." She leaned into him, because as she'd said last night, she was letting herself lean a little. "So, how was your day?"

He stiffened, even though the somewhat pleasant smile remained on his face.

"Shit liar, remember?"

He scratched a hand over his hair. "I…punched Granger."

"What?" she screeched, pulling back from her leaning. "You *punched* him?"

"I know. It was…bad. But he was there this morning, being a dick. I lost my temper. Pushed him. Captain caught us, then I punched him." He held himself so tense and so rigid, as if he'd done something wrong and was about to be punished.

Which didn't make any sense at all. "I'm so, so, so jealous."

He expelled a weird breath—almost like a laugh. "You'll likely get a chance." He shifted so they were facing each other, his hands on her shoulders, that serious expression he used so much—too much, really—on his face.

"I know he deserved it."

"I did it basically in front of the captain. In uniform."

"Oh." *Oh.* And over her, no less. That was not good. To put it lightly. "Write-up?"

He pursed his lips and nodded. "Franks was fair. More than, really. I think he knows Granger's got something up his ass, but still, it's... I've never been written up before. I've never done anything wrong in uniform before."

"There's a first time for everything?" she offered weakly, and then leaned her good cheek against his chest. "I'm sorry."

"I don't know why *you'd* be sorry, Tess."

"Because I'm not stupid and I know you'd only hit him if he said something gross about me."

Marc didn't respond, and she squeezed her eyes shut. "I don't know that this is worse, but the situation keeps getting...more. More everything."

"Well, *I'm* sorry for adding to it."

"You know what? No. We're both done being sorry." She looked up at him, trying to keep her face angled enough so he wasn't staring at the nasty bruises. "*We* haven't done anything wrong. Granger and my dad are the assholes."

She wanted him to smile, but he didn't. Not even the slightest curl to his lips. "It's going to be okay," he finally said, so seriously, so resolutely that she wanted to believe him. Willed herself to believe him.

But there was the little fact that going back to work

was going to be far more complicated than she'd ever wanted her work to be. "I've never dreaded going there. Not once in ten years." She leaned against his chest, because it was a solid place to lean.

"Don't think about it yet." He ran his hand over her hair. She was a little overemotional from all the upheaval of the past day or two, but she wanted to believe this thing between them could last. They could get through whatever work would be like once she went back, they could deal with the jokes and innuendo, they could deal with figuring out how they could have something serious.

God, if she was going to lose her reputation, she was at the very least getting Marc out of the deal.

"So, what were you planning on making for dinner?"

She shook away the thoughts of a future that was just too uncertain. "Hey, I *can* cook. I just choose not to cook froufrou diet food."

"Uh-huh. What's on the menu?"

"Pasta and tomato sauce?"

"Oh, Tess." He shook his head, all adorable and clucky. "I'll cook. Let me shower and change." He brushed a kiss against her temple and stepped out of the tiny kitchen.

"Everyone knows, don't they?"

He paused, and she couldn't see his face to make out his expression, but she knew. Oh, she knew. And she knew what was next. The dread at going back dug deeper. Embarrassment over her father was one thing, but all the crap she'd have to take now…

Then Marc turned. "I think you underestimate some of them. They respect you, Tess. I'm not saying it'll be easy, and we all know Granger's a dick, but Captain said…" He drew his hand over his mouth, expression pained the way it always got when he was searching for the right words.

Marc was always on the search for the *right* words. Sometimes she wished he'd just give her honest ones, even if they sucked.

"He said that you're the best officer he's ever had, and that you remind him of his daughter. He hoped you were well. The fact that he cares is important, Tess. It'll protect you some."

Tess swallowed at the lump in her throat. Captain thought of her as a daughter? That was…a little too much. Considering what she knew. "His daughter died."

"What?"

"My first year. His daughter died in a car accident." She blinked at the stinging in her eyes, cleared her throat. "I was the one who told him. He…" She'd never told anyone that Franks had cried on her shoulder, even though who could blame him? His seventeen-year-old daughter had died.

She'd cried herself, and offered an awkward hug to a man who was her superior when she'd only been a few months off field training. She'd known he'd appreciated it, that it was part of the reason he'd been somewhat easy on her when it came to stuff with her father, but she'd never known she'd reminded him of his daughter.

"See, Tess. It's things like that. You know these people—you've made them your friends. I'm not saying a few won't be assholes. They will, it's inevitable, but mostly you have an entire department that knows exactly what you do for them—or what you *would* do for them."

She looked up into his sincere expression. She was emotionally wrung out all over again, but there were good things leftover from this one. Even though it was painful, even though it was sad, it was good, too.

There were good things left. A lot of good things. "I'm making pasta with tomato sauce, and you can't stop me."

A corner of his mouth quirked. "All right, you're the boss."

She didn't feel much like the boss, but she did at least feel some equilibrium.

CHAPTER TWENTY-ONE

WATCHING TESS WINCE after she laughed was two parts comforting and two parts painful.

She'd made her terrible pasta à la tomato sauce and had only allowed him to contribute a salad. But she was smiling and laughing and conversation had been light.

Except for all the wincing.

"If that's not better tomorrow…" He trailed off because he had no idea how to finish that sentence. What was he going to do? Force her to go to the hospital?

Yes, you should. You absolutely should.

She glanced at the clock. "It's fine. I can take some more ibuprofen in a half hour. A nice bruise always hurts worse the second day."

He wanted to say something else. Something a shade angrier, but someone knocked on his door. Sure, Stumpf had said he'd call first when he retrieved Tess's keys, but maybe he'd gotten busy and forgotten.

Marc stood and went over to the door. When he

looked through the peephole, he thought about pretending they weren't here. "It's, uh, my sister."

"Oh, you want me to…" She nodded toward the bedroom door.

He knew he shouldn't want Tess to disappear, but he did. He didn't want to figure out how to introduce her to Leah, how to explain things had changed. Perhaps even more, he didn't want Tess watching his interactions with Leah and…interpreting things.

"You want me to go." She slid off the chair, and though he supposed she was trying to act unaffected, she was angry. Or worse, hurt.

"No, it's fine." He pulled open the door, determined not be the one hurting Tess.

"Hey, bro." Leah wrinkled her nose. "Yeah, that sounds terrible. I just wanted to see if—" For the first time her gaze caught on Tess standing next to the little table in the corner.

"Sorry." Leah's brows drew together before Tess turned the injured side of her face away. "I didn't mean to interrupt."

"No, no interruption. In fact, I have a phone call to make. Don't go. I'll make myself scarce." She was already heading for the bedroom by the time she said the last words.

The door closed quietly and Marc looked down at Leah, having no idea what he was supposed to do. Part of him wanted to go after Tess, but he couldn't leave Leah standing here.

"Normally I'd leave anyway," Leah said, not budging from the entry to his door. "But I need to talk to you and it's hard enough to escape Mom's clutches once. Twice will be impossible. At least if I want Jacob to keep speaking to me."

Marc still didn't say anything, but he stepped out of the doorway and let Leah in.

For needing to talk to him, she didn't say anything at first. She stood in the middle of his living room, looking hard at where Tess had gone.

"Is she okay?" she finally asked, her gaze meeting his.

He wasn't sure what he should say, so he just gave Leah the truth. "She was attacked."

"Badly?"

"Just...her face." He scrubbed his hands over his own. "Jesus. As if that makes it less terrible."

"I know too many women who've had to go through that." Leah let out a gusty sigh. "Shit, the world kind of sucks. Every time you think your own problems are bad, you get a little perspective, huh?"

Marc wasn't sure he'd had time for perspective, but he understood Leah's meaning all the same.

"Your crap's pretty bad too."

"Gee, thanks."

"A faulty heart is nothing to screw around with."

"Don't I know it, but it's not faulty anymore." She tapped a palm to her chest. "Healthy as a horse. Minus the asthma. And the allergies."

He almost smiled at that. Sometimes he forgot

how much he liked Leah. Not just because she was his sister and because he had to, but because she was honest. Forthright. She didn't hide from her feelings.

Not the way he did.

Uncomfortable topic. Time to move on. "So, what brings you here?"

"Remember that party I told you about? The spring potluck thing that's tomorrow night? Come." Leah glanced at where Tess had gone again. "She looked pretty comfortable here."

Marc only offered a nod.

"Oh, don't go all silent on me. Mom was practically giddy at some pretty girl being in your apartment for dinner the other night. You're seeing her."

Again, he nodded, which caused her to scowl, which almost made him smile. Because she was interested and pushing and it was...new. Nice.

"Bring her. It'll be something normal and fun to do, and, trust me, no one will say anything about her face. Not in that group."

"Will Mom and Dad be there?"

She hesitated, but finally nodded. "Yes."

"You so sure Mom won't say something about her face?"

"Maybe it'd be good for Boss Lady to feel like someone is overzealously interested in her and her eligibility for marrying a crazy person's son."

"Her name is Tess," Marc said, shifting uncomfortably. This was all so weird. Talking about Tess as if she wasn't in the next room. Words like *mar-*

rying. "And I think the only marriage Mom cares about is yours."

Leah lifted her hand, hesitated, then rested it on his elbow. "They kind of suck at seeing us. The real us. But we both kind of suck at showing the real us, I think. So, I just…" She dropped her hand then tugged at her ponytail. "Can't believe I'm saying this, but give them a bit more to go on."

"Are you telling me to cut them some slack?" It was too ridiculous to be offended by. Not all that long ago he'd been telling Leah the same, only not quite so nicely.

She scrunched up her nose. "Hard to believe, huh? Can't say I expected to be doing that about four months ago."

"Yeah, me, either."

"I hate having to contemplate all this weird stuff we have between us, but the fact of the matter is we're all going to be living in the same town soon, and we might as well be happy about it. You have to give them something. Something of you. Or things keep being the same. I know, unfortunately, some of why Mom and I get along better is because of Jacob being in my life. But it's also because we spent some time together and opened up a little. You've barely seen them."

"They've barely asked. And I'll remind you, I've spent plenty of time with them in my thirty-two years."

"Give them a reason to ask, Marc." She looked at

him plaintively, which he couldn't remember ever seeing from Leah. "I know they haven't made a lot of effort to see you on this visit, but they think they owe me some making up for lost time, and they think you understand that. Tell them you don't. Tell them you're upset about the ring, which Jacob refused, by the way. Nothing can change when you're pretending like this. Trust me. I know."

He didn't know how to argue with that, even if he didn't agree with it. He couldn't combat the strange bubble of hope rising up inside of him, making him wonder if Leah could possibly be right. He just needed to give them something to go on and they'd be able to…not treat him like nothing.

"I'll…come."

"Ask Boss—er, Tess, too. Okay?"

"I will." If Tess wasn't too angry at his pause over her not meeting Leah. "She may not want to, but I'll ask." Maybe it would be good for her, for them. After all, they didn't need to pretend anymore. Everyone at work knew. "And I'll let you know."

Leah smiled and when he moved toward her she stepped back. "I already told you. No hugs."

"Oh, now you did it. I have to hug you. Obnoxious older brother prerogative."

She held out her hands in protest. "Don't touch me, Creepo McGee."

"I'm going to hug you, Leah. You're my own flesh and blood."

She grimaced but put her hands down, and he gave her a quick, if a little awkward, squeeze.

She shuddered. "Bleh. So weird."

"Family, Leah."

"Don't care. Weird." She stepped toward the door, but stopped. "Thanks, though. You're a good brother."

He didn't feel like one. Even moving here and all he'd done, it had been for his parents, not for Leah.

"I know someone who went through something similar to Tess. I don't know if she'd want to talk about it, but if Tess needs someone to talk to, I can ask."

"Thanks." He took a deep breath, attempted to let some of his gratitude actually show through. "Really, thanks."

"Anytime, bro." She shook her head. "Yeah, I really can't pull that off. I should go. Let me know about the party."

"Yeah." He didn't know that he particularly wanted to go, but it didn't feel right to say no. Maybe it would be good for Tess and him to be around people who weren't their coworkers. Feel at least temporarily that things could be normal.

If he could smooth things over. No, not if. He would smooth things over because they loved each other. There were things they both kept to themselves, kept separate. Her father. His family. They both just needed to accept it. And they would, and it would be good.

"You didn't have to disappear."

Tess looked up at Marc standing in his bedroom doorway. His expression was blank. For all the support and comfort and damn sweetness he'd offered her the past few weeks, that expression was getting increasingly…frustrating.

It made her feel as though there were always things he'd shut out. Always things he'd pretend didn't bother him or weren't important. It made her feel as though she were on open display, but he was under lock and key.

Imbalanced. As though he had all the power. She didn't like that feeling at all.

"Sorry. I don't really feel like being around people when my face looks like this. Besides, you didn't want to introduce us. I'm not going to force you."

"I didn't mean that you should be sorry. I just meant that you didn't have to go. If you wanted to go, that's fine. I just needed to…process the question."

She looked down at his comforter, wanting to change the subject. Luckily, he did first. "Did you really have a phone call to make?" Marc crossed the room and slid next to her on the bed.

"I was getting a little antsy, so I called Stumpf." Tess picked at a thread on the comforter. "He said he got waylaid on a call, so it'd be another hour or so."

"I can call someone else."

"So could I." She winced at the snap in her tone, but he'd probably think it was her face hurting. And get that blank look. She couldn't decide if it meant he was angry about everything that had happened or angry about her not going to the hospital or some other emotion she didn't know.

Because he didn't tell her. Because he kept it all to himself. Because he didn't want to introduce her to his sister. He wanted to keep his family and her separate.

"Is everything okay?" he asked. She was a damn open book.

She wanted to laugh, but there was no levity in her. Nothing felt okay when he was like this.

She knew nothing about his life, his family. Oh, she knew *him*, that he was a good decent guy. That he liked hockey and reading and quiet. She knew who he was, *loved* who he was, but she didn't know *about* him. And it felt gross. Sure, she'd walked out of the room because she'd gotten self-conscious about her face, but he hadn't wanted to introduce her to his sister. "Will you tell me why she stopped by?"

He was quiet for ticking seconds and she had this sinking sensation he was going to brush it off, pretend it was unimportant, be impossibly blank and break her heart.

"She invited us to a party."

"Us?"

"Something her work friends are putting together. She was trying to get me to make friends, and then she put two and two together with you being here and invited you, too."

"Oh." Some of the fear in her dissipated, not that

she had any clue what strange weightless feeling took its place.

"Oh. Is that a good *oh* or a bad *oh*?"

"I'm not sure. It's just an *oh*."

"Oh."

That was why she was sunk. Even when she had little moments of irritation with him, he dissolved it all. With a laugh, with something sweet, showing who he was, even if he didn't emote every feeling.

He did make her happy—why did she have to feel at times as if she needed more? "Do you want to go?"

"Part of me thinks the idea of going to a party like that sounds like torture."

"And the other part?"

"Thinks it might be…good. It might be good to take you out and not pretend." He rubbed a hand up and down her arm. "A date would be nice."

"I guess we can do that now, huh?"

"If you want to."

"And what do *you* want?" She tried to catch his gaze, but it was trained on his hand rubbing up and down her arm.

"Whatever would make you happy."

How could something so sweet make her kind of want to smack him? Because it was great, amazing even, that someone would want to do whatever would make her happy. She'd been on her own, basically, so long, that had never been something she'd been given.

And yet being in love with Marc, caring about him, wanting to build something with him meant—

Whoa. Just because they were out in the open at work didn't mean they could exactly do any building. There were still rules once relationships got to…a certain point.

A complication she wouldn't have to deal with if she'd been able to keep her hands and her heart to herself.

His hand stilled on her arm. "Are you sure everything's all right?"

"Yeah." She slid farther down on the bed, closer to him. Complicated as it was, having someone to fuss over her was still way better than dealing with this alone. "Just antsy and cranky. So, when's this party?"

"Tomorrow."

She winced at that. "I would like to do something fun and out of this damn apartment building with you. I'd *really* like that, in fact, but—" she gestured at her face "—not sure I'm up for all the staring."

"Leah did say…" He squeezed her arm and released it. "She made it very clear no one would say anything. Made it seem like someone she knows went through similar."

Tess didn't know if that was reassuring or not.

"My parents will be there. I can't make the same promises for my mother. She'd never be rude, though. Overzealous, but not rude to your face. No doubt she'll make me uncomfortable, if that holds any appeal."

She smiled at that. "Tell me the truth here. Do you want me to go? Do you want me to meet your family? Formally. And don't give me the *if I want* crap. I want to know what *you* want. Because five seconds ago you had to think *really* hard about just introducing me to your sister."

He was quiet for a while, blank thinking face and all. "Smile. Frown. Emote." She poked him in the chest and got a frown.

"It's not my first instinct, Tess. I can't magically change because you want me to."

"Try. A little." When she put a finger to his chest this time, she traced the logo on his T-shirt. "For me."

"I would very much like you to go. I'm conflicted about you meeting my family. Not because of you, because of them."

He could be so earnest when he let himself be. That was the man she wanted to see more of. "Why?"

He rubbed a hand over his face. Tensing, but he wasn't blank. That was a start.

"My relationship with them is weird. Not bad, but weird."

"Okay, considering you've seen the aftermath of my parental relationship, I would think you wouldn't need to be embarrassed."

"It's not about being embarrassed, it's just…

stupid. My family issues are small and inconsequential to yours."

"I don't want you to compare."

"You don't want me to compare. You don't want me to be blank. What *do* you want from me, Tess?" He sat up and away from her, breaking any physical contact.

"I want to *know* you. I keep seeing glimpses, but then you clam up and I don't know if I'm seeing who you think I want you to be or actually you."

"How can that not be me? If it's what I'm doing. How is it not me?"

She…didn't know. It was only a feeling, this sense of vague dissatisfaction when he got all *whatever you want*. Wasn't that *supposed* to be what she wanted? Someone to treat her like a princess?

Gross.

"I want you to be happy. *That* makes me happy. How is that wrong?"

She didn't know, couldn't put it into words. Maybe it wasn't even important. She wanted to forget she'd ever said anything, wanted to forget anything complicated. "Let's put it aside for now. I'm too tired to argue with you. You know what I'm not too tired to do?" She slid onto his lap. Sex was easy, good. She wanted easy and good more than anything else.

"Are you sure you're up for it?"

As much as she liked his concern and support, she hated him treating her as if she might break.

She hadn't broken in thirty-some years, she wasn't breaking today.

"I got clocked in the face, not stabbed or shot."

He ran his thumb over the mark on her arm from where the bottle had cut her a few weeks ago. The scab had mostly healed, but there was still a visible scar.

Marc pressed his mouth to it. "You don't know how much I wish I could fix this for you."

"Ah, Captain Quiet returns," she joked, because otherwise she might cry.

"Not funny."

"Not wrong. You want to fix everyone else. Some displaced sense that you can and should. You know what you should worry about doing, Marc?" She cupped his face, hoping the affectionate gesture would ease the sting of her words. "Focus on you a bit."

"Why? I haven't got anything wrong with me. I told you, my life is very uneventful. No great tragedies."

"What happened with your sister when you were kids had to have been difficult. Maybe not a tragedy, but I am here and alive and no tragedy has befallen me, Marc. My father was sick, and maybe it hurt me a little more than your sister's sickness hurt you, but we can't keep some kind of checklist about who had it harder or who gets the sympathy."

His jaw clenched, and he all but scowled at the spot on her arm his thumb was still moving against.

"It's not easy for me to…" He cleared his throat. "I'm not used to too many people caring what I think or feel."

"Get used to it."

His mouth relaxed, but when those hypnotizing amber eyes met hers, his expression was still very serious. "For how long?"

She didn't know what to do with that question any more than she knew what to do with the reality of the situation.

So she kissed him and hoped the rest would come in time.

CHAPTER TWENTY-TWO

MARC WAS SICK to his stomach. Pulling up to MC on a pretty spring evening was nice enough. The big house, as they called it, was in fact big. Everything was shiny and well kept since they ran the restoration business from here and used it as an example of what MC was capable of.

The view was fine. But the cars in the lot, the people milling around the green, freshly mowed side yard. Those were the things that filled him with dread. People were definitely not his forte.

Tess looked beautiful, though. Sure, she was wearing more makeup than usual and it didn't completely cover the damage to her face, but her excited smile was genuine as she looked through the windshield at the house before them.

He'd missed that about her before in their quiet, hidden moments. Tess liked people, liked being around them. She was good with people and small talk and *doing* things.

Well, that made one of them at least.

"It won't kill you. Won't even maim you."

He pulled the keys out of the ignition. "Yes, I believe I'm well aware of that."

She reached over the console between them and pressed her thumb against his forehead, making a scowling face he supposed was mimicking his own. "Your forehead says otherwise."

"I'm not good at this stuff," he grumbled. "You recall my small-talk skills when we met."

"Oh, I thought that's just because you were irritated about having the hots for me."

"Yeah, well, that, too."

She laughed, bright and loud, and he was gratified she could, and would. She'd been beat down yesterday, with every right, broody and unhappy. Even the light had been undercut by a constant watchfulness, slight irritation with the nicest of gestures.

He didn't get a sense of that today at all. So if a little party with his sister's work friends changed that, he'd go to a million of them.

If that made him a rather sad piece of shit, so be it. It was indelibly worth it. She was worth every word, every emotion, every frustration he had to swallow down. He climbed out of the truck at the same time Tess did.

"This place really is gorgeous. It's a small town, but I haven't spent much time in this part of it."

"You grew up..." He trailed off. He shouldn't be bringing up her father when she was looking happy and eager.

Because though her eyes were on the group of people they were walking toward while her hand slid into his, some of that joy was gone. "Grew up in a house down by the old Jolly factory. Dad used to work there. When they left Bluff City, Dad lost his job and never found a new one. Lost the house. I was just starting at BCPD at the time. Got him the place he's in…was in…well, you know. Anyway." She turned to him and grabbed his other hand, stopping their progress across the yard.

"Tell me something about where you grew up."

Even though it was mostly a deflection of topic, he saw underneath. This was more of the *I want to know you* stuff he needed to get better at. The whole *emoting* thing and not shutting down, as was his initial instinct. Always.

"Um, well…" The problem was, he had no idea what to say. No idea what she wanted him to say.

"Anything. What color was your house? What kind of neighborhood did you grow up in? What posters did you have on your walls?" She squeezed his hands.

"Yellow. Middle-class suburban. Kirby Puckett."

"Who's Kirby Puckett? Like, a swimsuit model?"

"Baseball player."

She wrinkled her nose. "Why did you have Kirby Puckett the baseball player on your wall?"

"It was Minnesota in the early '90s. No boy my age didn't have Kirby Puckett on their wall. Half the girls, too, including my sister. Who is coming this way."

Marc hadn't spotted his parents' van, but the prospect of Mom, Dad, Leah, Jacob *and* him and Tess all being together was enough to suck any levity right out of him. Tess would see it—the pathetic part of him he'd only hinted at to her.

That he was still desperate for his parents' love and attention, even knowing he'd never get it. That he was bitter about their fawning over Leah and Jacob all the time.

But he didn't have to dwell on that anxiety as Leah approached.

"You actually came."

Marc forced a smile at Leah. "I said I would."

"I know. And you always do what you say, but still." She turned to Tess. "Hi, I'm Leah. I know we haven't been formally introduced yet."

Tess smiled brightly. "Tess. It's very nice to meet you. Thanks so much for extending the invitation to me. It's a beautiful evening for an outdoor potluck."

Jacob approached and cleared his throat when Leah didn't say anything. Finally, she rolled her eyes. "Right. Tess, this is Jacob."

"Her live-in boyfriend." Jacob smiled as he shook Tess's hand. "Things normal people share in introductions don't always make their way out of Leah's mouth."

"Normal people do not share live-in, you weirdo."

"Ah, love. Isn't it grand?"

Leah made a gagging motion, but she was grinning from ear to ear. Marc didn't understand their relationship at all, but he was glad they had worked things out. Despite their verbal sparring almost all the time, they both were happy together.

More and more he was understanding how much that added to a life. To have someone just to share it with. Even if he wasn't quite first, even if he didn't have a say, having Tess to love was worth it.

TESS HAD LOST track of how many people she'd met, or how many questions Marc's mom had asked her about the most random collection of things, from inquiries into her religious choices to subtle comments regarding her health. Not in a way that made it seem as if she was asking about the bruise on her cheek. No, this was stuff like the history of cancer in her family.

Luckily, Marc and Leah had saved her from a question she had no idea what to do with on more than one occasion.

Despite the interrogation, Tess was fascinated. Fascinated by a mother who, well, cared. Maybe Marc thought he wasn't as important to his parents as Leah was—and she could even somewhat see it based on how they all interacted—but his mother *cared*. She was here. Interrogating his girlfriend.

Funny to even think of herself as Marc's girlfriend when everything had started so secretly. But it wasn't a secret any longer and she could be his girlfriend. The fallout at work was going to suck, but she didn't have to worry about that until at least Monday.

Marc was deep in conversation with his father and a bearded guy—Henry, maybe? Mrs. Santino was thankfully distracted by the adorable little baby crawling around. So Tess could finally sneak to the dessert table that had been set up and get a brownie that looked a lot more homemade than her usual box stuff.

"Make sure to get as many of those brownies as possible. Once Jacob and Kyle get over here, all bets are off."

Tess smiled at the brunette. Grace, she hoped she was remembering correctly. Because she was Jacob's sister and engaged to someone. Kyle, maybe. That would make sense.

"Will do."

"You people and your chocolate," Leah muttered, approaching from the other side. She picked up a snickerdoodle.

"Jealousy doesn't suit you, Leah dear. We can't all give up chocolate just because you're allergic."

Leah muttered a curse under her breath then turned to Tess with a weird smile. It actually reminded Tess of Marc. Kind of forced, but enough acting skill to make it look real.

"I hope you're having a good time."

"So you're as bad at small talk as Marc?" Tess asked sweetly.

Leah's smile went to an authentic grin. "Oh, good, I like you. I don't have to pretend."

"Leah's way of showing love is ridiculing incessantly," Grace piped up, a bite of brownie disappearing into her mouth.

"I have years to make up for when it comes to ridiculing my brother. Help will be necessary."

"Years?"

Leah raised an eyebrow. "He hasn't told you…"

"I mean, he's insinuated some things. I guess I didn't realize…"

Leah shrugged. "There was about a decade there without much contact. I lived here, they lived in Minnesota and I wanted to keep it that way." She glanced toward Marc and her father, then her mother. "I think we're still working our way toward being a real loving-type family, but we're trying. Even Marc. Most of the time."

Tess opened her mouth to press more, to ask a million questions, but really they were questions for Marc. Questions she shouldn't *have* to ask.

She was getting pretty sick of it.

She took a bite of brownie, then the phone in her pocket buzzed, producing a genuinely nauseated feeling.

It's probably someone from the department.

She ignored it.

"So," Tess said brightly, having no idea where she was going with this line of conversation, "Marc told me you're an electrician. That's a really interesting field of work." That Tess knew absolutely nothing about.

"Aside from the whole dealing-with-customers

aspect, it's pretty much a dream job. Luckily Jacob takes care of most of the customer crap."

"What do you do, Tess?" Grace asked.

"She's a police officer," Leah said before Tess could answer. "She's even my brother's superior. It's all very sordid."

Grace chuckled, but shook her head. "See? Ridicule. Don't pay attention to her. But, oh, you should join our book club!" Grace said, nodding toward Leah. "There's always room for more."

"Yeah! You could probably blow us all out of the water, but you should definitely come." Leah nodded. "If you want. It's a good group. Always nice to get out and do something."

Blow them out of the water? What did book clubs have to do with being a cop? "I'm confused."

"Oh, right. Our version of book club doesn't exactly involve books," Grace said with a sheepish smile.

"What does it involve?"

"Guns," Leah said, as if it was the most normal thing in the word to have a book club about guns.

"Well, that *is* different."

"We go to Shades gun range once a week, weather permitting, and do target practice. Susan over there—" Leah pointed to a tall redhead holding the baby that had been crawling around earlier "—she's a part of it, too."

"It helped," Grace said simply, and that, coupled with some hints she'd gotten from around the party, was enough for Tess to get it. Grace had gone through something similar to what had happened with her and her dad. But she had been introduced to Grace's parents at one point, so her...incident couldn't have been exactly the same.

Or was it similar enough? Tess didn't know. It was all uncomfortable, really. She knew it was meant to be some kind of comfort or commiseration, but regardless, the idea of getting together with other women and doing something sounded good. Though she occasionally went out with some of the dispatchers, considering all her direct coworkers were male, she didn't have a lot of female friends.

She smiled at the two women in front of her. "I'd like that."

"Good. You can give me some dirt on my brother. The guy's a fortress." Leah sighed as Marc headed toward them. "And here he comes. Like he has some kind of radar I'm finally going to get some information to make fun of him over."

"Any dessert left?" Marc asked, easily slipping his arm around Tess's waist. Well, *that* she liked. Maybe all that dissatisfaction from not knowing much about his history was unfounded. Maybe it was an offshoot of not really knowing what to do with her life now that her father was basically out of it.

And everyone at the department knew she and Marc were together. The world hadn't ended yet. It was as if her whole life had been flipped upside down, and yet everyone was acting as if it was business as usual.

Jeez, she was tired.

"Thursday nights," Leah said with a wink. "Book club. I'll harass Marc for your number later."

Leah and Grace walked off with their desserts and Marc gave her a quizzical head tilt. "Book club?"

"Ah, yes, they invited me to join their book club."

"I guess you won't be reading any biographies of Lyndon Johnson."

She smiled. "No. No, I do not think so."

He helped himself to a brownie, his arm still around her waist. "You are a hit with my family. Mom's practically salivating over that baby like you'll…" He trailed off, cleared his throat. "Um, I didn't mean it like—"

"No, I know." They walked to a few chairs that had been set up under a big tree. "I'm pretty sure she interrogated me on the health of my uterus."

Marc choked on a bite of brownie. "She did not."

"Okay, she didn't come right out and say it, but I got the sense I was being interviewed for my ability to offer her grandchildren."

A few reddish spots appeared on Marc's face. "She's…"

"Deeply concerned about her child's future." Tess reached over and gave his knee a squeeze. "You don't have to be embarrassed. I think it's nice, if a little weird and uncomfortable."

He made a kind of grunting noise, but as he leaned

back in his chair, his arm came to rest on the back of hers. One thing she would never get tired of. He might shut himself off, but he never failed to touch her, smile at her, kiss her.

Words might be hard for him, but affection wasn't, and Lord knew she could use some affection in her life.

So she tilted her head to his arm to lean against it. She surveyed the group around them.

Almost everyone was in pairs, and even from her brief introductions she could see differences in the relationships. Grace and Kyle were sweet together. Smiles and hand-holding. Whereas Jacob and Leah were all teasing all the time, and yet there was an undercurrent of genuine affection that was obvious to anyone—probably even Marc. Mrs. Santino led Mr. Santino around a bit like a dog on a leash, but he didn't seem to mind.

She glanced at Marc from the corner of her eye as his parents approached Leah and Jacob. He looked relaxed, toying with the ends of her hair. Almost carelessly, as if it was just a habit he'd picked up.

She leaned into him, searching the sky for the first star to wish on. Silly and foolish, but she'd all but missed out on a childhood of silly and foolish, so why not employ a little now?

"I don't know if it's the right time or place for this," he said after a few minutes of pleasant quiet. "But I did want you to know…" His eyes seemed to take in all the couples around them, too. Susan and her wife with their little baby, Henry and his bubbly girlfriend.

"When Franks brought me into the office yesterday he mentioned that if our relationship went, uh, legal, I believe was his term for it, one of us wouldn't be able to work at BCPD anymore. At least not as an officer."

"I know that, Marc. We don't have to talk—"

"I know it's too soon to think about, maybe even too soon to talk about, but I just wanted you to know that if it came to that—I'd leave. We…still have a ways to go, but I didn't want you wondering. BCPD is yours, Tess. You belong there, and I might like it there, but I could like it somewhere else just as well. I'd never expect or ask you to leave."

She swallowed at the lump in her throat, that he'd offer, that his fingers never stopped rubbing the strands of her hair between them.

"It's not a big thing. Just the truth."

She swallowed and forced herself to turn to him. "It *is* a big thing."

He opened his mouth to argue, but she leaned over and pressed a kiss to his mouth instead. "And I appreciate it."

He smiled. "Good."

And it was good. She was getting her good. Some well-deserved good. Nothing was going to take that away. Not a damn thing.

"COME ON, SLEEPING BEAUTY." Tess was cashed. They'd spent most of the evening in the yard of MC, watching the stars come out, talking—not even all small talk. By dessert Marc had managed to feel almost comfortable with the people he only barely knew.

With the help of Tess.

Who had promptly fallen asleep on the way home and was now having a hard time waking up. She'd had a hell of a few days.

"I'm going to have to carry you."

She mumbled incomprehensibly. He slipped his key ring over his finger, then reached over and unbuckled her seat belt. He did his best to pull her out without knocking any body parts against the top or side of the truck.

"I can't believe you're carrying me," she muttered. But she rested her cheek on his shoulder, and he kicked the door closed.

He adjusted her weight, trying to make his grasp around her knees more stable. She expelled a breath against his neck.

"You'll never make it up two flights of stairs."

"Well, now you've challenged me," he said, trying hard not to sound out of breath. "And if you're so awake, you can pull that door open."

She chuckled and reached for the door. It wasn't easy to keep her in his grasp when she did that. But he managed, and he was going to manage it up those stairs. Really. He was. Because he could.

"Put me down, Santino. You are not going to drop me down those stairs."

He tightened his grip. "Damn right I'm not." The first flight wasn't even hard.

Then he started sweating. But he forced himself to their floor without dropping her or having a heart attack or anything.

"You're dying."

"I am getting you all the way to my bed."

She pressed her mouth to his neck. "And then what are you doing to do when you get me to bed?"

"Okay, knock that off. I can't do this with an erection."

She giggled, then wiggled. "Let me down."

"No, no, no. Got this far." He shook his fingers so the keys jangled. "Unlock, please."

"You can't even talk in complete sentences, but you manage to say please." She shook her head. "And carry me. You're crazy." But she unlocked the door and let him carry her inside.

He kicked that shut then turned. "Dead bolt," he instructed.

"Somehow I think you would still insist on locking the dead bolt even if I was standing in the middle of the room naked, ready to go."

"Wouldn't want anyone to walk in."

She snorted. "You are a bit paranoid, sweetheart. Someday I'm going to come home to, like, an infrared gun safe."

Marc made it to the hallway with slow, halting steps. His arms were starting to shake, but he was going to do this. Because he liked the sound of *someday* and *come home to*.

Finally, he dumped her on the bed.

"I think you've worn yourself out too much for any extracurriculars." But she flipped open the button of her jeans, unzipped, and despite his arms feeling like jelly, he helped her pull them off.

Her phone dropped out of her pants and he bent to pick it up. He handed it to her, but her eyes were closed, one arm flung over her face, chest moving up and down in steady, even breathing.

He kissed her forehead. "Go to sleep, honey."

"No, I want to…" She made a kind of humming noise, her head sinking deeper in the pillow, and then she was out.

As much as he would rather have ended the night on a slightly different note, this was good, too. Because Tess was in his bed, and she knew that even if they weren't *at* the future, he was interested in it.

He walked to the bathroom to change and brush his teeth, setting Tess's phone on the nightstand as he passed. The screen lit up. A word in the illuminated text stopped him in his tracks.

1 missed call from County Jail.

The urge to go into her phone and erase evidence of that call was so huge, the only thing that stopped him was the fact that when he swiped his finger across the screen it asked for a passcode and he didn't have a clue. He wasn't going to try and guess her password.

That was too much. Besides, it could be for work. But they would have left a message. If it had been a collect call from a prison, though, leaving a message wouldn't have been an option.

Marc took a step away from the phone. And then another. This wasn't his business, and she wouldn't like it if he tried to tell her what to do. Tried to interfere and erase something from her phone.

Crossing a line. He didn't want to cross lines with Tess. He wanted to give her what she wanted.

What about what you want?

Funny it was Tess's voice in his head saying that. Funny it was the first time he couldn't manage to get what he wanted out of his head.

CHAPTER TWENTY-THREE

TESS WOKE UP to an empty bed and sunlight streaming on her face. At first she thought maybe Marc was at work, but she quickly remembered he had the day off.

She smiled. Her first thought on waking up had been wondering where he was, knowing she was in his apartment. Things had gone so fast, she supposed she should have some worry, but it was rare. The worry only popped up when he closed himself off.

She stretched and snuggled into the bed. Good. Good. Enjoying the good. Maybe he'd gone for a run or something. She glanced at the clock. Almost nine. Wow, she'd slept in. Considering she'd conked out last night before they could even end the evening properly.

She would have to make it up to him this morning. Humming to herself, she got out of bed. She crossed to Marc's dresser, a weird giddy feeling centering itself in her stomach. Without much discussion or commentary, they'd moved some of her clothes and whatnot over to his place after Stumpf had retrieved her keys the other night.

Which made her think of the party last night and Marc saying if things got to the *legal* part of a relationship, he'd step down from BCPD. It made her feel warm and fuzzy and teary all over again.

What was she supposed to do with that? A man who would do all these things for her. It defied reason.

She grabbed some clothes, but her phone buzzed before she could head for the bathroom. She frowned, trying to figure out where it was until the sound drew her to the nightstand.

She glanced at the screen.

Incoming call: County Jail.

It could be for work. It could be unconnected to the call she'd received at the party last night—she'd never even looked at who that had been from. This could all be so innocuous and unimportant and the diving feeling in her gut could be…paranoia.

Her finger hovered over Accept. Even if it was Dad, that didn't mean she had to listen. Or had to not listen. Maybe it was important. *Maybe he needs you.*

Someone cleared his throat and Tess turned to see Marc standing in the bedroom doorway.

He looked so grave. As if he could see the screen and read her mind. As if he knew every weak thought, every desperate word telling her to help, to fix this.

His expression went blank as the phone stopped buzzing. "I made breakfast," he said simply.

"Okay," she said, wincing that it was a whisper and not a breezy morning greeting.

"I'll get you some ibuprofen."

"No, it's—" But he'd already disappeared out into the main part of the apartment.

Hold on to the good. Fight for the good. God, she was tired of fighting for every little thing. She liked the easy. So much of what they had was easy. Why couldn't it stay that way?

Not how life works.

Steeling herself for, well, life, Tess grabbed her clothes and went through the shower. If she practiced a few speeches to tell Marc what was what, well, so be it.

Of course, when she entered the kitchen he was blank as ever and overall pleasant. "I made French toast."

"Wow, that seems very unlike you." When his mouth quirked up, she sighed. "You somehow made it healthy, didn't you?"

"Sit. Eat. Take the painkillers."

"It's feeling a lot better today," she said, allowing him to nudge her toward the table. She sat and he placed a plate with French toast and two little pills in front of her. Followed by a glass of orange juice.

Then he squeezed her shoulder and kissed her temple. "I'm very glad to hear it."

How could this be any more perfect? It was

picture-perfect. Hot guy making her breakfast. Taking care of her. Caring about her.

But the blank expression somehow ruined it. How did he do that? Make everything seem wrong when it should feel absolutely right.

"I didn't answer."

He paused whatever he was doing in the kitchen before grabbing his own plate and sliding across from her. "It was from the jail again?"

"Again?"

He looked down at his plate. "I picked up your phone last night. I happened to see…"

So it was Dad. Had to be.

"Tess."

She looked up to find him staring at her intently. "It's probably him, but…I didn't answer. So…" So what? She'd thought about it. Considered it. Might have if Marc hadn't cleared his throat. So there were no *so*s. Not really.

"Tess. I think…" He looked down at his plate, then rubbed his hands over his face. He was certainly emoting right now. Frustration and a controlled kind of anger.

"Say it. Say whatever you're feeling. Please say it." Because she wanted this moment to feel real, not like some scene out of a movie. Even if it ended up being bad. She needed some honesty.

"Don't ever answer it. Let it ring forever. Because, Tess, that man is a monster, and I'll be damned if I stand around and let him put his hands on you again."

In the blink of an eye, she wished for the movie, the blank, because that was the last damn thing she wanted to hear.

MARC PUSHED AWAY from the table. He couldn't stand to look at the disappointment on Tess's face. That, that right there, was why he didn't share every feeling, every past mistake, every thought.

People didn't like to know. People didn't *want* to know unless it agreed with what they felt. He should have kept his mouth shut, pretended everything was fine. Accepted his role as second in her life.

He did it so well with his family. They never had a clue. Except, well, maybe Leah a little bit, but still. *Still.* He needed to get better at all this acting.

"He's... What he did was wrong, but he's not a monster. He's sick."

"No, Tess, Leah was sick. People with cancer are sick." He should stop. Leave it at that. Find a way to push all the feelings down and ignore this. Accept his place.

Nothing could end well if he kept talking.

She stood from the table, following him into the little living area. She stood in front of the couch she'd convinced him to buy and resolutely said, "Alcoholism is a disease."

He'd worked too many cases seeing the victims of alcoholism to feel much sympathy for a disease

FALLING FOR THE NEW GUY

people chose, that always seemed to hurt the loved ones more than the "sick" person.

Don't say it. Don't say it. Don't say it.

"He doesn't mean to hurt me."

It broke whatever last control he had, whatever he'd hoped to contain and ignore and pretend away. Because he couldn't pretend it was okay for her to think that.

"He tricked you into coming to his apartment in the middle of the night, in the dark—using suicide and fear. He waited for you and then hit you with something hard enough to leave a mark that's still there, bright and colorful on your face."

She lifted her chin, not backing down for a second. His anger spurred hers on, because of course it did. Anger and yelling weren't the answer. Pretending things were fine was the fucking answer.

"I'm not saying it was right."

So why did she have to keep saying things that eradicated a lifetime of keeping his mouth shut? "Then what are you saying?" he asked. No, it was a demand.

"He's sick. And he's not perfect, but he's my father. He deserves my help. I'm the only one who can help him."

"People like your father are worthless assholes who can't get their shit together for their own flesh and blood. He attacked you! He hurt you, and not for the first time. My God, how can you defend him and run to his aid again, Tess?"

"He's my father." Her voice cracked and wavered. "Alcoholism *is* a disease and that's not defending him, it's stating facts. I'm fairly certain I've read a few more books on it than you have, even with your extensive library."

He could see it, too. Her poring over twelve-step books trying to find the magic cure to fix a man who repeatedly treated her like nothing, or worse, a punching bag.

God, it killed him. She killed him. This whole thing killed him because he was sixteen again, confused and trying so hard to be what everyone needed and failing.

Someone else's *disease* was making him miserable again, and he was choosing that like some kind of fool who couldn't learn a lesson. Why had he ever thought he was good at this? He'd never been good at it—his parents just hadn't bothered to notice.

"He didn't beat me, Marc. This right here is new. It's the first time he's ever—"

Because he was angry and hurting and so damn pissed at himself for falling in love with someone who'd put him in this damn situation he'd thought he could handle because he was so fucking good at it, he yelled.

He hated himself for yelling. Hated himself for this whole thing, but the emotions were out of his control now. Out of his reach. "Why are you lying to me? There's not just your face. You also have a mark on your arm. And that's just in the month

I've known you. He's hurt you twice. Harasses you almost daily."

"The first time was an accident," she said. "I know my face wasn't, but the times before—"

"You have to know what you sound like." The victim of repeated abuse. How many domestic calls had he worked? *You don't understand. He loves me. He didn't mean it. It'll be okay.* "You have been a police officer too long to believe this bullshit."

"It's different."

"Why?"

"Because I am all he has, and I am the reason—" She stopped herself, eyes filling with tears. "I know…" She cleared her throat, some of the certainty and fight leaving her posture. "It's not my fault. It's not."

She didn't sound nearly as sure of that as she had when defending her father, making excuses for him.

"You have done everything in your power since you were a kid, Tess. A *kid*. At some point you have to accept that you can't fix it. You may be all he has, but he doesn't deserve you. Not an inch of you."

Her throat moved as if she was attempting to swallow but couldn't. "He's all I have, too," she said in a wavering voice.

His own throat clogged. "Do you really think that?" he forced out. Because if she didn't think she had *him*, what the hell was he doing so wrong? Bending over backward to be what she needed. Couldn't she see that?

He'd thought she saw it. Appreciated it. That even if he came in second, she at least gave a crap that he was trying to give her what she needed.

But she thought an alcoholic abuser was all she had.

"It's just that…" She took a deep breath and let it out. "I know you're here, and you love me, and you'd do so much for me. You take care of me, and it amazes me how you do, *that* you do. But you're still someone I've known for such a short period of time, and the fact of the matter is you could hightail it tomorrow. He is my father. I am his daughter. That can't be changed."

"Taking care of you, loving you, saying I would quit my job for you, that's less important than time and biology? What has that man ever done for you?"

"He's why I'm here." She shrugged. "I lived. He kept me alive all those years before I could take care of myself. A lot more than my mother did."

"They're both shit. Worthless. And so damn stupid for not taking care of you the way you deserve to be taken care of. Do you have any idea how strong you are? To have gotten through that? To keep trying to help people? Fuck, Tess, you're a goddamn saint, but sometimes you have to walk away."

"You don't get to decide that for me."

"No." Amazing how quickly the blankness swept back, anger leaking out of him completely. Anger could gallop beyond his control, but hurt? He'd been practicing too long not to hide that. "No, I suppose I don't."

"The next time he calls, I am going to answer. And if I decide to go see him, that's not something you have any say in."

He stared at the couch instead of her. "All right."

"Don't—" But she stopped herself.

He knew what she was going to say. *Don't be blank.* But she stopped herself because that's exactly what she wanted. Blankness and agreement with whatever she wanted. That's what people wanted from him; anything else was…pointless.

"You should eat your breakfast. It's likely cold by now."

She blinked then looked back at the table. Their plates sitting nicely across from each other. Like a picture or a painting. Not real.

Her gray gaze met his and he thought for sure she was going to say no. Walk away. He'd spoken his mind and that ended whatever shot he thought he'd had at making this a real, lasting thing.

Instead, she opened her mouth and said, "Okay," and walked back over to the table. "Cold French toast can't be very appetizing." She slid into her chair, took a visible deep breath and looked up at him.

He couldn't decipher what her expression meant, what *this* meant. All he knew was it was pretend— an even bigger pretend than he'd been affecting up to this point.

Even as he walked over to the table and took the seat across from her, he wasn't sure he wanted to pretend anymore.

EVERYTHING WAS WRONG.

Tess hated to be overdramatic, but, seriously, everything was all screwed up and she didn't know what else to do except go along with it. Pretend it was fine. Take a page out of Marc's book and mask the shit out of everything hard.

Except there was this perpetual lump in her throat, and her phone felt like a dead weight in her pocket. Every move, every word felt like tiptoeing across thin ice.

And when the ice broke, Marc would disappear. *Sometimes you have to walk away.* Marc had said that regarding her father, but the words kept rattling around as if they meant something more, something bigger.

It was fundamentally against everything she believed. Walking away didn't accomplish anything except hurting the people you left behind. Whether or not her father deserved that hurt was a separate issue.

She couldn't walk away. It had less to do with her father and more to do with her. Because how could she live with herself if she did exactly what her mother had done? Abandoning him when he needed something.

Why couldn't she figure out what he needed? That would solve all of this.

"Tess."

She looked up at Marc, realizing she'd been standing in front of the farmer's market booth for minutes without...doing anything.

Except thinking and brooding.

"Can we go—" She almost said *home*, but today seemed to illustrate they didn't have a home. Not together. "Can we go?"

He gave her a Marc nod. Barely noticeable. Blank.

The lump in her throat fizzled, made it harder to breathe. What was happening? How had everything gotten so messed up?

They walked to his truck; he placed his bags in the backseat. Then he drove. Back to their apartment complex. Silence choking every second of the short drive. Tears burning her eyes.

What was happening? One little argument, disagreement, and suddenly they were strangers. Acting like worse than strangers, pretending to care.

Her care wasn't pretend, but everything else was.

They got back to the apartment. Marc grabbed his groceries. They trudged up the stairs. Silence. Silence. More silence. Keys out. Locks unlocked. Step inside.

He carefully locked the door behind her. Said nothing. Didn't look at her. Didn't ask why she'd wanted to leave.

It was all so fucking wrong.

"I'm going to go see him," she blurted, not sure where it came from. When she'd come to that deter-mination. She just couldn't do this pretending-like-he-didn't-exist thing.

It didn't mean she forgave him or thought what he'd done was right. It only meant that she had to see him. Talk it through. Try to find some answers, and if Marc couldn't see that...

God, she didn't want to finish that thought.

Marc paused, though he didn't turn to look at her. He simply paused, then continued walking to the kitchen and placing the things he'd bought on the counter.

"I have to."

Again, no response. No words. No looks. He started unloading his bags.

"Marc."

"Yes?"

"I..." She stepped forward and then stopped, ex-asperated and hurt and confused and, oh, fuck, all these damn feelings. "Aren't you going to say any-thing?"

"No."

"Why not?"

"You told me what you're going to do. What does it matter what I say? You don't want to hear what I have to say, Tess. You're going to go. Go." He said it all so calmly, evenly. Not a hint of snap to his tone. Nothing.

"And that's...just it?" Of course her voice was

all high and squeaky with emotion. "Go? You…
That's it?"

He finally turned, slowly, carefully. All measured
calm, so *him* it made her want to push him. And that
made her feel kind of sick to her stomach. Violence.
Wanting to enact it on someone she loved.

So gross.

"What do you want me to say, Tess?"

Her chest got tight, her lungs all squeezed and
crunched. She wanted him to say he understood.
That he'd support her. That she could come back afterward and they could go back to last night, when
she'd felt good was finally a thing she was going
to get.

Even knowing he couldn't give her that, at least
not authentically, she wanted it. The pretend. God,
she wanted him to make her believe it was okay and
he'd be there.

No matter what. No matter what. He wouldn't
walk away because she wasn't doing what he wanted.
No wonder she left, Tessie.

Marc wasn't her mother. He wasn't abandoning
her. This wasn't…like that…but oh, how similar the
pain felt.

So much so, she couldn't say what she really
wanted to say. *I want you to love me, support me,
always be there.*

Because that's all she'd ever wanted, and she'd
really thought she'd found it, but suddenly it was
leaking out of her fingers.

Because of Dad.

Or was it because of herself?

"Can't you let me handle this and understand that I know what I'm doing?" It was somehow easier to push those words out. "Trust it'll be okay. I'll be okay. You trust me, right? It'll be okay. I can't abandon him. I can't do that. Even for you. So, please, find a way to understand."

He was quiet, staring at some point behind her, shoulders tense and everything about him…untouchable, unreachable.

But his throat moved, and for all his pretending, he wasn't unaffected. "I can't do that," he said, his voice coming out rough though the rest of him remained blank. "I've spent my life pretending I'm okay with things I'm not okay with. I can't do it anymore, Tess. Even for you. I tried, I did." He cleared his throat, still not meeting her gaze. "But you can't have it both ways."

She hated that she was crying. That he couldn't bend for her, give her this. When he'd given her so much, so many things she'd never had, and now he was taking them away because he couldn't let her…

She didn't want it both ways—she wanted him to understand. To see. And he was refusing to open his mind to a world that was not all black-and-white, right and wrong.

"Goodbye, Marc. You can…put my stuff in a box, leave it at my doorstep or something." Because she didn't have the strength or wherewithal or whatever the crap she needed to go through his apartment and eradicate herself from it.

Just the thought…

"Tess, we still have to work together."

Of course, work. He certainly wouldn't be stepping down now, would he? And, oh, weren't they going to make a lovely source of gossip? "Goody," she muttered, walking out the door.

She'd always prided herself on ending relationships maturely. She didn't feel like being mature right now. Or nice. Or Ms. Strong Woman Who Could Handle Anything. She felt like crying and throwing a fit and, damn it, why the hell not?

So she slammed the door behind her as hard as she could.

CHAPTER TWENTY-FOUR

MARC STARED AT the closed door. The sound of it slamming shut reverberated in his ears long after it was actually done.

There was a scaring pain in his chest, a ball lodged in his throat and a heat behind his eyes he refused to acknowledge.

It wasn't a surprise, exactly. Their painfully awkward breakfast and increasingly uncomfortable farmer's market trip hadn't ever been leading up to any amazing moments of super coupledom. Certainly hadn't been the kind of day he'd pictured after the party last night.

Why couldn't things have stayed like that? Why'd he have to open his mouth? Or why'd she have to be so...

He wanted to punch something. Hard. Really, really hard. He settled for giving the couch—the couch Tess had picked out and talked him into buying—a kick. A hard fucking kick.

Good. The pain was good. Bring on the pain and actual feelings.

How could she visit a man who would bash her

face enough to leave bruises and marks? When was laying your hands on someone you were supposed to love ever okay?

He wasn't so callous that he blamed her for thinking she could help. Hell, that's what abusive men did all the time, convinced women to think there was something they could do to change them. He had witnessed it routinely in his years as a police officer. And Tess had grown up with that man making her believe she somehow was all he had, all she had.

He didn't blame her for thinking there was something she could do. He only wished there was some way he could convince her the man she called a father didn't deserve it. Not her love, her attention, her sympathy.

There were men, men like him, who would give it all to her. Without asking for too much in return. He just wanted to be with her, because she was strong and fun and made him feel like a person.

Until this morning. Then he'd gone back to feeling like a useless rock, and it was so damn hard to go back, knowing what the alternative was.

Too damn hard to know he'd have to stand by and watch her go back to her father again and again, be hurt again and again, while he waited in a stupid suit with a ridiculous meal going cold.

He turned away from the door. It hurt that she could believe her father was all she had. Even knowing she'd had a lifetime of one man's voice in her head and all they had was about a month. Intellectually, he understood all this.

What he didn't understand was how to fix it or change it, and honestly? He was so tired of trying to fix and change people. So tired of being the strong, sturdy rock hoping to be seen.

He wanted something that wasn't keeping his mouth shut, or ignoring his feelings. He wanted something that wasn't someone else's disease making him have to take a number with the people he loved.

It was selfish and childish and probably wrong, but he'd reached a breaking point. Caring hadn't mattered. Why not try not caring? Last time he'd done that, he'd gotten Tess.

Now that he was pretty sure he'd lost her, why not try it again? Live for himself, for what he wanted.

He might not feel better about life, but this was better than the morning had been. Better to hurt and be angry and kick a couch than force blankness and stiffness and act as though he was nothing.

He was tired of being nothing. Tess had given him a glimpse of something, and it made the nothing parts impossible to live with.

When someone knocked on the door, such a myriad of emotions swelled in his chest he couldn't get a handle on them all. Hope and apologies and more angry words and refusals and just…everything.

The bottom line was, he had no idea what he wanted, how to verbalize it, how to make her see all he wanted was her. Her and her safety and well-being. And if she couldn't choose that, he wasn't sure he could go down that road again.

"Marc!" Pounding followed his mother's voice and all the feelings mashed up in his gut sank into disappointment. Sadness.

Not Tess. Not hope.

He opened the door, and while his instinct was to go blank, to pretend, he didn't have the reserves built up. His mother smiled up at him and he only frowned.

"We come with lunch," she said, holding up a few bags. Dad, Leah and Jacob stood behind her. Only Mom seemed oblivious to his mood; the rest of them were looking at him as if he'd grown a third head.

"Well, are you going to let us in?"

For a moment, just a flash of a second, he thought about closing the door. Shutting it right in all their faces. Tune out the past world, tune out maybe even a little bit of his present world. Maybe he could suitably disappear and exist somewhere else. Somewhere outside all this fucking baggage.

But Leah's whole life was a testament to the fact you couldn't outrun your baggage. She'd tried. And here she was.

So he stepped out of the doorway and let his family and Jacob inside.

Mom poked around as she meandered her way to the kitchen. "Your lady friend isn't here?"

"No, Mom. Tess is not here."

"Everything okay?" Dad asked, patting his shoulder.

"Fine and fucking dandy."

"Marc Paul Santino!" Mom slapped the bags down on the table. "Since when do you use that kind of language around—"

"Mom, maybe we should go," Leah said, giving him a considering look. As if she could see he was on a very dangerous precipice.

"Yes, please do. I'm not in the mood for company right now." And certainly not in the mood for pretending he was. Yeah, he was done with that bullshit.

"What's going on? What don't I know?" Mom looked from Marc to Leah, and her gaze stayed there, because of course it did.

Tess was ruled by her father. His family was ruled by Leah. He was always the damn odd man out.

He was never going to matter.

"Believe it or not, nothing is going on that concerns you. Or Leah. Or anybody. Except me. This thing only concerns me. Who would have thought?"

"Goodness, you're in a mood today. I do not like it one bit. We've come all this way to have a nice visit, and here you are being downright rude."

Marc laughed. He couldn't help it. Couldn't help that the laugh sounded nasty and bitter. He couldn't help any damn thing.

Apparently he was losing it and it felt...freeing?

A hell of a lot better than trying so hard. He was tired of working so hard.

He was tired, plain and simple.

"I do not see what is so funny, young man," Mom snapped.

He managed to sober enough to talk. "No, no, of course you don't." He grabbed his phone, his wallet, his keys, and then he turned and looked his mother directly in the eye. "Mom, you do not see anything that does not start and end with Leah."

"Marc, I know I said honesty, but maybe not—"

He gave Leah a withering glare. "And we should do everything the way you want us to, right, Leah?"

Jacob made a move to step in front of Leah but she didn't let him. Still, Jacob's face was grave and steely, and of course he had to speak up. Because he was fucking Jacob. "Marc—"

"Ah, the sworn protector of Leah's precious feelings." He was being such an unrepentant asshole and it felt good. This rising heat of anger and letting it spew out instead of swallowing it all down felt amazing.

"Because that is the bottom line of this family. Leah. What Leah needs or wants or thinks she wants but really needs, and I'm sick of it. I'm done with it."

He strode to the door of this dumb apartment he hadn't even wanted. Hadn't wanted to move here and change his life but he had and it had somehow turned good and now it was all shit. "The saddest part of all, the whole ridiculous part of this whole family is that Leah's probably the only one who understands that sentiment."

Then he did something he'd never done. Despite his mother's protests, his father's demands and Leah's pleas, he walked right out, not giving a flying monkey they wanted him to come back and talk.

He stomped down the stairs, jerked the building door open, stepped outside and something warm and wet plopped onto his head. At first he thought it was rain, but the sky was sunny and blue. He looked up to see a bird's nest right on the awning above the door.

A bird shit on his head. Yeah, that was pretty much the cherry on the sundae of this fucking day.

TESS STOOD OUTSIDE the county jail. She needed to go inside before visiting hours were over, but actually being here, knowing people inside knew her, knew what had happened, she felt sick. And torn. Of course, that wasn't any different than what she'd felt this morning. Everything was all mixed up and even things she was sure were right didn't feel so right.

Being here didn't feel right. Though her bruises and scratches didn't ache nearly as much today, standing here, knowing her father was inside because of that, they throbbed in time with her accelerated heartbeat.

Sadly, any thoughts of leaving didn't feel right, either. Oh, damn Marc for getting in her head, for making her think of every woman who'd been beaten and excused her abuser. Because she'd shaken her head at those women, complained with her coworkers about those women.

Here she was. That woman. Telling Marc it was different. It *was* different, but…

She closed her eyes, let out a breath and then drew one in. The fact of the matter was, she was here. She would go in there and talk to him. See if there was anything he needed, and…go from there.

It didn't mean she was excusing his actions.

It didn't.

She did the breathing thing a few more times, trying to fight back the tears and loneliness creeping through her.

This was what she had to do. For herself. For her own sanity. So she'd do it. She went into the jail building and walked through the process of checking in.

It was very strange to be on this side of things. Not dropping off prisoners or picking them up. No, she was visiting. She was one of *those* people, and while she couldn't remember ever judging *those* people, she'd always known she wasn't one of them.

Now she was. Once she checked in, she was led to a little visiting room with separating glass and phones to pick up. It was surreal. Like a TV show. She'd never had reason to be on this side of things, and could hardly believe she was here. This was real and not some joke.

When her father was ushered in by a guard, she

had to fight the urge to bolt. She didn't want to do this. Moreover, she didn't *have* to do this.

He's all you have. Made all the more certain by being here. Did that mean she'd chosen her father over Marc?

God, this was all so wrong.

But she sat in the chair across from Dad and picked up the phone, propelled by a force she'd probably never understand.

"Tessie, I'm so glad you're here." His voice was raspier than usual, and his hands shook holding the phone. "I'm so sorry. I'm so sorry. Everything's all mixed up."

Her hands shook, too, but not from alcohol withdrawal. No, they shook because she had no idea if she was doing the right thing.

"I just wanted to make sure you're okay."

"I need to get out of here, Tessie. I can't think in here. I can't… I'll get better. I promise. This time. I promise. Just get me out of here."

"Treatment?"

He faltered for a moment. "Sure, sure. Whatever you want. Just get me out of here."

Which was not reassuring, or believable. It was crap, and she swallowed down the need to tell him so. Because it didn't matter.

"I need you to get me out of here, Tessie. Everything will be fine if I can get out."

Tess didn't say anything as he fidgeted and pleaded. Finally, she pulled her phone out of her purse and pulled up the picture she'd taken of her injuries when they'd looked their worst. She held the screen to the Plexiglas. "This is what you did to me."

He didn't look at it at first, but she didn't waver. She kept the phone screen up there until he finally glanced.

His face crumpled. "I'm sorry, Tessie. I'm sorry. I didn't mean to. I just… It's the liquor. And…and… I'm all alone. It's so hard. It's so hard and—"

"Enough," she said quietly, evenly. He didn't stop sniveling, but he did stop trying to excuse it away. "I'm tired of your excuses. I have had enough of your excuses and your blame. The only way you're going to get better is actual treatment."

"But—"

"I will not stay by your side for another round of Beat Tess Up and Make Her Feel Like Shit. I have a tiny bit of self-respect left, and I won't let you take it away." She wasn't sure where it came from—not those words or the truth in them, but as she spoke, holding up that picture of what he'd done to her, she felt stronger with every breath.

"The only way you keep me in your life at this point is going to some kind of facility that treats your alcoholism. I'm not recanting my statement, because you hit me. With God knows what. You blindsided me like a common criminal, your daughter. Your own flesh and blood, the *only* person who has stood by you. This is your breaking point. Treatment, or

I'm gone. Regardless, you're dealing with the consequences of your actions."

"I'm not going to one of those places. I'm not staying here. Why aren't you helping me? Why aren't you fixing this? You're all I have."

Words that so often cut her down and drowned out reason didn't hit so hard when they were all strung together, said by a sober man in a sad little jail visiting area.

No, she didn't feel much like taking those words to heart right now. She finally dropped her phone in her purse and hung up the jail phone receiver. She could see Dad's mouth moving, and she was pretty sure she made out the words *don't go.*

On a deep breath, she picked up the receiver again, but she didn't hold it to her ear. She only spoke into the mouthpiece. "When you're ready to change your mind, when you're ready to get professional help, I'll be there. But I won't do this anymore."

Without letting him make any false promises in her ear, she hung up again. Then she walked out.

She didn't cry. She didn't shake. She had been strong and reasonable without abandoning him. She'd done the right thing. Maybe it wasn't the perfect thing. That was life.

She drove back home, that sense of rightness propelling her all the way to the parking lot and out of her car. She faltered a little bit seeing Marc's truck and patrol car sitting right there, meaning he was home, but that was a little stumble. A little blip.

A much bigger blip when she reached the top of the stairs, and he was turning the key in his door, pushing it open.

Please don't look, please don't look. She paused at the top of the stairs, holding her breath, but before he stepped inside, he glanced over his shoulder.

He looked...weird. And this was weird. Why was this happening? They shouldn't be apart. Not because of her father.

She could tell him. Tell him that she had given Dad an ultimatum. Not carte blanche for forgiveness. She could tell Marc and maybe they could come to an understanding. A compromise. It didn't have to be black-and-white, see Dad or not see Dad.

She opened her mouth to do just that. Tell him that this morning had been a mistake and if he'd listen he'd see that they didn't need to break up over this.

Her heart wanted that, downright yearned for it, but her mind remembered. He didn't trust her to be able to go visit her father and set those limits. Maybe he didn't have reason to, maybe it was even fair that he didn't have that trust in her.

But it was what she wanted. So she didn't say anything. She walked to her door, unlocked it, went into her apartment and closed the door behind her.

And she was alone. Completely and utterly alone.

CHAPTER TWENTY-FIVE

MARC STOOD IN his living room, staring at the door, trying to work out how the hell this was going to work.

Tess would be back today, unless she'd changed her plans. Which meant they'd have to share a car. Which meant they'd have to ride in to the station together. Which meant...

A lot of uncomfortable things.

Chief among them that he had no earthly clue what had gone so wrong. Sure, he'd said he couldn't accept her going to visit her father, and she obviously had, but out of the heat of the moment, he had no idea what any of that meant.

Except, no more pretending, right? He didn't want to act as though he was okay with her going back to a father who'd treated her like less than garbage.

So instead he was going to act as if he didn't love her and desperately want her back. Yeah, that made a lot of damn sense, didn't it?

Finally, because he couldn't risk being late, he put his hand on the knob and turned. Open door. Step outside.

See Tess.

Feel like death.

Her gaze immediately slid away from his and she put her back to him as she pulled her door closed. "I'm going to take my patrol car in for roll call," she said, locking her door. "I'll meet you there."

"Okay." Even though it wasn't. It was completely *not* okay. It was a crap thing to do considering there had never been a time they'd gone to work separately.

So, right. Pretending. Again. No. No, he wasn't doing that. "Actually, it's kind of a shit thing to do, if you really want to know."

She squared her shoulders and turned slowly. Her gray eyes didn't meet his, but at least she looked in his direction. "I have a meeting with Franks after our shift. I don't know how long I'll be. It makes sense to take separate cars."

"Sure."

"You want to read into it, be my guest. But I'm still your field training officer, and I'm still going to do my job to the best of my ability. I've never let anyone get in the way of that." She walked past him and to the stairs.

She seemed to think he would. Get in the way. Make this hard. Apparently she had no clue, which meant all this love bullshit was just two pathetic people making crap up to make themselves feel better.

He swallowed at the tight feeling in his throat, tried to take a steady, even breath through the constricting in his chest. But it all lodged and lingered. Hurt. More and more hurt.

Why had he ever come here and let all this happen?

He had no answers for that, so he trudged down the stairs. After all, he wouldn't let anyone get in the way of him doing his job, either. Because he wasn't a jackass *trying* to make her life harder, unlike certain people she wanted to choose over him.

You are a childish prick, Santino.

Being a childish prick didn't feel quite as freeing as it had yesterday. Today it felt heavy and restricting. Depressing, really.

He just wanted to be happy, and telling everyone where they could shove it wasn't fulfilling at all. Of course, the truth wasn't fulfilling and pretending wasn't fulfilling, so he had no idea where that left him.

Tess's cruiser was already turning out of the lot when he got into his. So stupid. Driving to the same damn place, and he really doubted a meeting with Franks was what was keeping her from sharing a ride.

They still had to spend eight hours in a car together. Not just today. A majority of days for only a little less than two months yet. Unless she was going to talk to Franks about changing that.

Christ, this sucked.

But he drove to the station because what else was there to do? Even if he didn't pretend he was fine, there was no *action* he could take. There was only working.

Unless you apologize.

But that was the problem. He didn't know what he was apologizing for. Not wanting her to be hurt by her father? Should he really have to apologize for that? He wanted her to be safe. That should not be the cause of a damn breakup.

Marc pulled into the station. Roll call would be fifteen minutes of people figuring out pretty damn quick that everything they'd just found out about him and Tess a few short days ago was over. Honestly, he didn't even care enough to be embarrassed. He couldn't work up embarrassed when his gut felt as if it was tied up in heavy knots.

So damn heavy.

He walked into the station, trying to greet anyone who greeted him but keep a low profile. Basically, his goal today was to find the old Marc Santino. The one back in Minnesota everyone had been sure was a robot.

He didn't have time to drop his stuff off in the locker room with all the dawdling he'd done this morning, so he stepped into the roll-call room and found the first seat he could, shoving his bag underneath the chair.

Franks went through the normal, and Marc kept his eyes focused on him. If anyone was trying to figure out the situation with him and Tess, he wouldn't give them anything to go on.

Oh, pretending again. What a joy.

Fifteen minutes of getting caught up with what was going on in Bluff City and then it was time to face the real music. Seven hours and forty-five minutes in a car with Tess. The countdown could begin. Well, once he put his crap away.

Tess left the room before he did without a word. He had no idea if that meant he'd meet her at the patrol car or if she was going to find a way to not have to do this.

He didn't have a clue about anything anymore. So blank wasn't even pretending—it was straight up not knowing what to do.

He took his bag to the locker room, wincing when he saw Berkley and Granger. He'd thought he'd escaped having to hear their comments when they hadn't made a peep at roll call, but then again, Franks had been there. Now they were changing out of their uniforms after having worked the midnight shift.

"Trouble in paradise already?" Berkley said. It didn't sound as mean-spirited as if Granger had said it, but it still rankled. But he wasn't going to comment. What was there to say?

"Maybe he found out he doesn't like wearing the skirt in the relationship," Granger said with a smug-ass grin.

Marc could respond to that. A few choice words were on his tongue, the memory of punching Granger satisfying. There were a lot of things he could do. Unfortunately, all the responses felt shitty.

In fact, today, all he'd felt was like shit. Shit for losing it with Mom and Dad. Shit for everything with Tess. Not that it was his fault, exactly. But it still ached like an open wound.

He didn't know what that meant. How to fix it. He'd never been in a relationship that meant this much, and certainly never put some line in the sand he didn't know how to cross.

So he walked away from Berkley and Granger. Didn't even flip the asshole off when he said something about him being a pansy.

Marc wasn't going to waste any more energy on some dickwad with an attitude problem.

He was his own dickwad, and he had to sort that out.

TESS DROVE AROUND Bluff City for a full half an hour after Marc dropped her off at the station at the end of their shift.

She was being cowardly, and she *hated* that, but she also hated seeing him and smelling him and being so damn close she could touch him, and she'd gotten that for almost eight solid hours, so…this was some kind of reward.

Now she was sitting in front of the building in her car and she could go be alone in her apartment and wonder if he'd try to make things right and wonder if she should try to make things right and wonder if Dad would ever change his mind about treatment and…

Her phone buzzed and she tensed, but when she looked at the caller ID, it was a number she didn't recognize. She debated a few moments before finally answering. "Hello?"

"Um, hi, Tess? This is Leah…Leah Santino."

"Oh." What the hell? "Hi."

She cleared her throat. "So, hi. Yeah, um—jeez, Grace, be quiet. Hey, so Grace and I were wondering if you wanted to come to the book club thing with us tonight?"

"Um, I guess you don't know that—"

"No, I know. I mean, I kind of figured things weren't great when Marc kinda lost it at us yesterday, but you know."

Lost it at them? Marc? He hadn't lost it at her even when things ended between them. Oh, there'd been a little blip of emotion, an argument, but nothing more than them coming to an ultimatum.

No screaming, no tears—not in front of each other, anyway.

Which, wow, what did that mean?

"O…okay."

"The thing is, you can still come. I mean, we want you to. Or whatever. If you wanted to. If it wouldn't be weird. For you. I won't be weird." There was a pause then a snort. "Grace's right. I won't be any weirder."

"Well, I—"

"Tess?" The voice was different this time. "Hi, this is Grace."

Her head was whirling. Surely she couldn't go hang out with Marc's sister. Even if she'd agreed to it at the party. This...them...everything had changed. "Oh, well, hi."

"What Leah is trying to say is, regardless of what's happening with Marc, you're still welcome to come. We want you to come."

"Why?" She shouldn't be so skeptical or so questioning, but she had no idea why these women who had met her only briefly would want to extend the invitation.

"It's just..." Grace sighed into the line. "Whatever is going on with you and Marc doesn't have anything to do with our invitation. I know what it's like to go through...hard stuff, and only a few things were more helpful than Susan and Leah letting me join their little group. I know we don't know each other, but knowing you've had a similar experience, it's hard for me not to get nosy."

Someone said something—Tess assumed it was Leah in the background—but Tess could only make out Grace telling her to be quiet.

"So, you'll meet us at Shades at six?" Grace prompted.

Tess looked up at her apartment complex, at Marc's truck and cruiser parked in front of it. All she felt was lonely and sad, and she'd had enough of all that.

"Okay. Yeah. I'll come."

"Great! We're excited to induct another member. See you then."

Tess clicked the phone off and walked up to her apartment. No Marc sightings—thank goodness. She changed and ate something, trying not to feel the little pang that no one was cooking for her anymore.

That had been so nice. He'd acted as though it was nothing, cooking for her, but she'd never had anyone do that with any kind of regularity and, well, crap, she missed it. As much as she wanted it to be about the food and not having to cook or clean up herself, it was about someone caring enough to make the effort.

But that missing would fade and heal. Because it wasn't enough to ignore the fact he couldn't agree with something she thought was important. It wasn't enough to go on with his blank face or to do whatever they'd been doing at the farmer's market.

That was way too painful to forget just for a few delicious meals.

What about the other stuff?

No, no thinking about that. She got her gun from her utility belt and packed it in its case and some ammunition in a bag. If nothing else, she'd get some weapon practice in tonight, since she'd been neglecting that the past few months when everything had started to get so…busy with Dad.

He hadn't called today. Which was good. Maybe he was considering what she'd said. Considering treatment. She might not have come to the conclusion Marc wanted her to—that her dad was worthless and never going to get better—but at least she was starting to accept she couldn't help him. Not alone. He needed professional help, and she couldn't keep ignoring that or pretending it wasn't the only way.

The niggling idea she should tell Marc that and try to make some compromise, come to some understanding, sneaked under her breastbone and pressed against her heart. But...

She'd asked him to find a way to understand and he'd said no. Because he'd spent too much of his life pretending. Which meant he'd never understand and she had to cut her losses. He equated understanding with pretending, which meant he was never, ever going to understand.

She blinked at the tears in her eyes. She was not crying over Marc Santino anymore. Nope, she was going to go do something that was good practice for her job. With people who seemed interested in her.

No one gives a shit about you, Tess.

She shook away that voice. A woman's voice. Sometimes she thought maybe it was her mother's, but mostly she knew it was her own faulty, irrational subconscious. One she didn't listen to because it was full of lies. So many lies.

With one last check to make sure she had everything she needed, she stepped out into the hallway. And, of course, there was Marc.

Paying a *pizza guy*. What the hell? Maybe it was his version of drinking himself to oblivion. Eating terrible, greasy food. Which meant maybe he was as upset as her. Which meant maybe she should...

The pizza guy thanked Marc and then headed for the stairwell and Tess was caught staring. She looked away. *Oh, you coward.*

"Tess."

Which made the cowardice worse. The leap in her heart that he was saying her name and the very fact was...

She didn't know what to do. Her whole life had been a series of figuring out difficult situations and she straight up did not know what to do when it came to Marc.

"I'm going shooting with your sister," she blurted.

"Oh."

"It's not about you. Just so you know. She and Grace invited me and it's...nothing to do with you." It was coming out all wrong. Kind of snippy when she only wanted him to know he didn't have to feel weird about her being around Leah.

"Great." He started closing the door, and she wanted to know why he'd said her name in the first place, but...

Oh, hell, maybe this was her punishment for never having an awkward high school breakup, because she felt about sixteen with all the uncertainty going on in her head.

She squared her shoulders as Marc closed the

door. She was going to take a few lessons from *Lethal Weapon*. First, she was too old for this shit. Second, she would deal with her problems by firing her gun more times than necessary.

Bolstered with purpose, Tess went to her car and drove leisurely toward Shades. It was outside of town next to one of the conservation areas. Though she tended to go to the indoor gun range in town, where she got free ammo from the department, the laid-back atmosphere of Shades would be nice.

She wasn't feeling too supercop these days, anyway.

When she pulled up to Shades, two other cars were there, three women standing in front of them laughing and chatting.

Suddenly and acutely, Tess wished she hadn't come. This seemed so intimate. So friendsy. Lately everything with Dad had taken up so much of her free time that all those friendships she kept at arm's length anyway had faded even further.

Amazing that she hadn't noticed how much this particular round of Dad's decline had affected her life as it was happening. But now that she looked back, wow. Yeah, it had been pretty bad.

That's what Marc had walked into. The tail end of that. No wonder he felt the way he did. Maybe she should cut him some slack and try to explain...

Oh, you stupid heart, shut up. Shut up.

"Hey, guys," Tess greeted, overbrightly, as she

stepped out of her car with her bags. "Thanks so much for inviting me."

"Anytime. The more the merrier." Susan offered a smile and after a few more pleasantries they started walking to one of the target areas.

Being in law enforcement, she was surrounded by people who owned and carried firearms. Still, it *was* surprising to find three women who all had their own guns and routinely practiced shooting with no occupational need for doing so.

"This is quite a book club, I have to say," Tess said, hoping she wasn't the cause for the kind of awkward silence going on. "You all got guns because you've been...threatened?"

"Ah, no," Leah said, focusing very carefully on loading her Glock. "I think we all have different reasons for it, I guess."

"Mine was for protection," Grace said, taking a little Glock with a design painted on it out of its case. The design matched the tattoo on her arm—an orange-and-red diamond thing. "It's helped me feel safe when I felt threatened. I'm not sure it really did anything to keep me safe, but I'm responsible with it, so I feel like that's okay."

"Right."

"It helped. It wasn't just the attack part, but the guy getting out of jail afterward, you know? There's a lot of factors when that kind of thing happens to you." Grace slid her a glance out of the side of her eye. "I'm sure you deal with that in your job."

Tess had a feeling Grace was trying to draw her out. But she was doing it carefully enough that Tess didn't feel uncomfortable with it. Awkward, sure, but it felt kindhearted. As if Grace was trying to offer commiseration, not force her to renounce any and all contact with her father.

Which Marc hadn't exactly done—but maybe he had. Oh, jeez, could she just stop thinking about damn Marc at every turn? This was not about him. Even if his sister—with their sibling resemblance— was standing a few feet away from her.

"He was my boyfriend, kind of. Weird situation. A few dates, I tried to break it off, then..." Grace shrugged, lining up the sights of her gun and then pulling the trigger. "You know. Coma."

"That's...much worse." Tess swallowed. She hadn't worked on Grace's case, but she had heard enough about it to remember it now.

The guy had gotten out of jail and stalked her. Tried to kidnap her. Yeah, nothing like what Tess had to deal with. Feeling too shaky to take her turn with the target, she stepped out of the way so Leah could step up. "I... My experience was just, you know... No hospital." Oh, gross, she was a police officer, trained to deal with difficult situations and terrible information, and she was stuttering like some kind of moron.

"A guy knocks you around, it's wrong. Period," Leah muttered, stepping forward and taking a shot.

"Well, sure, but…" Tess took a breath. "My father's an alcoholic. It's different."

The three women all looked at her with matching wide-eyed surprise. "Your father?" Leah asked.

"I…" She'd assumed Marc had filled his sister in on all the details. Apparently not. Now she felt like a complete idiot, with a bright red face to boot.

Susan took her turn at the target. "I think we can all agree, whoever, wherever, it's crap. The end."

"Here's to that." Grace nodded and took her turn.

All three women looked expectantly at Tess. She took a breath and stepped forward to take her turn. It was such a surreal experience, talking about this with other people, even if it wasn't in detail. Even if she didn't know the other people that well.

So she breathed until she had control of her limbs, and they spent the rest of the next hour taking turns shooting and talking about Grace's fall wedding, and both Susan and Grace poking fun at Leah over her relationship with Jacob.

It was nice. Nice to be able to move on from the uncomfortable moment, nice to practice an important skill for her job and nice to engage in some girl talk that didn't make her think about Marc.

Too much.

At the end of the hour, just as the daylight was

beginning to fade, they began packing up their guns and heading for their cars.

"Thanks for inviting me, guys. It was a nice distraction." From Dad. From Marc. From being so alone.

Yeah, not a bad way to spend the evening at all.

They said their goodbyes, but as Tess put her key in the ignition, Leah tapped on the window. Tess rolled it down.

"Hey, look… You know, whatever happened with my brother…" Leah winced. "Damn, I hate sticking my nose where it doesn't belong, but he's not a bad guy. I think sometimes he's trying so hard to be the good guy he messes stuff up."

Tess swallowed the lump in her throat. "I think you're right, but…"

"No, you don't have to explain. I just wanted to get that out. Thanks for coming, Tess. I'm sure we'll be hounding you to come next week, too." She smiled and waved and walked back to her car.

Tess didn't have a damn clue what she was supposed to do with any of this. All she knew was she needed to figure it out before it drove her absolutely nuts.

CHAPTER TWENTY-SIX

MARC STOOD OUTSIDE Leah's house, leaning against the hood of his truck, trying to figure out why he was here and what he was going to say.

He only knew that he couldn't fix what was going on with Tess. If she wanted to keep going back to her father, what could he do to stop that? He wasn't a therapist, nor could he tie her up in his apartment, so there was nothing he could do.

But with his parents, with his *family*, there were things he could and should do. His outburst had felt good at the time, but it hadn't been fair. Because you didn't go from pretending everything was fine to imploding without giving the audience any warning.

Leah *and* Tess had tried to get that idea into his head   that he needed to tell Mom he didn't like being ignored, that he needed to open up about how it hurt. Instead, one day it was fine, the next he was walking out on them in his own apartment.

Yeah, he was a dick. That's what he needed to fix.

He stepped forward and stopped when Leah's garage door began to rise as her truck pulled into the drive. Ah, so she was back from shooting with Tess. Apparently he should have manned up a little sooner.

Not that Leah didn't need a bit of an apology, too, but his parents deserved the big one. Still, maybe it would be good to do it all together.

A family. Deep down, that's what they all wanted. If only they didn't all go about it so differently.

"Hey," Leah greeted, stepping out of her garage and looking sheepish. "Was there a dinner I didn't know about?"

"No. But I thought I should come talk to Mom and Dad before they leave."

She nodded, looking at the house.

"And apologize."

Her gaze finally met his. "Yeah, I think they'd like that. Yesterday was kind of…"

"Shit."

"Yeah. That." She shook her head. "Look, *I* understood yesterday to an extent, but I think that's because we had our moment over Christmas. For them it—"

"Came out of left field. I get that. Took me a bit, but I do get that." He scrubbed a hand over his face. "Everything's kind of gone to shit lately and I'm not sure how to fix that."

"Make up with your girlfriend?"

"Leah."

"Come on. You were so cute together at the party. You were smiley. *You.* That has to mean something, and she seemed…"

"She seemed what?"

"Aha! See, you're still interested, so it can't be all bad. Remember when Jacob and I were kind of doing the breakup thing and you were all weirdly encouraging of not letting one little disagreement keep us apart?"

Yes, he did remember. But that had been different.

"You know I'm not mushy about love and crap, but you *were* happy. I know there was a big stretch of time where we didn't really know each other, but I don't remember ever seeing you full-on happy."

"One apology at a time, huh?"

She pointed a finger at him. "So you *were* the screwer-upper. It's always the guy."

"You were not faultless with your stuff with Jacob."

She waved that away. "We're focusing on you right now. One apology at a time? Well, let's speed this one up so you can get to the next." Leah started propelling him to the door.

It meant something, that she was invested, that she was saying stuff. That she was here, pulling him toward the door. Enough to say things he normally kept to himself.

"I appreciate the effort you've been making."

She stopped abruptly, moving away from him. "O-oh, well—"

"I wasn't exactly kind over Christmas and I've kept my distance since I moved, but I want you to know I appreciate your effort. And more, I like you. As a person and as a sister."

She stared at him openmouthed for a few seconds before giving him one final push toward the door. "Save the gushy stuff for Mom and Dad, jeez."

But as he opened the door he could see her blinking a little rapidly, and she even managed a mumbled, "Thanks. And, for what it's worth, I like you, too. Brother, person and all that."

"Enough to tell me how to fix this?"

"Parental fix or romantic fix?"

He opened his mouth to say *parental*, but instead "Maybe both" slipped out.

Leah grinned. "Mom and Dad first, then. That'll be easy." They stepped inside. "I know they tend to focus on me, but they think you're a saint."

"It has quite honestly never felt like that."

Leah paused in the entryway, studying him. "I never in a million years would have believed this when you all showed up on my doorstep in December, but I think this whole moving-here thing is the best damn thing that could have ever happened to this family."

"Yeah, I'm not sure *I* believe that."

She gave him a stern look. "It sucks in the interim, I'll give you that. But you know this is going to make things better."

He glanced into the house from Leah's entryway. Better? This might be what he had to do, but the sick feeling in his stomach wasn't convinced things would get better. Maybe for her, but considering she'd barely talked to the family for a decade, that wasn't hard to make better.

But if there was some way he could voice his feelings to his parents, maybe there was hope that…well, that he could live his own life without feeling guilty for not giving them everything they wanted. Maybe if he had a solid grasp on his own life, it wouldn't be so painful when Mom went in full-on Leah mode.

"It's hard not to think, shit, Tess's dad is the one that did that to her face and here we are upset that our parents don't treat us the way we want," Leah said. "I hate false equivalency crap like that, because regardless of starving people and three-legged dogs, I should be able to feel bad or complain sometimes, but at the same time, it's a bit of perspective, you know?"

"I know." He did. Tess had hated when he'd compared or belittled what was going on with him because hers was worse, but maybe that wasn't exactly the kind of perspective Leah was talking about. Perspective and ignoring that he was unhappy with his family life were two different things, he realized.

It was starting to become abundantly clear that perspective was exactly what he needed to be happy.

He was really, really ready to be happy. Which meant taking action, moving forward and figuring out what he wanted. Somehow balancing that with what the people he loved wanted. Surely there was compromise to be had without completely ignoring himself.

He followed Leah into her living room, where Mom and Dad were sitting on the couch, Mom all but shoving a magazine in Dad's face and asking him about some color.

"Mom. Dad."

Dad looked up with his angry face on, which was very rare these days. He stood up between Marc and Mom. Which made Marc feel like even bigger shit.

"Well, young man, I hope you're here to apologize," his father said gruffly. "You made your mother cry."

"I am. I do. I absolutely apologize for the way I behaved yesterday," Marc forced out in a grumbly voice, knocked flat by the fact Dad was lecturing him and he'd made Mom cry. That was not... him. He'd never incurred their displeasure. Sure, not much praise, but he'd never been in trouble. Not since he was a little kid.

"Come on, Marc. Say it like a human."

He knew Leah's attempt at humor was supposed to lighten the mood, but it didn't work. Familiar guilt and shame curled up in his gut. He couldn't really be what they needed. Never had been. Never would be.

But Mom smiled. "It was a good apology. Succinct but genuine. Besides, Leah said you and Tess might have had a fight and that might have been the cause of your bad mood."

"We...broke up."

Mom waved a hand in the air. "Nonsense. I refuse to accept it. The grandchildren you two would make me." She clasped her hands to her heart. "Now, what do we need to do to fix it?"

"He needs to apologize," Leah piped up.

He glared at her and she laughed. "Sorry, you being the center of attention is too much fun for me not to be a part of."

"I came to apologize." He looked around, trying to get his bearings. "How are we past that already?"

"Because, my goodness, Marc, you almost always do the right thing. I can't remember the last time you disappointed me. One little outburst, caused by a broken heart, is easily forgivable."

Marc blinked. Was that…praise?

"Now. Let's talk Tess. Surely you know better than to let one disagreement be the end of anything. You wouldn't even be alive if your father and I had done that, let alone Leah." Mom got off the couch and started ushering him to the door.

"Mom—"

"Don't pretend they weren't important things to argue about. You were there when things were particularly bad between your father and I."

What was happening? "I—"

"Now, you will go make things right with that girl. Flowers are a nice touch. But the most important thing is words and meaning them, of course."

Suddenly he was standing in front of the door.

"Mom, I'm not sure I can live with what she wants me to live with."

"Love isn't everything, honey, but it's a heck of a lot." She gave him a squeeze. "I know you both think I'm overzealous on the finding-a-spouse thing, but it's only because having someone to share your life is huge. It's gotten me through so much. I want the same for my children."

"I…" He looked at the door, but it was his easy out. "I haven't been happy."

"Oh, don't I know it. You think I wanted to move you here just because? I thought a change of scenery, maybe making some friends might help. Having your sister here was a good start, but you didn't even need her. You met Tess all on your own."

"You wanted me to move here because of Leah."

Mom rolled her eyes. "Well, of course, dear, but not only because of her. Your father and I have been worried about you."

Worried about him? They never did any of the things they did to Leah to him. No incessant calling, no unannounced visits. "You never said…"

"Said anything? Honey, I've wanted you to find your own way, not just do whatever your father and I told you. That's why we told you less and less with every passing year. We wanted you to find your life. Your father and I knew you needed a…change. A spark. And getting us all in the same town meant all four of us would get something we wanted."

"I thought you cared only about Leah. I don't

mean only, but…" He felt as if his head was spinning and none of it made any sense.

Mom put a hand to her heart. "Marc." She blinked rapidly, eyes shiny with tears. "How could you ever doubt that we cared about you?"

"No. Not…that. I just…" Christ, couldn't he get a full sentence together without stuttering? "Everything was about Leah. Never me. I have always come in second."

Mom kept blinking. Her hand moved from her heart to her mouth. "I know Leah needed more attention, but you never…" Mom took a deep breath. "Her illness took a toll on all of us, especially before and the year right after the transplant. Maybe we didn't give you as much attention as you needed or deserved."

"I didn't mean it that way."

Mom pursed her lips and fixed him with a stern glare. "I think that's exactly what you meant." Some of her tenseness slumped. "And maybe you're right." She glanced back at the living room where Leah and Dad stood, both with their hands in their pockets, shoulders hunched, eyes on the floor.

"I know I've acted more like a chicken with her head cut off than a rational adult the past few years, trying to bring Leah back into the family. Trying to make us a close, tight-knit family again. I've dropped some balls."

"Mom—"

"If I ever… No, I can't even say *if.* You're right,

I— Not that I've ever cared more about your sister, but that because of her health I showed her more attention, and I dropped the ball when it came to *showing* you how much you were loved and needed."

"Please don't cry." Because the tears were too much paired with the words and the look on her face, clearly saying she thought she'd failed. She hadn't. Not really. They all had.

"You never said anything, but I should have seen it."

"I should have said something."

Mom sniffled, pulling a handkerchief out of her back pocket. "I'm your mother—I should have seen that you needed something from me."

"Not if I pretended—"

Dad cleared his throat, causing everyone to look at him. "I hate to break up all the self-blame," he said in his low, gravelly voice, commanding all the attention in the room since he so rarely strung so many words together. "But I think we can agree we've all made mistakes. And that we all need to be more open and honest and understanding with each other."

Mom's expression transformed from distraught to immediate joy. "Yes. Yes, Dad's right. The important thing is, we're here, on the edge of a new beginning." She wiped her tears, straightening her shoulders as she shoved the handkerchief back into her pocket. "If Dad and I can move here by the end of the year, if you two decide to settle down with the lovely people you've found in this town, well, that's a nice new beginning. Don't you think?"

Dad nodded, then Leah, then Mom fixed him with a look.

A nice new beginning. He wasn't sure…oh, hell, maybe he wasn't sure, but that's what he wanted. What they all wanted. And they were all probably determined and stubborn enough to make it work.

"Yes, I think so."

"Good." Mom took a deep breath and then clapped her hands together. "Now go get your girl. Maybe you *won't* give me adorable grandbabies with her. Sweet little ones to spoil." Mom let out a dramatic sigh. "I'll deal with that. What I won't deal with is you continuing to be unhappy. I thought I was doing right by giving you space." She shook her head. "But if you want me to start being more proactive, like I am with Leah, I can do that, honey. I just never thought you wanted or needed it."

"Can we find a happy medium?" he managed, his voice thick with too much emotion.

"I think we could very much work on finding a happy medium. *I* will work very hard to find a happy medium. With both of my children, whom I love more than life itself no matter how poorly I sometimes show it."

"You're—" When Mom fixed him with a *don't you dare argue with me* glare, Marc cleared his throat. "I will work very hard on that, too."

"Good. Now, speaking of happy…" She hurried over to her purse in the corner. Then pulled out the little white box from a few weeks ago.

"Mom."

"I was wrong to offer it to Jacob," she said. "Maybe you're not ready to use it with your young lady, and that's fine...I guess." Another dramatic sigh, and then she touched her palm to his cheek. "I got a little...fixated on getting my girl married and I made a big mistake, overlooking what you wanted." She furrowed her brow, looking down at the floor. "Maybe I've done that more than I realized, but we're going to fix that." She met his gaze, nodded. "We are."

Marc took the box. "I'm not ready to—"

"It doesn't matter. It's yours. Do whatever you like with it." Mom gestured to the door. "But regardless of using it, you need to go make up with that young lady who put such a big smile on your face."

"I don't know..."

"Of course you do. You're very good at knowing. Now, apply that to getting."

Marc finally nodded and enveloped his mother in a hug. "I love you, Mom." Because he did. Even with all they still needed to come to terms with, he'd never not loved her.

She squeezed him hard, and if he wasn't mistaken she sniffled. "I love you, too, my sweet, strong boy."

It didn't magically fix everything. There would still no doubt be days he felt as though he was being overlooked or underappreciated, but they'd started a foundation of him figuring out how to express rather than fold in on himself.

Mom and Dad had backed away because they'd wanted him to make his own choices, and somehow he'd clung harder to the choices they wanted him to make.

How screwed up was that? He scrubbed his hands over his face, trying to make sense out of anything.

"Flowers," Mom said matter-of-factly, pulling the door open. "Sincere apology. And then tomorrow night a big family dinner before we have to go back to Minnesota."

Marc opened his mouth but no sound came out.

"Go on. Don't make me do it for you."

Which was enough impetus to get his feet moving. Out the door. Onto the porch.

"Good luck, honey. If it isn't too late, make sure you let us know how it goes."

"Right. Sure. Right."

"Marc?"

He turned to face his mother, trying to get his thoughts into a coherent line—to get his *life* in a coherent line.

"Just be honest, and yourself. Don't overthink it. Honesty makes everything fall into place when it comes to love."

Love. Which he was terrible at. Honesty, too. But…well, maybe it was time to get better at them.

TESS DIDN'T PARTICULARLY like to run in the dark, but if she had any hope of sleeping tonight, she needed this workout. And while it wasn't her favorite way of doing things, keeping her gun strapped to her rib cage under her T-shirt at least made her feel safe.

She made it back to the apartment complex after a long run through the nicer part of town, breathing heavily, sweating profusely despite the cool spring night.

She stood out front, stretching and trying to catch her breath. She hadn't gone as far as she'd have liked to make her entire body a mass of quivering exhaustion, but it wasn't half-bad.

Headlights hit her in the eye, and she winced and flung her arm over her face. Once the car was off, she lowered her arm and almost laughed. Because, honestly, how could she not have known? Apparently she and Marc were the only two people to ever come or go in this place.

Marc walked toward her, carrying a bulky shopping bag, and what she should do was look down or turn away or anything but watch him and ache for the damn jerkwad she couldn't figure out what to do about.

"Hi," he greeted, standing right in front of her. Not moving on. Not looking elsewhere. No, his eyes were directly on her.

"Hi," she offered in awkward return, cringing when a drop of sweat dripped off her forehead. Of course he'd want to talk to her when she was disgusting and sweaty.

"Do you think we could talk?"

"About what?" She didn't want to discuss work or taking separate cars or—

"Us."

Oh. He looked so earnest, so…like he needed this. Wanted it. All that yearning and hope she wasn't sure was smart or stupid little-girl fantasy overrode every cautious bone in her body.

"Okay." She hadn't a clue what they could possibly talk about, but if he wanted to, maybe…

Maybe.

CHAPTER TWENTY-SEVEN

MARC WALKED UP the stairs to his apartment, trying to steady the racing of his heart. He'd wanted more time to plan out what to say and figure out the important beats to hit. All the ways to give her what she wanted without totally losing sight of what he wanted.

But she'd been there, and how could he ignore that all he really wanted was her? He just had to be honest.

That's what got you here in the first place.

He frowned at the door as he unlocked it, walked stiffly into his apartment, straight to the kitchen counter so he could set down the heavy bag of books he'd bought. When he turned to face Tess, she was locking his door. Sliding the dead bolt.

It twisted up in his chest. He knew she wasn't as careful as he was when it came to that stuff, but she was doing it because she knew that's what he preferred. And shit. Shit. Shit. He needed to make this right.

Her eyes met his, then her gaze slid away. "Um, so I'm kind of gross." She gestured at herself. "If we could kind of move this along so I could take a shower."

Beads of sweat dripped down her face, her neck. She wore an oversized T-shirt, darker around the collar from sweat.

"Why'd you go running in the dark?"

She rolled her eyes. "Look, if you're going to start the Tess-can't-take-care-of-herself bullshit again, I'm out of here."

"I've never thought you couldn't take care of yourself."

She shook her head and made a move for the door. "My ass."

"Wanting you to be safe is not the same as thinking you can't take care of yourself. How many times did I step back and let you take care of something?"

She whirled around. "But you didn't want to!"

"So what? There are a lot of things I don't fucking want to do and I do them anyway because that is what you do when you love someone! You make sacrifices and mistakes and all sorts of dumb shit."

She crossed her arms over her chest. "You're an expert on love now?"

"No, no, I'm not an expert. I'm a mess. An idiot. I have no idea what I'm doing. I only know I *do* love you and I don't want this to be over because we disagree about how to handle your father."

"But he *is* my father. He's always going to be. We can't ignore it or pretend it isn't this big thing we don't agree on."

She was right, but he had to believe that if she was here, if she was willing to talk about them, it didn't have to be that black-and-white. As black-and-white as he'd been looking at it, as black-and-white as he'd viewed his whole life.

There was such a thing as compromise, and that didn't have to mean sacrificing *everything* he felt. Or her sacrificing everything she did.

He pulled out the books he'd bought, much to the weeping of his budget. "I got you some books."

"Books?"

"I know you said you'd read a lot about this topic. But—"

"I don't want the twelve-step books, Marc. What's that supposed to do? It doesn't matter because when I went there and visited him I told him I wasn't coming back unless he got treatment. Because, whether you want to believe it about me or not, I'm not some pathetic little girl under his thumb who can't understand reason or...whatever."

"I never thought you were pathetic. Never."

"Well—"

"What made you think I thought you were pathetic? What did I ever say or do that would make you think that?" And now he was yelling. Why were they getting angry? That wasn't the point of this.

She frowned at him, her eyebrows all scrunched together. "I was not the one who went all *I can't do this*. That was you."

"And I was wrong and confused and didn't know

how to deal, okay? I'm glad you went and told him that. I wish you'd—"

"Wished I'd what?"

"Told me! Involved me! Let me in. *That* is what I'm trying to get at. I want to be a part of your life. I don't want to swallow my disagreements but I also don't want one thing we disagree on to be the end of us."

"You said you couldn't deal with me letting him in my life because he's such a monster. Well, he's not a monster. I believe a lot of shitty things about my dad, but I'll never agree with that."

"Okay."

She threw her hands up in the air. "What do you mean, okay?"

"I mean, okay. That's fair. These books I bought are about managing relationships with abusers *and* alcoholics. It's not about...I know you want to fix him, and I'm not sure I'll ever think that's possible. But I do want to be by your side while you try to make it the best relationship it can be."

She stared at him, openmouthed, but didn't say a word. Just stared.

So he pressed on, because that had to mean something good. God, he hoped.

"I want to be your partner. I think that's what I was missing or didn't understand with my parents and my sister. I was never an active participant in helping. I did what everyone wanted me to do. I let her sickness and her running away run my life, even though I never needed to let it do that. Yes, I was there. I was a foundation, but nothing else. I never spoke up. I never told anyone what I felt or that I didn't want to do it. When you do that you lose sight of yourself and your wants, or at least that's what I did.

"That's not what I want with us. I want to work together. That means talking through things. No shutting down or getting angry.

"I want you. I want us. I'm telling you what I want, honestly. So…there. That's it. That's why I asked you to come in here."

He didn't know what else to say or do. So he waited.

Tess didn't know what to say. She couldn't move. Sweat kept dripping down her temples and her neck and her back and…

He wanted her. Them. He wanted to be partners. Suddenly she wanted to cry. She blinked hard because otherwise the tears would leak out like the sweat running down her back.

Jeez, she was a *mess*.

"Tess?"

"I…I need to take a shower."

"What?"

She awkwardly gestured to her shirt, backing toward the door. "I can't do this all sweaty and gross."

Marc stepped toward her and she felt the need to run even more acutely.

"Do what, exactly?"

"I don't know. Think, or…Marc." She pushed her fingers through her disgusting hair, making it fall out of its band and make her even hotter. "I don't know," she choked out.

"Okay." He nodded. "Okay. Maybe you want to take some time to think about it."

She swallowed and nodded and reached for the door. But when she turned the knob she remembered she'd locked it and that made her want to cry all over again.

What was she doing? This sweet, supportive mess of a man wanted to be her *partner* in fucking life and she needed to take a *shower*? She needed time and thinking and…no.

No, she didn't need any of that. What she *needed* was someone to be there, to care, to want to try even when things got hard. To come back even after they'd both walked away.

She needed someone in her life who didn't blame her or hurt her, even if he did disagree with her about important things. Because disagreements could be talked through, worked out, moved through.

She dropped her hand from the knob. She wanted him. Them. Just like he'd said, and there was no point in showering or trying to talk herself out of it. Like sleeping with him, like falling in love with him, she wanted something for *her*.

Because she deserved it. Because *they* deserved

it. Because…because it was good. Even when it was hard, it was still better than being apart.

She forced a step, then another and then, what the hell, she launched herself at him. He managed to catch her without toppling over, and his arms wound around her just as tight as hers wound around him.

"I want that. I want all of that," she said, holding on hard. "A partner. I've never—"

"Yeah, me, neither." He cleared his throat. "I think we've both made a habit out of doing things on our own, because we had to or because we didn't want to get hurt or whatever, and I think that's why we walked away over something that didn't really need to be walked away over."

He was right. So much of not knowing what to do had been the very fact that fighting for something that could continually hurt her was too much. Too much like the things that beat her down.

But even though Marc would always be capable of hurting her—that was kind of the nature of love— she knew he wouldn't try to. He wanted her to be happy. Regardless of the fact that she couldn't ever hate her father or think he was a monster.

"You are really, really sweaty," Marc said on a laugh. But he didn't let her go. Maybe he didn't, like, tear off her clothes, but he did hold on. And holding on was exactly what she needed.

"I love you," she said, as emphatically as she could force the words out.

His grip tightened. "I love you, too."

It wasn't exactly a fairy tale, but it was better than that. Because it was real. Real sweat and tears and love.

And that was good.

EPILOGUE

"CHRIST, THIS THING weighs a ton," Marc grumbled.

"You're the one who didn't think we could take it apart and move it," Jacob grunted as he, Marc, Kyle and Henry maneuvered Leah's work shed into the backyard of the house Jacob had renovated. Between a truck, a few dollies and sheer muscle, they'd managed to get it to the back corner of the yard.

"Okay, right here," Jacob instructed.

Though they'd taken everything out of the shed, moving it had been no easy feat.

But now they were done.

"Who wants to help me put all the crap back in?" Jacob asked cheerfully.

"You are on your own," Kyle replied. "I have to get back. I promised your mother I'd be there to help load up all the presents Grace gets."

"Marc, Henry?"

"I've got to go pick up our cat from the vet."

Jacob groaned. "Marc, you're my only hope. And she is your sister."

"Yeah, yeah, yeah."

The other two men said their goodbyes and Marc

helped Jacob put all of Leah's tools and whatnot back into her work shed.

"She'll like it, right? Even though I touched her stuff?"

"You're asking me?"

Jacob linked his hands on the top of his head, looking around the inside of the shed. "She'll say yes." He nodded, sounding anything but sure.

Marc shook his head. "You're really nervous? You two have been drawing this out forever. Mom has her own special sigh for when she's thinking about you two living in sin, *not* getting engaged."

"Yes, well, tell that to your sister."

"Eh."

Jacob dropped his hands. "Thanks for your help, man. Don't think we'd have gotten it back here without you."

"Anytime."

Jacob started walking him back to the front. "I'll drop you back at your place. Grace should be able to keep Leah busy until then."

"I texted Tess to come pick me up. Don't want to ruin your grand fall into matrimony."

"Thoughtful of you. Of Tess. Speaking of drawing things out, wedding bells do tend to breed more wedding bells."

"I don't think my mom's heart can take more than one wedding at a time."

"Which means you've *thought* about wedding bells." Jacob slapped him on the back and Tess's car pulled up with just about perfect timing. Because while he and Jacob had built a kind of friendship in the nine months since he'd moved to Bluff City, he wasn't interested in anyone teasing him about marriage and Tess.

It was too important.

"Heya, hot stuff," Tess called out of her unrolled window. She was in a dress and makeup after Grace's bridal shower this afternoon, and Marc could not wait to get her home and out of it.

"Now, Tess, I'm happily taken," Jacob responded, pretending to tsk. "Marc will have to do."

She grinned. "The beard blinded me for a second. You'll have to forgive me."

Jacob rubbed a palm over his chin, his grin only dying when Tess offered him a "Good luck." Yeah, the guy was scared shitless.

"You really don't have to be nervous," Marc said with a shrug. "She'll love it."

He patted Jacob's shoulder before climbing into Tess's car.

"That was sweet," she said, waving at Jacob before pulling out onto the street. "Both of you. Very sweet."

"How was the party?"

"Really fun," she said brightly. Almost too brightly. She chewed on her lip. "Dad called."

Marc rested his hands over hers. "Everything okay?"

She shrugged. "He wants out of the treatment

center. I said I didn't approve of that. He yelled. I hung up on him. The usual."

"I'm sorry."

"Yeah. But, you know, I got to go back into the party and see how happy Grace was and it went a long way in putting it into perspective. There are a lot of things to be happy about, even when that's not."

She smiled, and even though there was a hint of sadness behind it, it wasn't a fake smile. "I have you and a job I love and some really great friends. So I'm happy."

"Good." He was glad she could be. She'd been so excited when her father had agreed to go into a treatment center last month, but it wasn't as easy now as either of them had thought it might be.

But she had him, and they'd approached it like a team, and he liked to think that made it at least a tiny bit better for her.

Life wasn't perfect, but they were happy.

Wedding bells do tend to breed more wedding bells.

The truth was he *had* been thinking about wedding bells. Jacob dropping the bomb he thought Leah was finally ready to be proposed to hadn't started that thinking. In fact, it had almost put it on the back burner. Because he didn't want to steal Leah's thunder.

But that didn't mean he couldn't start getting the

wheels rolling in the right direction. "You know, I think…I'm going to put my two weeks' in tomorrow."

Tess hit the brakes a little hard at the stop sign. "Your two weeks'?" She looked at him, wide-eyed.

Marc nodded. "Yeah. See what Franks has to say about maybe transferring me to the jail. If it would be a conflict. If so, I'll figure something else out."

Her eyebrows drew together. "A conflict? What are you talking about?"

Marc rested his arm across her shoulders, grinned. "I guess you'll just have to wait and be surprised."

She blinked at him, then back at the road, then at him again. "Well," she finally managed, eyes looking suspiciously teary. "Well." Then she cleared her throat as she finally started driving again. "You should probably give Leah a little time to enjoy… things first."

"I will. But, you know, Jacob's not exactly waiting for his sister to be married to pop the question to Leah."

Tess blinked even harder. "Oh, hell," she muttered, pulling to the side of the street.

"What are you—"

She flung her arms around his neck and then pressed his mouth to his. "I love you," she said against his mouth before pulling back and grinning at him.

"I love you, too."

She was smiling. She was happy. *They* were happy, and it'd go a long way in dealing with anything that wasn't.

* * * * *

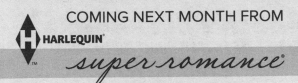

LARGER-PRINT BOOKS!

HARLEQUIN *Presents*

PASSION GUARANTEED SEDUCTION

GET 2 FREE LARGER-PRINT NOVELS PLUS 2 FREE GIFTS!

YES! Please send me 2 FREE LARGER-PRINT Harlequin Presents® novels and my 2 FREE gifts (gifts are worth about $10). After receiving them, if I don't wish to receive any more books, I can return the shipping statement marked "cancel." If I don't cancel, I will receive 6 brand-new novels every month and be billed just $5.05 per book in the U.S. or $5.49 per book in Canada. That's a saving of at least 16% off the cover price! It's quite a bargain! Shipping and handling is just 50¢ per book in the U.S and 75¢ per book in Canada.* I understand that accepting the 2 free books and gifts places me under no obligation to buy anything. I can always return a shipment and cancel at any time. Even if I never buy another book, the two free books and gifts are mine to keep forever.

176/376 HDN F43N

Name	(PLEASE PRINT)

Address	Apt. #

City	State/Prov.	Zip/Postal Code

Signature (if under 18, a parent or guardian must sign)

Mail to the **Harlequin® Reader Service:**
IN U.S.A.: P.O. Box 1867, Buffalo, NY 14240-1867
IN CANADA: P.O. Box 609, Fort Erie, Ontario L2A 5X3

**Are you a subscriber to Harlequin Presents books
and want to receive the larger-print edition?
Call 1-800-873-8635 today or visit us at www.ReaderService.com.**

HPLP13R

ReaderService.com

Manage your account online!

- Review your order history
- Manage your payments
- Update your address

---

*We've designed
the Harlequin® Reader Service
website just for you.*

Enjoy all the features!

- Reader excerpts from any series
- Respond to mailings and
  special monthly offers
- Discover new series available to you
- Browse the Bonus Bucks catalog
- Share your feedback

Visit us at:
ReaderService.com

RS13